BETRAYED

Gabby Skeldon

Rhianne,

Thank you for Beta'ing (haha)
It's only 'write' (haha) that you
own a physical copy!

Love,
Gabs.

BETRAYED
Copyright © 2022 by Gabby Skeldon.

All rights reserved. Printed in the United Kingdom. No part of this book may be used or reproduced in any manner whatsoever without written permission except in the case of brief quotations embodied in critical articles or reviews.

This book is a work of fiction. Names, characters, businesses, organisations, places, events and incidents either are the product of the author's imagination or are used fictitiously. Any resemblance to actual persons, living or dead, events, or locales is entirely coincidental.

For information contact:
Front Cover Design by : Saint Jupiter (@saintjupit3ergr4phics)
Editor: Gabby Skeldon (gab@authorgabskeldon.com)
Formatting: Gabby Skeldon (gab@authorgabskeldon.com)
ISBN:
First Edition: June 2023

For Danny.

1

"Do something cool." Asher says for the hundredth time this morning.

We're in the library, where we spend most of our time nowadays. It's beautiful in the soft afternoon light, sun streaming through the tall stained glass windows, painting the books with red and blue and gold. It's much more homely than it was when I arrived six months ago. Lots of cushions and throws to keep us comfy on the long nights of research. Today I've been practising spells, the others excitedly suggesting tricks they want me to try.

My magic has grown tenfold since I claimed it in the cave. I've learned spells to grow and heal, and how to mix potions and ointments that work. I can cast protection charms like shimmering gossamer spider webs that fall around the twins if they're threatened. After months of endless practice, I'm really becoming a proper witch.

But I'm not the only one who's been busy. Willow,

BETRAYED

Asher, Ren and I spent three solid weeks collecting ingredients and mixing potions— faery repellants, if you will— to send to the other Templars and knights' estates. Things they might use to fortify their strongholds in case of an attack. There have been a few since we sent the Evil Faery Queen screaming to the depths of her realm. *Spies.* Sir Tristen has reported multiple sightings in the North, Peter Lucan and Matthew Gawain complaining of the same down South. It's been long and tiring work, getting them to listen, to take action. Every single night, I fall into bed exhausted.

"Cool like what?" I ask.

Asher's laying with her head dangling over the side of the couch, the tips of her orange braids trailing on the floor. She swings into a sitting position, upsetting Willow, who has her head in a book called '*Flora and Fauna: Natural Remedies for the Intermediate Witch.*' "Like something really cool. Proper magic."

"As opposed to that fake magic I'm always doing?"

"You know what I mean."

"I've got an idea," Willow interjects.

"Not this again." Ren says. I've been lounging against him, but now he shrugs me off and sits up straight. "Do we have time with everything else?"

"The next full moon is tomorrow. If we miss this one, it'll be at least another month until we can try again."

For the last few weeks, Willow has been insistent that I summon my familiar. It's deep magic, something that will sap a lot of my energy, and Ren's right to be concerned. In two days, the knights will return to the Templar. A meeting to re–group and update them on our progress. Not that there's been much.

Since Lore woke up, she's struggled to remember anything about her life before. For the first few weeks, she could just about recall Lux, Joth and Ren, but everyone else was a blur. Shadows. Slowly people began to return to her, slivers of memory forming foggy pictures, but she still doesn't *really* remember. I can't even imagine how awful it must be, everyone knowing you but you knowing nobody. Not your own twin, not even yourself. But she's learning, and has shown some improvement thanks to Willow's patient, patient tutoring. Lore always forgets me, though, and it pierces my heart like a glass shard.

I was hoping I'd have something to share with the knights, at least a small step forward in restoring the queen. But all the enchantments we've found require an advanced spell caster, someone who's got experience meddling in people's minds. One wrong move and I could do irreparable damage, and I'm not skilled enough or foolish enough to attempt it.

"The sooner you summon your familiar, the better, according to the books. You're supposed to *bond,* grow your magic *together.* That's the whole point of having a familiar." Willow urges.

"And it would be pretty cool." Asher says.

All three of them are looking at me. Waiting to see what I think. And all three of them are right. It would be cool to do a proper spell to test how far I've come, but the timing isn't great. We have a lot to do, and this may be an unnecessary distraction.

Maybe that's exactly what I need.

"Let's do it." I say.

Willow jumps out of her seat, clapping her hands.

"Are you sure?" Ren sends, assessing me.

"I'm sure."

He's worried I've been pushing myself too hard these past few weeks. He says I need to slow down and take a break.

BETRAYED

That I'll burn out. Asher agrees with him, except she thinks I'm hiding something. Keeping a secret from them that's weighing me down.

She's right. I am. But I don't let that show on my face as I kiss Ren's cheek.

"You'd better eat something first, then." He says. "You've been practising all morning, and you know magic needs energy to work."

It's true. From what we've been able to find in our books, it seems my ability to cast spells is directly linked to my body creating usable energy. The more fuel I consume, the easier it is to draw on my power. My stomach growls as if to annunciate his point.

"You two can get snacks." Willow says pointing at Asher and Ren. "Make yourself useful while Merle and I set up."

"Yes, ma'am!" Asher jumps to her feet with an exaggerated salute. "Come on Du Lac, duty calls."

"We won't do any of the fun stuff without you." I say, grinning as Asher tugs Ren out of the door.

Once we're alone, Willow clears a space in the piles of books on the floor and sits cross–legged, motioning for me to join her. She hands me a battered notebook with a butterfly on the cover. It's full of scribbles about the spell, working out the right words and exactly what tools we need. There's a lot of literature on the subject, pages and pages of notes to trawl through.

"So we've got the candles and the oil, the herbs, the salt," Willow ticks the list off on her fingers as she counts, pushing the ingredients towards me. Nearly all the spells we found use a pink or white candle as part of the ritual, as well as scented oils and various dried herbs.

In the end, we chose to use witch grass for its links to

4

animal magic, passion flower to attract friendship, rose and sunflower for energy and protection, and strawberry leaf for success and good fortune. I grew what I could myself, but Asher went to find sunflowers and rose petals at the local market when they didn't bloom as expected. Last week, Ren, Lore and I spent an afternoon drying and chopping everything in preparation. Now the concoction sits in a little glass jar, waiting to be awoken by my magic.

I take the candle and the almond oil, squeezing a few drops into my hand. The spell says to rub the oil into the wax, coating it entirely. As I'm finishing up, Ren and Asher reappear, arms loaded with sandwiches, coffee, and cake.

"Etta sent you this," Ren says, placing a muffin in my greasy hand. It has cream cheese icing and a little carrot shaped sprinkle on top. "She says it's got raisins in, just how you like."

"I'll go down and thank her later." I respond, spraying crumbs everywhere as I shove the cake into my mouth. "So *good.*"

"Be careful!" Willow shrieks. "You're making a mess, and this is important!"

Asher, now perched in the armchair behind Willow, rolls her eyes and I can't help but laugh.

"Now go and wash your hands." Willow pushes a tub of salt towards me. Its sea salt, untreated, as raw as it gets, also bought from the market. According to our research, it's used for cleansing. It should purify my magic as it leaves my body, ensuring I summon my familiar rather than something more sinister.

"Yes, boss."

When I'm back from using the little bathroom across the hall, scrubbed and ready, the others are sitting in a circle, all cross–legged. I fold in beside them, being careful not to touch anything with my newly cleansed fingers. In the centre of the

BETRAYED

circle is the pink candle, shimmering like a blossoming rose petal, the mixture of herbs scattered around the base. Once I'm comfy, Willow leans forwards and smudges a finger of oil across each of my eyebrows. Eyebright to help focus my magic, to make it more powerful. Around the circle lay crystals, tiger's eye, onyx and green amethyst.

"Are you all ready?" I ask.

They nod in unison, tight–lipped and wide eyed. The air seems to have taken on a thick, heavy quality, thrumming with something vital and alive. They've seen me do magic before, of course, and wield much stronger power, but somehow this is different. It's deep magic, magic of blood and bone and creation. A once in a lifetime opportunity. Something they will never see again. I clear my throat and there's the grating sound of a striking match as Ren lights the candle.

I close my eyes. Having spent hours writing and memorising them, I know exactly what words to say. I wait for a moment, concentrating completely on the task at hand, allowing everyone to settle. I've dreamt about her, my familiar. Her shadow and the colour of her fur. I focus on that image now, flashes of grey, black, and soft fawn. Of deep, ringed eyes that shine turquoise and gold. It's almost as if I can feel her waiting for my call. Exhaling, I begin:

"Where I go, you go,
What I need, you provide.
Whatever your form,
Come now to my side.
Bound by blood,
In mind and soul.
Come forth my creature,
Make this half whole."

The hum of my magic wraps itself around the words, tasting them, bringing them to life. I open my eyes to the candle flickering and the crystals jittering in their places. The others are staring, eyes glued to the herbs which suddenly burst into flames. When they've burned away to nothing, the rest of the instruments go still.

"What happens now?" Asher asks after a few moments of silence.

"We wait for the full moon tomorrow night. We'll probably have to go outside to find it. To the faery rings." Willow says the last tentatively. We don't go out there if we can help it. It's too dangerous. But their magic draws things to them. It's quite likely they'll draw my familiar too.

"Do you think it worked?" Ren says, squeezing my fingers.

"We did everything right. I'm hopeful."

In reality, I'm more than hopeful, but I don't want to get *their* hopes up. In the last second, before the herbs disappeared and the candle flame guttered, a name was whispered in my ear. The name of my familiar. *Aila.*

I spend the rest of the day in the library with Willow. First recounting the details of the spell and how excited we are that it went to plan, then turning our attention to the prophecy Merlin gave me. We've been working on it ever since Lore woke up, trying to attribute meaning to his cryptic words. The trouble is that there's too *much* meaning, so it all means nothing.

A few weeks ago, we changed our focus to prophecy itself– the delivery of it, the recording of it, how the events played out in real life —with the hope we'd learn something new. We think we've cracked part of the first line; '*When enemies come disguised as friends',* referring to the fae's ability

BETRAYED

to take on other people's identities as Morgwese did with Shelby and the unidentified Royal did with Mum.

At the thought of her, there's a twinge in my chest. A tightening of the muscles in my throat. It's easier now to accept what happened, but thinking of her still hurts. It's like there's two separate parts to my grief, completely different but also co–dependent.

There's *rational grief*, which understands the inevitability of death, that it comes to us all and we can't control it. That part knows Mum is gone and that I must move forwards. It knows what happened was horrible, a tragedy, but her death can't dictate what remains of my life. It understands there's only one way to get over it. To keep rationalising. To forget. It'll be okay because it has to be. It's really as simple as that.

Emotional grief knows none of these rules. Sometimes, I'll be reading a book and a word will remind me of her voice. Or I'll think of something to tell her only remembering at the last second she's not here to tell. Those parts are the worst, and there's nothing to be done about them. There's no warning when they'll hit. When I absentmindedly wonder what Mum's doing, whether she's heard from Aunt Hazel and Ali, and then I remember she doesn't exist anymore.

People say 'never' all the time. Things they'd never say or do or believe. But *never* is an entirely different beast when it's applied to somebody you will *never* see again. And it's unbearable. Just time, stretching out infinitely. One day, I'll have been alive for longer without my parents (unless Morgwese has her way) than with them. I won't remember how they looked or sounded. They will be lost to me forever, and it's a bitter pill to swallow.

"'*The lines of blood will break.*'" Willow muses, snapping me back to the present. I'm glad she's looking down at her notebook instead of at me, giving me time to wipe my eyes. Ren and Asher are playing chess in the corner, well out of the way. "Well, they didn't *break*, did they? You used the Templar's bloodline to cast Morgwese and Elaine back. We're stronger than ever."

"Yes. But it could be a warning, not something that's already happened. See, in the next line, '*the tied will come undone*'. It's another thing referring to separation, of being cut."

"Hmm." Willow sighs, the fluffy end of her ball–point pen wobbling as she jots down the word. This is what we're trying now, breaking it down into keywords and similar themes. So far we have: *betrayal, death, fire, madness,* and now, *separation.* "It's not looking good for us, is it?"

"Best to just end it all now, I reckon." Asher says as she puts Ren's king in checkmate.

"There's still '*hope*'," Willow smiles and adds it to the list.

"But only after burning flames, or whatever it says. Looking forward to that, are you?"

"Stop it! It might just be metaphorical. A lot of prophecies are."

"Let's go eat." Ren says, getting out of his seat and coming to my side, offering me his hand.

"Good idea." I can't help grinning at him. He's so lovely. Shadows from the fading light emphasising the sharpness of his jaw and the soft bow of his lips. I still can't believe how lucky I am.

"Come on then, Etta's making stew and I don't want to miss it. Then I've got to see Joth."

"Have fun with that. I'll be going straight to bed." I say, looking into his eyes, hoping he gets the message that I want to be alone.

In the aftermath of Morgwese's banishment, we stayed

BETRAYED

together every night, and we try our best to do that now, but it's not always possible. Sleep is something we've all lost. In between nightmares, bouts of insomnia, and endless, endless tasks, it's difficult to find time to rest.

And don't forget about your midnight visitor. I think to myself.

Yes, that too. That's the real reason he can't stay in my room tonight. The secret I've been keeping from them for months.

"That's the most sensible thing you've said all day." He grins and kisses my temple.

Asher purses her lips and gives me a stern look. She's onto me, as per usual. I want to tell them, I do. I don't keep anything from them, I never have. But on this point, I'm sworn to secrecy. I have my orders.

We file downstairs behind Willow, who's back to excitedly chattering about my familiar. Lux, Lore, and Eyrie, a now permanent addition to their team, already have plates in front of them when we sit down. Asher ruffles her sister's hair affectionately before Eyrie shoos her away.

Lux gives me a grim smile from his position opposite. That's all his smiles are nowadays, grey and concerned, not reaching his eyes. He's never been as openly excitable as Lore, always more pensive and brooding, but his sister's change has hit him hard. He has purple circles under his eyes, his cheeks thin and pale. I want to reach out to him, to squeeze his fingers or ruffle *his* hair, to let him know I'm with him, that I understand. Instead, he turns away from me and goes back to trailing his fork through his dinner.

When we've finished eating, I make my excuses and head upstairs, kissing Ren goodnight before I go to my room. There's no use trying to sleep when I know I'll be woken again

10

at any moment, so instead I read through one of my history books until my eyes are sore.

As the clock strikes midnight, I wonder if I've misread the signs. Maybe my visitor won't be coming after all. I'm about to switch off the lamp when taps begin to echo on my door.

Tap–tap, tap–tap–tap, tap–tap.

Not a very intricate secret knock, but one that's served us well. I get up and go towards the sound, my heart sinking with each step. When I finally get there and pull back the heavy wood, I'm met with watery eyes and sniffles.

"Come on, Sweetheart, come in. It's all right." I say, opening my arms. "It's all right. Don't worry."

Lux steps inside, wrapping his own arms around me, sobbing into my jumper.

2

The next morning, I wake up feeling groggy and disoriented. Usually, it doesn't take long to calm Lux down after his nightmares, but last night was particularly bad.

We all have them, lingering terrors from the night of Lore's attack. My dream is always the same. Joth comes to the hall, waving his arms and calling my name, telling me that Lore's awake. When we get to the room, I know something's wrong. Sometimes it's Lux's face that gives it away, other times it's Lore. When she turns to me, she has blue rings around her eyes and rows and rows of sharp teeth.

Lux's nightmares are different. When Lore was unconscious, he could hear her sending messages, pleading to be woken up and let free. I could hear her too when I placed my hand over theirs. The sweet hum of Lore's magical spark connecting with my own. We thought it would stop when she woke, but we didn't account for part of her still being gone. Lux says he can hear her, in the small hours of the morning when he can't sleep:

"It's so dark down there, and so cold. I can hear Lore crying, but I can't get to her. Crying all the time—"

I shudder and climb out of bed, making my way to the bathroom to shower. I've tried to convince him they're just nightmares and Lore isn't stuck anywhere, but he doesn't believe me. Maybe she *is* stuck. Waiting for me to rescue her. I think some reassurance from Joth or Ren might help, but he's sworn me to secrecy. He doesn't want them to see, the others, the knights, how badly he's coping. Instead, we've resorted to herbal teas and meditation, light sleeping potions and breathing exercises. He's a little better, and most nights, when I check everyone's auras to see if they're safely tucked in bed, he's asleep. But sometimes, he needs someone to chase the terrors away.

While my spell casting powers have grown a lot since I claimed them, they've not advanced nearly as much as my telepathic abilities. I can send messages with my mind and watch other people's memories like films. I can also 'project' memories, just like I did with the vision Merlin gave me all that time ago.

I suppose I've got him to thank for what's been happening to me recently.

I keep having visions. At least, that's what I think they are. They feel different from memories, like I'm really, truly *there*. And they're always about the future. Some things I've seen have actually happened, like Mona dropping a whole tray of tea in the hallway. Mostly I can't make sense of the snippets, or I can't remember them properly. All I *do* remember is it being cold. Cold to the bone. And sometimes I hear a woman

BETRAYED

laughing.

I'm quite confident that these flashes hold the key to fixing Lore's amnesia, that they're a message pointing me towards the answers we seek.

From my late night studies, I know visions can be induced, but it's dark and mysterious mind magic. Dipping in and out of memories past is one thing, jumping to glimpses of the future is entirely another. It's a little less risky than searching for Lore's memories, and I'd be the only one to get hurt. I did manage to find a spell, one that will allow me to search through my dreams and enter the vision I want. It takes a lot of power and I'll need help from the others. But I haven't had the courage to ask them yet, especially with Ren and Asher sulking. I know they don't understand what's happening with Lux, that they're worried, but I literally *can't* explain. The oath I swore crippling me.

I've asked Mona what she thinks about the visions. She's different from the others. Hard and unforgiving in her judgement of things. She's as smart as a fox, and as sly as one. She understands that if there was a choice between Lore and me, I'd always sacrifice myself, that I'm willing to die to bring her home. Mona thinks we can do it, but only as a last resort.

On the bright side, having a familiar is supposed to help. I might be able to draw on her power, or use her as an anchor. At the thought of her, a warm shiver of nerves runs down my spine. The spell has to have worked and I can't wait to meet her.

As I rinse the suds from my hair, I cast my mind out into the Templar searching for Ren. Everyone in the Templar has a very specific aura and colour associated with their brain, and once I know them, it's easy to locate who I want. Like Asher, her light pulses bright and blue in one of the rooms above me. Probably the library, as she's with Willow, whose own light is a healthy mix of green and yellow. Ren's is blue too, but much darker than Asher's. Sometimes his aura is streaked with red and black. I've told the others about it, and we've spent hours analysing what they might mean, what secrets about their personalities they hold. After a moment of searching with no luck, I turn the water off, wring out my hair and towel myself dry. He must be in the greenhouse.

My greenhouse is a recent addition to the Templar grounds, something that Joth and Ren had built for me for Christmas. I'd been studying the books from Merlin's cave and found one on herbalism. I wanted to try out all the potions and medicines and needed somewhere to grow the necessary ingredients. On Christmas morning Ren led me through the halls with my eyes closed and into the garden, and all of them, Mona, Etta, Benji, Asher, and Eyrie, Willow, Joth, and the twins, had been waiting next to a glass shed with a red bow on the door. Inside were all the plants and tools I'd asked for. It's by far the best Christmas gift I've ever received.

That's the last truly lovely day I can remember. When no one's smiles came with shadows under their eyes, when our laughter wasn't full of hollow notes. The last time the muscles in my neck didn't ache and the skin on my hands was soft, and yet to see the hundreds of hours of potion making, weeding and spell casting.

I pull on my leggings, jumper and boots, and head out into the hallway. It's still cold enough for condensation to collect on the windows. At least there are signs of winter ending. The bright shine of new green through the frost, the white sunlight tinted with yellow and gold.

I sneak out of the kitchen door and over the flagstones to the entrance of the greenhouse. Much to Lux and Lore's dismay, the glass isn't actually green. It's clear and held up by a sturdy frame of wood from an Ash tree. Ash, Willow says,

BETRAYED

has magical properties associated with healing, which is what most of the plants are for. The inside is full of wooden work benches, trellises brimming with colourful flowers, and stacks of pots and gardening equipment. The beams are strung with fairy lights, and there's even a couple of soft bean bags thrown in the corner for anyone who wants to relax.

I push open the door to find Ren leaning over a tray of dried lavender, dutifully trimming the buds from the stems. Today we should be able to make a new sleeping potion we've been waiting to try.

"Oh, of course," he says, grinning and straightening up. "You've missed all the boring stuff, again."

"Sorry." I wrap my arms around him. Sliding my palms up to his shoulders and around his neck. "Thank you for doing it."

"It's no problem." He kisses the top of my head. "What's next?"

"The valerian." I pull away from him, motioning to the plant pot on my left. Growing in it are the long stems of the beautiful plant, sprouting bunches of tiny pink buds. Some flowers are open, the petals turning white towards the edges. "Dig around a little. We need the root."

He picks up the pot and searches in the soil while I turn my attention to setting up the small cauldron and chopping board. Asher proudly presented me with the black pewter monstrosity on Christmas day, her addition to the greenhouse.

"*You're not a proper witch if you've not got one of these.*" She'd said. *"And don't worry, I've got a top quality broomstick in mind for your birthday."*

When I'm ready, Ren offers me the bundle in his palm. It looks like a tiny potato that's been left in a cupboard too long, shrivelled roots sticking out at odd angles. I take it from him and chop it into pieces, scooping them onto the edge of the long silver blade and dropping them into the pot.

"Do you think we're ready to meet with the knights?" Ren's voice breaks the quiet. It's a question I've been expecting, but wishing he wouldn't ask.

We've been in what feels like hundreds of meetings, all of them blurring into one. They always ask the same questions. *What of Morgwese? Of Lore's condition? How will we restore her? How will we protect ourselves?* Then there's all the other stuff. All the queries in relation to their land, the law review that's necessary but an absolute pain in the—

"Merle?"

"Sorry." I say, brushing my hand through my hair. "You know where we're at. We don't have anything new for them." I go to the trellis against the far wall. The beautiful faces of the passion flowers stare up at me. They're the most exotic plants we've grown. I pluck one of the heads and twirl it in my fingers. It has white petals, spines of purple and blue growing from its pale yellow centre, lime green pistils sprouting from it. Nature's answer to the archery board. I take it to the workbench and slice it like the valerian. "I don't feel Morgwese or sense her magic. Lore's getting better, but not fast enough. She still doesn't have her old memories. You already know I'm at the end of what I can do for her with magic." I break off, guilt pounding against my rib cage, the knife trembling in my hand. I hate it, that I can't do more, that I still can't *fix* her.

Ren, as always knowing exactly what I want without having to ask, first places two sprigs of mint on the chopping board in front of me, then wraps his arms around me, disarming me of the wobbly knife. He takes the buds of lavender he separated earlier and adds them to the mix. "Mer, six months ago, you had no idea any of this even existed. *Since then,* you've banished an evil faery queen, settled tens if not hundreds of trivial disputes. Together we've got Lore to where

BETRAYED

she's building new memories, mostly remembering them—"

"She never remembers you though, does she?" A horrible, spiteful whisper whistles around my mind.

"—And that's just the stuff you've done for other people! What about how far you've progressed with your magic? And with everything that happened before, you didn't have time to grieve."

I squeeze my arms around my middle. "There's no time for that. We've waited long enough to act. Half of them still believe it's over." And mostly I don't trust the knights, not really. As individuals, the knights are loyal enough, but the unit is dysfunctional. They've got too much power. Power that should be reserved for the king and queen.

Even so, I've grown to like some of them more, Lydia Geraint and Greg Tristen being among my new favourites. Since Christmas, Lydia's been visiting the Templar regularly, more involved than ever before. She recently announced that she and her fiance Oliver are expecting a child. Everyone's ecstatic at the news. It's the first time a baby's been born within the Templar's circle in almost two decades, the last being Owen Lamorak, who's now seventeen. Joth has been fussing over her duties, not wanting any unnecessary stress to be placed on mother or baby. We've given her a permanent room, and she's able to come and go between her own estate in Scotland as she pleases.

Ren sighs. We've talked about this before. Without a plan, we can't fend off their apathy. "There has to be something we can do, something we've overlooked. Water, please."

I close my eyes and imagine the cauldron filling half way with clear liquid. The energy it takes to complete the task makes my head spin. I should've eaten breakfast. When I open my eyes, Ren is frowning.

18

"There is something," I say. "But you won't like it."

"Do I ever?" He cocks an eyebrow, staring down at me with a smirk.

"Tonight we're going to find my familiar, and when she gets here, once we've properly bonded, I'll be able to use her to amplify my magic." I take a deep breath. "I want to induce a vision. I've been having them, or snippets anyway, and I truly think they have the answers we need."

"It's dangerous, messing with stuff like that."

"Yes, I *know* it's dangerous!" I edge my way past him, pacing the floor. "But I'll practise first, and I *can* do it. I know I can. And it's better than leaving Lore where she is, better than what's going on with–" *Lux,* I almost say before clamping my mouth shut.

Ren rolls his eyes and turns his back to me, hurt flashing across his features. I've tried to persuade Lux to let me, but the answer is no.

I lean back against the workbench clenching my fists in frustration, watching him assemble the stove, placing the pot on top. With a flick of my finger, I light the flame and he can't help but smile.

"Look," I say, before Ren can open his mouth. It's true that I can't *tell* him about Lux's night terrors, but I might have a bit of wiggle room. "Do you remember the oath I swore to? Before I went into the cave?"

"It's basically the same thing we all swear to–"

"But it's not exactly the same, is it?" I take hold of his hands. "Knights swear to serve and protect, and to uphold Templar law. I swore to the same thing, obviously, but there's an extra caveat to mine."

"Which is?"

"'*Upon bestowment of your powers, you'll be bound to the Pendragons,*'" I say, quoting Joth's words exactly. I know

BETRAYED

them by heart, after all. I've spent hours thinking about how I might get around them. "*'To serve them and keep their secrets until the end of their lives or yours.'* Do you understand what I'm saying to you? To serve them and *keep their secrets*."

His eyes widen. I can almost see the cogs whirring in his brain. "Oh." He says. "*Oh.*"

"So please believe me when I tell you, I don't want this. But my hands are tied."

"Is it Lux or Lore? Or both of them?"

I give him a long, hard stare. He sighs again, scrubbing his hand across his chin. "Is it serious?"

Now it's my turn to sigh. I shouldn't say anymore, but it's cruel not to ease his mind. "No. Not really. They aren't in danger."

"All right." He slides the collection of ingredients onto the edge of his knife before dumping them into the now bubbling water. When he turns back to me, he's smiling. "Tell me more about these visions.

3

REN

I can't fault the logic of Merle's plan. She paces as I stir the potion– a sleeping draught that promises no dreams– occasionally flicking her hazel eyes to meet mine. The sunlight glints off the gold in them and makes her skin glow. She's beautiful, always, but I can tell she's worn out. She has been for months, even if she doesn't see it for herself.

It amazes me how she's constantly able to adjust, to take things in her stride without question. Nothing is too much. There's no task too great. Whether Willow needs assistance in the library, Joth wants to discuss defence plans, or Mona needs help to change a bedsheet, she's there. Ready and waiting to *serve*.

Asher's seen it too, I know that. The dark circles under Merle's eyes, her ragged nails, how thin she is. Asher was the one who figured out Merle was hiding something, too. She knew before I did. We've tried to help, to share the load. But

BETRAYED

what use are we? Lowly knights, compared to her, the true heir of Merlin Wyllt?

"So?" Merle says. She has her arms crossed over her middle, one hand playing with the pearl rosary that has long since replaced the ring at her throat. "What do you think?"

"Let me get this right." I put down the wooden spoon so I can check the points off on my fingers. "You want to cast a spell so you can go into your dreams and try to find the right vision? Not only is this spell extremely difficult to cast–"

"Not *extremely*—"

I hold up my hand, and Merle quietens. "You'll use your familiar to anchor yourself here and draw on its power if you need it—"

"Then I'll find the vision. It'll tell me the answers and solve all our problems." She scowls, rolling her eyes and putting her hands on her hips. "I know it isn't perfect, Ren. It's reckless, and I might not be powerful enough, and my familiar might not even show up! But we're running out of time."

"I know we are." I say. "It's worth telling the others. Willow can help find a spell." I hold out my hand to her and she takes it. Squeezing her fingers, I pull her close and wrap my arm around her shoulders. She smells good, like lilacs and honey, but feels brittle under my touch. As if she might shatter. I know she's close to the edge, how much pressure there is to perform her duty. And it's an endless duty, it turns out. Endless and thankless. "We'll work it out. If that is the only way, so be it."

"All right." She says.

It wasn't exactly the right thing to say. I never seem able to find them, the words I need when I need them.

"Come on, the others will be awake by now, probably eating breakfast–"

"I could definitely eat."

22

"There's a surprise." I plant a kiss on her forehead and pull her through the door into the cold.

Asher and Willow are already in the hall, and have saved us seats directly across from them. They've loaded up plates of pastries and mugs of coffee. It's been extra helpful having them here. Now we're officially friends. Willow and I never paid much attention to each other before Merle arrived. She was always working, buried in piles of books and scrolls, and I was always babysitting the twins. Teaching them sword skills and how to climb trees. I never minded it, really. I didn't even realise I was lonely until Merle came along.

Then there's Asher, who we probably wouldn't have got through the last few months without. As soon as she realised Lore's memory wasn't coming back, she requested that Amalie Percival take charge of her estate in the North so she could stay. She's strong and brave, and loyal to a fault. I couldn't have asked for a better person to glue us all together. Asher has even brought Willow out of her shell.

The knight in question looks up from her breakfast, shining a quick smile at Merle before pushing a plate of food under her nose. It's also nice to have a knight on our team whose opinion actually holds some weight around here.

My reputation is tarnished and has been since before I was born. I've been working for years to cement my seat, to pay back in good deeds what Lancelot did in bad ones. He was accused, and unfortunately, actually guilty of committing high treason. Adultery with the queen, saving her from execution, and abandoning his knightly duties for a life of love. It was agreed upon my arrival here, by the knights already in residence, that I would commit to ten years of impeccable service as a squire and if I complete them without a hitch, I'll wash away the sins of my ancestors and start anew.

BETRAYED

Between mouthfuls of eggs, Merle whispers her plan to Asher and Willow. Willow listens attentively, as always, her fingers tapping on the table as if they're itching to be writing notes. Asher keeps her face still, eventually turning to look at me. We aren't telepathic like Mer is, but I don't need to read minds to tell what she's thinking.

And you've agreed to this, have you?

I shrug. *Do you have a better idea?*

"We don't know if your familiar is going to show up. No point planning until then. Not if it all depends on that." Asher finally says.

"*Of course* it's going to show up!" Willow swats at Asher's arm before taking Merle's hand. "You did everything exactly right. Of course it will."

Thank god someone's got a brain cell. I think, catching Willow's eye, giving her an encouraging grin. Where Asher's pragmatism and wicked sense of humour have been excellent for problem solving and lightening the mood, it's Willow's gentle words that seem to bring Merle back to us. She always knows exactly what to say. They share a quiet and sensible way of going about things, a calm in the storm of demands and duty. It's safe to say that subtlety isn't something Asher understands too well.

"I didn't mean that." Asher sighs. "But I don't want you to get your hopes up. Let's just take it one step at a time, shall we?"

Merle tips her chin up, their eyes meeting. I know they're talking, words we can't hear. After a few moments, she nods.

I'm glad a steady peace has settled, especially since I have somewhere else I need to be. I drain the last of my coffee and push back from the table.

"Where are you going?" Merle asks, twisting in her seat.

"I promised Lore I'd hang out with her this morning."

She nods. Usually we spend as much time with Lore as possible, helping her remember her life before Elaine's attack. We've made progress, but it's slow. She knows who I am and who Joth is, who Lux and Eyrie are. We've spent the last six months painstakingly going through all the details of her previous life. She hasn't *remembered* much, a few snippets here and there, but she's learning. The cruellest part is that she always forgets Merle, no matter how many times we explain who she is and why she's here.

"All right. Take her some pancakes if she's not had breakfast. She'll like that."

"She certainly will." I lean down and kiss between her eyebrows, the tip of her nose, her lips. "I'll find you when I'm done."

Lore's waiting patiently for my arrival, sitting in the hall outside her bedroom door. She's grown an inch or two, her long legs spilling out into the hallway. I was thirteen when the twins showed up. I remember Joth pulling me into his office and explaining that we'd be having two babies come to live with us, twins, very important, who I could think of as my cousins. Part of my duty was to care for them, and even though it's been my duty, I've enjoyed every single moment of it. They're my siblings, kids I've taught to read and write, to walk and climb trees.

I miss Lore all the time. She's always been so kind, so free with her smiles and stupid jokes. My partner in crime, the happy–go–lucky 'ying' to Lux's serious and noble 'yang'. Now, though, she's serious too. Gone. Trapped inside her own mind. I try to stay positive for all our sakes, but it weighs on me. Every time I look into her eyes, and don't recognise the person I see, a tiny piece of my soul withers.

"Ren?" she asks.

BETRAYED

I'm not sure if she's checking who I am, or asking whether I'm listening. "You're up early for a lazy bones."

"Says you."

"Watch it." I ruffle her hair, causing her to pull a face and bat my hand away. "No Lux today?"

"He says he's too tired. Didn't get much sleep last night."

Join the club.

We head back upstairs and into one of the vacant rooms we use for a classroom. There's still a table, a couple of plastic chairs and a row of yellow bookshelves. On the back wall is a large blackboard, covered in chalk scribbles and various photographs. Lore throws herself onto a large cushion we've stolen from the library. Her ash coloured hair is braided down her back, grey eyes reading everything on the wall. Learning, remembering? I really can't tell.

"Do we have to do lessons today? I'm tired. My brain hurts." Lore says, leaning back and closing her eyes.

"We don't *have* to do anything."

"Where's Mel?"

"Merle."

"Where is she? Didn't she want to see me?"

"Did you want to see her?"

"I like her, if that's what you mean."

"Is that what you mean?"

"You're annoying." She huffs. Then her expression goes blank. "I know I make her sad. Is that why she didn't come?"

"No." I sit down across from her. "And it's not you that makes her sad, Lop."

"You call me that because it's how I used to say my name."

"Do you remember?"

"You told me."

I nod. It's true, I did tell her. It stabs like a knife that she doesn't remember. When she first started talking, she was so excited to get her words out that sometimes she'd run them into each other; *whatchadoin? Comansee! Renquick!* Even her own name flowed into one: *LorPendragon.* So we ended up Renwick and Lop. Over the years it's died out, but I still call her that if she's anxious, which is most of the time nowadays. Much like Merle, she's got a permanent look of pensiveness on her face, as if she's somewhere else. I can't imagine what it must be like, memories slipping through her mind like sand through an hour glass. I see it sometimes in her eyes, if she doesn't laugh at an inside joke, or when Lux talks about things she can't remember.

"I make everyone sad—"

"We've talked about this."

Lore closes her mouth, her cheeks flushing a dull red.

We've talked about it many times. How we know it's not her fault, and she knows we aren't sad because *of* her, but because of what she's lost. That we love her and want to help, but it never changes anything.

Are you surprised? Do you think anything other than getting her memories back will help?

"Can I ask you something?" I say. I've been thinking about it all morning, whether it's a good idea, whether I should pry, but if Merle's hiding a secret for the twins, Lore might tell me what it is. "Have you asked Merle to do something for you? Or told her something she can't tell me?"

"What?" Lore wrinkles her nose and scowls.

"If there is," I proceed carefully now, the clouds of a storm brewing around her. "You can tell me about it. You can tell me about anything. I'll never be mad, I promise."

Instead of the thunder I expect from her, a sunny smile breaks across Lore's face. "I know that. I like Merle, I *really* do, but why would I tell her something secret and not you? You

BETRAYED

always know everything anyway." I study her for a minute. I can always see the signs of her lies; picking at her nails and shuffling her feet, but right now she's just looking at me with mild puzzlement. "Can I find Lux now?"

"Okay."

She gets up from her seat and walks towards the door, then she stops in her tracks, pointing towards a stuffed toy on the bookshelf. It's a grey dog with floppy ears and a loose button eye. "I got that with Merle. Before. He's called David."

"Did she tell you that?"

"No." Lore turns to look at me, her grey eyes glowing. "I remembered."

I find Merle back in the greenhouse, bottling up the potion we made earlier. A dark purple concoction that smells of lavender, chamomile, and sleep. It's not the first time Lore's remembered a small fraction of something, but it's certainly the biggest thing she's remembered without prompting, and it relates to Merle. It might give her some hope that finally we're doing something right.

"She truly remembered?" Merle asks after I've relayed the encounter. She looks better after eating something. There's some colour in her cheeks, dark tendrils of hair framing her face. I pull her closer to me, sweeping my thumb along the fine ridge of her jaw, angling our foreheads together.

"She truly did."

Mer kisses me hard on the mouth, wrapping her arms around my neck. I run my palm down the length of her spine, the fine muscles of her back tensing under my touch. Then she leans back, pressing her forehead to mine again. Smiling a dazzling beautiful smile that makes my heart ache. "That's wonderful news. Really it is."

It's made more wonderful by the fact it makes Merle so

happy.

I leave her to mix her potions, she's working on something dangerous now, a magic killing potion called *Letum de Mors*. She has to wear gloves up to her elbows. The potion's purpose is to close the faery rings, a last resort to banish magic from the very ground and seal them shut for good. We've tried it only once before, a single dark drop into the centre of the ring we banished Morgwese with. After the ground shook and threw up foul smelling sludge, we knew it was truly destroyed. Any hint of magic eaten up. That's why Mer has to wear the gloves. If it gets on her skin, it could seriously injure her. It's worth it, she says, to close the rings forever.

I grab a beanbag and take out my notebook, my research contribution to solving the prophecy. The line I'm supposed to solve is:

The mad will rule in the court of the dead,
the tied will come undone.

As with most prophecy, it means nothing. Or it could lend itself to a thousand different things. And it's almost always foreboding. So far, we think it means something about the twins' rule and Avalon.

The tied will come undone.

Maybe that's what's happening to us now, the bond we forged when we vanquished Morgwese, slowly unravelling into loose threads and frayed ends.

No, I tell myself. *Enough doom and gloom.*

I can't let it happen. I won't. Not now we've got everything to fight for. So I turn back to my book and begin my study again.

4

It's almost midnight when everyone's ready to head into the woods. It's still cold out, frost glittering on blades of grass, the air biting at any exposed skin. I pull my jumper closer as we step into the night.

I've had a strange feeling bothering me all day, an anxious tug on my heart. It's the same urge I felt when I made the blood wish, the desperate pull of the faery rings. Something is definitely out there. Waiting.

The full moon is high in the sky, its waxy yellow face shining down on us, turning my friends into silver shadows and dark lines. Willow is most nervous, her hand clasped in mine while we walk. Her fingers are shaking with anticipation, the hope she'll see magic come to life.

Ren and Asher aren't so excited, especially not after telling them about my plan to induce a vision if I'm successful in summoning my familiar. They're both dressed in dark coats and armed with iron daggers. The faery rings, whether or not

I like it, are a dangerous place. I always thought they were mine, mine and Dad's. But it was never so. Morgwese has tainted them, luring me in to do her awful bidding. They're right to be sceptical, I suppose, even if I'm sure it's safe. Tonight, those rings are mine.

I come to a stop, untangling my hand from Willow's. "Stay here."

"I don't think—" Ren starts, but Willow raises her now empty palm.

"She's the Heir of Merlin." She says the title with such reverence, as if Merlin has any say in what I do.

"I'll be fine." I go to Ren, squeeze his fingers, and kiss him lightly on the cheek. "I won't be long."

He grumbles but lets it go. Asher's watchful eyes meet mine and she nods almost imperceptibly.

"Be back in five minutes," she sends. *"I don't like it out here."*

I give her a thumbs up and step into the trees. I suppose it is eerie in the dark, especially if you don't know where you are. Branches loom overhead, casting dark and twisted shadows across the uneven ground. Moss, mint green and lacey in the light from my torch, hangs down like shimmering silver cobwebs, coating the night in mystery. But I *do* know these woods. I know every step I take.

I sense the first faery circle before I see it.

The ring is small and full of incomplete holes, its limbs stolen by the frost. She's here somewhere. My familiar. Waiting in the dark.

Twenty paces forward and I find the ring I want. It's always this one, the one I opened when I was a child, and then again six months ago. There are still lines in the ground surrounding it, shards of grass, darkened from my blood poking from the ground. The mushroom edges are a little

BETRAYED

dishevelled, broken stems and drooping tops. Inside the ring, however, is pristine, as if I never disturbed it. And right in the centre, waiting as promised, is Aila.

My heart swells as I step over the threshold, familiar magic enveloping me in lilac and lavender.

The small cat raises its head, luminous turquoise eyes staring into my soul. She's a lynx, I think. Soft lines of tan fur cover her face, freckles of black dotted around her pink nose. As she stands, I fall to my knees.

She's mine, made of my magic. I can feel her heart beating, the swell of her breath in my lungs. The tips of her ears have tufts of black fur stemming from them, tiny claws protruding from already huge paws.

There's still part of the ritual yet to perform. It wasn't in any of the books we read, or in any of Merlin's prophecies.

The thing people don't say in books is to do *real* magic – to control that dangerous beast and wield it as your own, to heal the sick, and create life –requires sacrifice. *Blood.* There's always an exchange, a willing gift from the witch in return for the use of boundless, endless, power. It's not like growing plants or reading tarot cards, that needs only a breath. A tiny thing for a tiny favour. But to create a familiar? A creature bonded to me and everything I do, something I have called into being, that I have *wished* for. Only blood will do.

This is something I just *know* now. Every so often, it's like there's someone guiding me along, giving me instruction. I've got to bind us. Make us whole. I reach into the pocket of my coat and draw out Dad's old penknife.

I peel open the blade and press its tip into the soft flesh of my forearm, just underneath the mark that Merlin left me. It's as clear as the day it happened and will never fade.

That, I've since come to learn, was my first Witch Mark, a tattoo of power, made through pain and inscribed on skin, a constant connection to blood and sacrifice. Merlin's sigil ties me to him as the Witches Knot I'm about to draw will tie me to Aila.

I've been practising the symbol for the last month, how to form the knot in one continuous line. The more I carve in one go, the stronger our bond will be.

I let out a breath and close my eyes, allowing my muscle memory to take over, following the loops and whirls of the knot. At least these cuts don't have to be deep, only precise. As the tip of the knife traces the lines I've diligently practised, I know I'm going to make it in one.

"Your name is *Aila*." I whisper into the dark. "And you are mine, and I am yours. Until death divides us."

The magic in me grows, swells until blankets us, invading every atom of our beings and weaving them together. Ice rages through my veins, but not enough to dampen the pain of the blade. To stop the burn of my skin as it tears or the line of hot fire that follows.

I open my eyes as I connect the lines, looking straight to Aila when it's done. She twitches her nose and takes two steps forward, then she sticks out her tongue, dragging its rough spines over the mark, sealing it with her own offering. Crimson colours the white fur around her mouth as she laps at the wound.

"Oh," I say out loud, startling myself. "*Oh.*"

As soon as she's finished, the Witches Knot sears into my skin, glowing orange and red. For a moment, there's no air, no smell of lilac or hum of magic. There's only agony. I double over with the force of it, screaming.

No sound leaves my mouth, the vacuum in the faery circle so complete that silence consumes everything. Then the world spins on its axis, my bones shaking, teeth chattering in my skull. This was a mistake, a terrible, terrible—

BETRAYED

In the next breath, it's over.

I'm thrown out of the circle and into the frost. When I shuffle onto my elbows, I find the cat staring at me. She's still a kitten, although slightly larger than she was a few minutes ago. She tips her head to one side, eyes searching mine. The fur around her mouth is still stained red. That will be fun to explain to the others. Speaking of–

"We should find them." I say out loud.

"Who?" Aila tips her head to one side.

The question comes to me devoid of actual words, but I can feel the meaning of it in my bones. Her thoughts are all over the place, finding their way to me in bursts of energy and emotion. We've read about this too. Animals obviously don't speak English, at least not at first. She might learn as I talk to her, but she might not. That shouldn't stop the connection growing between us though, we don't need to use words to communicate.

"Ren, Asher and Willow. They're just out there, waiting for us. Come on."

Aila tips her head the other way and curls her tail around her perfectly placed front paws. Not walking then. I roll my eyes and go to her, offering my hand for her to sniff. Then I scoop her up and she licks my cheek, purring. I make my way through the trees, but halfway back, there's the distinct sound of someone running towards us. Twigs snapping, brambles strewn aside. Then I'm met with Asher's face, eyes wide, breath whooping through her open mouth.

"Quick, you've got to come right now!"

"Why, what is it? What's happened?" I clutch Aila to my chest. Her tiny heartbeat has sped up, fluttering against her rib cage.

"There's been an attack on the Geraint house in Scotland. Oliver is dead."

Asher and I race back to the house in silence. We're both shaking. Hot and cold rivers run through my body, my stomach rolling with waves of grief and disbelief.

Oliver is dead.

Oliver is Lydia's fiance, her squire, the father of the baby about to be born.

Every time I open my mouth to say something, I close it again. I'm shocked beyond words, *stunned.* How can this have happened? We've been sending spells and potions to the knights for months, and I know Lydia's been using them. They work, we've tested them, over and over.

That can mean only one thing. Morgwese must be more restored than we thought. Already building an army to destroy us.

Everyone but the man himself is gathered in Joth's office, including Eyrie and the twins, Etta, Benji and Mona. Etta is dabbing at her eyes with a handkerchief, leaning on Benjamin for support. Mona brings her ice–blue eyes to mine as we enter. Rage burns there, the only sign of how sickened she is. There are no tears. It's not the first time in my short life as Merlin's Heir that I've believed Mona's wasted as a housemaid.

Lux's skin is almost as grey as his eyes, aside from the dashes of crimson across his cheeks. Eyrie and Lore sit together, Willow's pacing behind them, wringing her hands. Ren's deathly still, fingers clenching and unclenching at his sides. Knuckles white.

No one blinks an eye at the Lynx in my arms. I wish I could apologise to Aila. Her entrance wasn't supposed to be this way. She was supposed to be fawned over, able to stretch out in front of the library hearth, basking in the glow of the embers. The star of the show. Instead, I set her on the floor and send: *"this is important; you have to wait."*

BETRAYED

Aila tips her head to one side, studying me for a moment, then she flops down, curling into a ball and tucking in her tail.

There's shuffling from behind as Joth appears. His blue woollen jumper is pulled up to his elbows, exposing a dark pattern on his forearm. It's something I've never seen before and looks suspiciously like a Witches Mark. Each pair of eyes follows him as he moves to his desk.

"That was Sir Tristen on the phone. He's the closest to Lydia, and even though he'd departed for our Templar, he's sending some of his staff to her aid. Rab McGavin arrived some hours earlier–"

"*We* should send somebody–" Ren says. He's trembling all over.

"We *will* send somebody. But right now there's something else, the reason I called you all here." Joth reaches inside the neck of his jumper, pulling out a thin golden chain with a key hanging from the end. After removing the necklace, he unlocks the drawer of his desk, gnarled fingers reaching for a thick red book laying on a cushion of velvet. He carefully lifts it out and places it gently on the desk.

"Oh great." Asher rolls her eyes. "*More* rule books!"

"That's not just any rule book." Willow says. "That's *the* rule book."

"Confirmed and signed by George Bartholomew Kay." Joth adds as he folds back the cover. The pages inside are rough and uneven, much older than their binding. I've seen it only once before, and Willow told me she almost had a heart attack when *she* saw it. Inside are the signatures of all twelve original knights, inked carefully into the ancient paper.

Aside from the documents detailing Lux and Lore's heritage and my bloodline, it's the most important book in the Templar's possession. "There's a special protocol for times of war, when the kingdom is under threat. I can invoke the

36

ancient tradition of *Animus Nostras Salvari,* something that hasn't been done since we banished Morgwese."

"And that means...?" Asher asks.

Joth looks at Asher and then at me. His face is solemn, carved from stone. "*Animus Nostras Salvari,* to save our souls. When there is no other path, the law removes the need for absolute democracy. Only to be used if the threat is so great that it will quite literally claim our souls unless we take action."

"And *that* means?"

"When the king and queen or guardian," he sends a pointed look towards the twins, "feels the threat is significant enough, they can override the knights. They can make decisions *without* the knights. Any action that doesn't contribute to the legacy of the Templar or preserving the lives of the king and queen is to be saved for more peaceful times."

"So, this can all be over?" Lore asks, sitting forward in her chair.

"No." Joth shakes his head. "Unfortunately, it means it's just beginning."

5

REN

The room remains quiet as Joth explains what will happen next. The knights that haven't gone to aid Lydia will still arrive as planned, but the meeting won't go as they expect. Joth will announce the invoking of the law, a call to war. Something they can't ignore any longer.

At least Joth has done this before, hundreds of years ago. He wasn't a Templar guardian then, but learning the ropes from his father. I can't remember the exact reason he ages more slowly than the rest of us, something to do with the blessing associated with his family's service. He's looked exactly the same for as long as I've known him. Not that it matters. *All* that matters is that he's able to steer the ship through the oncoming storm.

Then, when he's finished speaking, it's time for bed.

For a long while, nobody moves, the weight of what's happened pressing down on us. It's almost too hard to breathe.

Then Merle shakes her head as if to clear it and bends to grab the kitten, patiently waiting by her feet. If there's one thing that can cheer anyone up, it's a soft and fluffy baby animal.

"This is Aila," she says, crouching in front of Lux, Lore and Eyrie, presenting the cat in her arms. "Would you like to help me make a bed for her? Get her settled in?"

While Merle is kneeling before all of them, she's staring at Lux. He's the twin with the secret then. His eyes are unfocused, staring at the floor while Lore and Eyrie eagerly nod at the offer to play with the Templar's newest addition. Merle smiles at them both, but reaches out to touch Lux's elbow.

"Here, Lux." She offers the kitten to him. "Would you like to hold her?"

He nods his head, as if he's in a dream or some terrible nightmare. But he takes Aila, who immediately balances her front paws against him and licks the tip of his nose.

"Do we get to keep her?" Lore asks.

"If we can persuade her to put up with our nonsense." Merle grins and drops a wink at the future queen. Then those hauntingly beautiful eyes turn to me, determined and full of fire. "*Joth says to stay behind. He didn't say why.*"

I don't want to arouse suspicion by turning to Joth. If he went via Mer's telepathy, it means he doesn't want the others to know. "*I'll come up, after.*"

For a moment, her gaze flicks back to Lux. But then she nods, biting her lip between her teeth in contemplation.

"I'm sure she'll get used to you eventually." Asher says when Merle takes too long to usher the children to their feet. "Now come on, the lot of you. Let's find this mongrel a bed."

"How dare you?!" Willow slaps at Asher's arm, her voice sharp, mouth suppressing a grin. "I'll have you know that 'mongrel' is one of the greatest feats of magic you'll ever

BETRAYED

encounter, Lady Gaheris. Shame on you!"

Merle looks at me one last time before following the rabble out of the door. Benjamin and Etta go next, Mona close on their heels.

"Mona," Joth says as she's about to cross the threshold. "Can I ask a favour?"

"O'course." Mona turns back towards us. "Anythin'."

"I'll announce the *Animus Nostras Salvari* to the knights myself, but as per our ancient etiquette," he pauses again, emphasising the sarcastic note in his voice. He's definitely been spending too much time around Asher. "It's to be communicated to the other Templar guardians in writing. You're the only member of this household truly familiar with the *Old Parlais*. I was hoping you would translate the decree for me?"

Mona's face flushes pink, emphasising the sharp cut of her cheekbones. "I'd be 'onored. Bu' am no' sure I can—"

"You're more fluent than Willow." I say. The Old Parlais is a written dialect used by the Round Table Knights of old, a special and secret way of forming words and letters. Initially, it was used to communicate important news, the Parlais undecipherable to anyone outside our organisation. The tradition has long since died out. Only Joth, the other guardians, Willow and Mona, know it. To deliver such strong news to the Templars will no doubt cause uproar, and Joth knows only the ancient script will do.

"All righ' then," she says, inclining her head towards me.

"I'll bring the papers to you in the morning," Joth smiles. "For now, bed. There's nothing else to be done."

Mona nods again and then leaves, closing the door behind her. Once we're alone, Joth motions to one of the comfy chairs by the fire, and then turns to his liquor cabinet to pour his usual measure of dutch courage, reserved especially for tough conversations. I don't doubt that if the children hadn't been present at the meeting, we'd have already started on the whiskey. When it's poured, the honey coloured liquid sloshing in crystal tumblers, Joth joins me in the adjacent chair, feeding kindling into the embers of the fire. He smiles as he looks up, deep lines around his sharp blue eyes. Even with his wrinkles, he looks better than he ever has, younger, more rested. It's since Merle's arrival, since he's been able to share his endless to–do list with her.

I thought I understood it, the weight of responsibility. I've always had them, duties to the Templar, training, caring for the twins, tasks that need to be completed. But there's usually been a reward, inching closer to becoming a knight, learning how to use a sword, being fast and strong and agile. Then there are the twins. Seeing them grow up and becoming their very own people makes everything worth it on its own.

It hits me like a thud, how expertly Joth has handled my education. Giving me enough responsibility to learn to deal with pressure, to problem solve, to excel, but never to drown. Shielding me from the greater problems as I shield the twins now. And it should be that way. Joth raised us. He's been the only parent I've ever known. It's natural for him to want to protect us. But he's not had to shield Merle, someone who isn't his child. Someone who has come into our world with the power to be considered an immediate equal. I would want to share the work, too. And it's not like Mer doesn't know how to shoulder responsibility.

"It has to be you that goes to Scotland." Joth says when he's satisfied with the flames. "I was going to talk to you about it before the attack. As awful as this tragedy is, and there's no doubt you'll be a great support for Lydia, it gives us an excellent cover for your true mission." He turns to me, assessing. It's just like him to have been planning behind the

BETRAYED

scenes, not letting anything slip until he's ready or forced. It was the same with Merle and Marcus.

I'd heard of them, of course. The wild Wilde's from across the tree line, always in the faery rings and causing havoc with the little folk. And I knew Marcus had disappeared. Before it happened, he and Merle used to stand in the trees and look towards us, whispering about who lived inside the 'other manor'. All those long years I saw Mer, sneaking over the field, throwing glances over her shoulder, trying to figure us out. Then one day Joth told me to introduce myself. It was time to find out if Merle was who he thought. To offer her the inheritance due.

"What do you mean, my 'true mission'?" I ask.

"There's an ancient legend, amongst the oldest of our kind, that when Merlin was a young man, still at home in the Welsh forests, he used his magic to grow a special tree. The tree was beautiful and like nothing anyone had ever seen, it sprouted purple and blue flowers before bearing sweet and delicious fruit." Joth spins the crystal tumbler in his hand, wiggling his eyebrows at me. "*So beautiful* was the tree, that a passing prince proclaimed it the work of God. Holywood. From that tree, Merlin carved a wand, the most powerful magical instrument in existence. He named the wand *Abrasax.*"

"And where is it now?"

"Nobody knows. Nobody truly knows if it ever existed. I knew someone who went in search of it, but she never found it. There are stories, and *I* have searched in every direction they point, but I stopped looking, resigning myself to the rumour that the wand's existence was only a legend–"

"But now Merle actually *is* the heir, and we might actually have to fight a faery army, it could be useful for us to have an all powerful piece of wood?" I raise an eyebrow, trying to stop the grin as it spreads over my face.

"As always, my boy, you're too clever for your own good. And you understand why it has to be you?"

"I understand."

Joth brings his eyes up to mine. They glisten for a moment, then they soften. "I always assume that these things go without saying, but when we're constantly on the edge of doom, you can never be too careful." A smile pulls at the corner of his mouth. "I'm sending you, Ren, because I wouldn't trust another soul on earth with this task. You are loyal, and quick, and you have served this Templar impeccably. I'm very proud of you. And there's only you I can trust."

I don't look away from Joth while he speaks, but I have to swallow the lump forming in my throat. "Thank you. I won't let you down."

"Oh, I know that." He smiles again. "Now go on, be with your friends. And you can tell Merle you're going to Scotland, but not about the wand. Not yet. The fewer people that know, the better. At least until we're sure it's real."

"I have questions to ask before I leave? Where will I find it? How will I know if it's there? I mean, you've searched for this thing for literally hundreds of years, I don't—"

"Ren." Joth leans forwards and puts a strong gnarled hand on my shoulder. "I'll answer all your questions, but for now, go to bed. Tomorrow will be better."

It's something Joth's always said to us if we're having a hard day or in a bad mood. *Tomorrow will be better.*

"Okay." I say, getting up from my seat. "Good night, then."

Asher's waiting for me outside Joth's office. Her back straight against the wall, hands hanging limply by her sides, eyes closed. Asher's appearance is somewhat deceiving when you

BETRAYED

compare it to her personality. She has a high, broad forehead, sharp cheekbones, and piercing green eyes that seem to reach into your brain and pluck out whatever's hiding there. There's no sense, in those strong and bold features, of the joy she spreads without even trying. Her clumsy jokes and sarcastic nature have often saved us all from falling completely into the abyss. She's brought Merle back from the edge more times than I can count, more times than I've been able to.

There's an unshakeable bond that's grown between them. It's always existed, right from their very first meeting. It's all I really remember from the party, that awful evening when everything spiralled out from under me. Asher swooping in, taking Merle under her wing, making her feel at home. A snap between them, a spark so bright it was almost visible. Sometimes I'm jealous of whatever it is they share, but mostly I'm grateful.

"What did the old man want?"

"He's sending me to Scotland."

"Understandable." A smile flashes across her mouth for just a second, then it disappears into a scowl. "This is a good thing, right? This law?"

"Can it be worse?"

"Somehow, probably."

"Out with it, Ash. Whatever you really came to say."

For a moment, I don't think she's going to say anything. But then she takes a deep breath. "I'm worried. I mean, look what's happened! Poor Oliver! The knights —I mean... they're not working *against* us per se, but they aren't exactly making it easy, are they? It's still not got through to them that we're in crisis mode! An evil faery queen is trying to murder us all in our sleep, and our very own queen is still missing." She taps her temple hard. Two quick raps with her index and second finger.

It's only a small movement, an action without thinking. Still, it grates on me. Doesn't she think I know what she means? We're all suffering from it, the horrible, anxious undercurrent that dictates our every move. I know she's frustrated, but it isn't Lore's fault. She's suffering most of all.

"They're trying to get back a sense of normality. Recover from—"

"Recover?!" Asher throws her hands over her head, exasperated. "There might be a war, Ren. In fact, it's *likely*! A war! A *magic* one. And if you hadn't noticed, we've only got *one* witch! Instead of letting her grow those powers we're most certainly going to need, she's filling out forms and learning land boundaries and settling budget disputes! And now this! Another thing to distract us from figuring out how to bring Lore's memory back. Because in that, Merle truly *is* the only one who can." Asher's breathing hard. For the first time, it seems she's reached her limit and everything's pouring out. "And there's something else, something else she won't tell me. Do you understand *that*? She tells me everything, *everything*. But not this and I—"

"I know something. Not *exactly* what—"

"How long have you known? If I've been worried out of my mind and you've been keeping something from me, I will strangle you." Asher's staring at me fiercely, brown fingers gripping at the air in front of her.

It takes a minute for it to dawn on me that she's not joking. Well, maybe she isn't actually angry enough to strangle me, but she is seriously worried. I narrow my eyes at her. There's something else going on, something that isn't this. Another thing pulling on her and unravelling her usually calm and collected threads.

"Ash?"

She starts as if she's only just realised how wound up she

BETRAYED

is. Then she lets out a long breath, waving away the question with a flick of her wrist. "Tell me what you know."

"It's to do with the twins, or *a* twin. Something they've asked her to do or asked her not to say, I don't know."

"If she told you that, surely—"

"That's not what happened. She can't *tell me*, or anyone, because it would break the oath she swore. She said hers is different from ours. We offer to serve and protect and be loyal, and so does she. But she also swore to keep their secrets."

"So she's hiding something for them? What?"

I've been wracking my brain all day, but I can't think of anything. The twins are different now, obviously. But they've been through a lot and they're getting to that age. "Lore didn't know anything about it. I don't think she was lying."

"So that leaves Lux. And Lore would cover for him *convincingly* if he asked her to."

"No. Well, she would, but she wasn't lying about this. I don't know what the problem is, but it's Lux."

Asher sighs and rubs her hand over her eyes. "I'll talk to Eyrie. See if she knows anything." Asher was in two minds about letting her younger sister stay here long term, worried about keeping her around Lore.

"*Not because of anything she's done,*" Asher told us. "*But because it's sad. It makes Eyrie too sad to see her this way.*"

But Eyrie had insisted on staying. I suspect it's just as much for Lux as it is for Lore. Eyrie is a little older than the twins, twelve to their eleven, and she's headstrong. She doesn't let Lore get away with any nonsense, or Lux dwell too much. She's great for them.

"Asher, are you all right?"

She sighs. "Yes. I'm tired and at the end of my rope. We just need a break..."

"We'll fix it."

Asher brings her eyes up to mine. They look clearer, but I'm still not sure she's been entirely straight with me. "Okay."

She says goodnight and heads off up the stairs and, thinking of Lux, I follow her. I wonder what it is, whatever he's hiding, whatever he wants to keep a secret. He's always been more reserved, a bit of a stickler for tradition and rules. When he was a baby, he'd sit on Joth's lap while he read tales of the knights. His expression would be solemn, listening so carefully to Joth's words.

Lore and I would sit and listen too, sometimes. Usually she'd get bored and pull on my shirt sleeve until I agreed to sneak out. Then we'd go running through the halls, into the garden, up to the Mews. Merle told me about their trip into the catacombs, that Lore had known exactly where to go. She's always been adventurous, but never really a secret keeper. She *could* keep them if she wanted. I know she can lie. But it isn't her way.

Well, it wasn't before.

Now she's different. Now, everything is different.

I don't wait for a response as I knock on Merle's bedroom door. She's sitting on the bed, chewing on her fingernails. Her eyes meet mine and she says: "Tell me. Tell me everything."

6

Ren, quickly and efficiently, explains exactly what Joth asked of him, even down to the wand named *Abrasax*, which he wasn't supposed to tell me about. I've been waiting with Aila. The kitten, who seems to grow larger by the hour, has been padding around my room. Testing out the furniture to find the comfiest spot.

"There was no point trying to hide it." He says. "I don't want to keep things from you."

I'm sitting cross–legged, staring at my fingers. Six months ago, my hands were lovely and soft, but now they're full of scratches, red burns and calluses. "I understand why Joth said it. It doesn't matter."

Joth knows, buried deep in my heart, is the promise that I won't rest until Morgwese is vanquished. He also knows the battle, when it comes, might not go my way. The fewer world ending secrets I carry, the better.

"It's awful. About Oliver."

"All of it's awful." I ruffle my hands through Aila's fur. "So I'm going to do it. Induce the vision. I know Aila only just got here, and it's dangerous to try, but we can't wait any longer." I'm not exactly asking for permission, but I want to know what he thinks, despite the fact it's already decided. Right now, a reluctant Willow and determined Mona are looking for the ingredients I need to cast the spell. I'm sure that those glimpses of dreams are the clues we've been searching for, that they'll point the way. Eventually, Ren lets out a sigh.

"You're right, it is dangerous. But we can't wait. Not now. I wish there was another—"

Tap–tap, tap–tap–tap, tap–tap.

The beats are light on the door. A tendril of unease uncoils in my stomach. I knew Lux would come after the attack. I knew he would need me.

*Tap–tap, tap–tap–tap, tap–tap.*More desperate this time, louder.

Ren raises his eyebrows at the noise as I get to my feet. It's a horrible trick to play, one that has shame burning in my throat. But the burden is too much to carry alone. And I have a plan for the king, one that requires Ren's help.

Tap–tap, tap–tap–tap, tap–tap.

"Answer it." I send.

Ren's brow furrows as he frowns, but then he slides to the end of the bed and goes to the door. I fall into step behind him.

As the door swings wide, Lux throws himself in, opening his arms for what usually would be me. He doesn't stop as he realises it isn't. He might not have realised.

Ren is fast, so fast, as he crouches to wrap his own arms around Lux's middle. So fast to pull him in close and smooth down his hair, whispering calming words in the boy's ear as he

BETRAYED

moves to the bed, sitting with Lux on his lap. Over the top of the blonde mop of hair, his eyes meet mine.

"What is this? What's happening? What's wrong?"

"Ask. Ask him."

I still can't say. The words are stuck in my throat, muted by my oath.

"Lux," he whispers, "Lux, whatever it is, you can tell me. I promise."

The boy takes a deep breath that trails out of his lips in bubbling sobs, then he drags in another gulp of air, and another. A few moments later, the heaving of his chest is slower, and he sits back, looking into Ren's face. Then his eyes find mine.

"Go on." I urge him. *"Ren loves you."*

After another shuddering breath he says; "Nightmares. *Night terrors.* Ever since Lore got hurt and I can't find her, I can't find her *anywhere.*"

As soon as he says the words, a tight band unwinds itself from around my middle, a weight lifted from my chest. I've heard it used in a metaphorical sense, but I can really *feel* a difference. Even Lux seems calmer as he leans back into Ren, sniffling into his shirt. Ren's mouth is set in a grim line, and he stares back at me as he smooths his hand down Lux's back.

"Explain."

"He made me swear not to tell. He doesn't want anyone to know. With Lore already... and the faery attacks... He's ashamed, and sad, and he misses Lore. He tried to make me swear a blood oath."

Ren's eyes widen for a moment, in shock or admiration I can't exactly tell, then he takes hold of Lux's middle and shifts him so he's sitting on the bed, Ren moving to his knees on the floor in front of the king.

"Your knife, the penknife, where is it?" Ren sends to me,

already holding out his hand of the blade.

"*What are you—?*"

"*Trust me.*"

And because I do, I take the knife from my pocket and hand it over.

Ren flicks open the blade, and without looking at either of us, he puts the sharp point to his palm and presses, drawing a thin red line across the skin.

"Lux Pendragon," he rises onto one knee so that he's close and looking directly into Lux's eyes. "I swear to you, not as a Knight of this Templar but as your brother, that I will spend what's left of my life protecting you from the darkness, that I will never judge or hurt you, that whatever demons plague you, *we* will hunt together. I swear you'll never face trouble alone, no matter what mask it wears, and you *never* have to feel ashamed. You are my brother. You and Lore are my family. I love you. Both of you. Always." He shows his hand to Lux, the thin line now dribbling with red. "I seal my oath with blood, and so, if you accept, we are bound. What do you think?"

Lux nods slowly and holds out his hand for the knife. Ren twists it in his fingers and passes it over. Lux cuts himself, and I wince as his skin splits. Surely it's an act of treason? Joth might certainly see it that way. Then he holds his trembling hand out for Ren to shake. It's enough to make tears start streaming from my eyes again. I've begged Lux to tell Ren for months, that he'd know what to do.

"Now, it's time for bed." Ren says, hooking one arm under Lux's knees, standing up as if the child is a bag of sugar.

"*Library, after.*" I send to him as he walks to the door. "*For the spell.*"

Ren's just over the threshold when he stops. He mutters something to Lux, too quiet for my ears. Then there's the

BETRAYED

thump of two feet hitting the floor. Ren turns back to me, eyes dark and sparkling. He takes my hand and tugs me towards him, running his other hand up my shoulder, cupping the back of my head, pulling me closer, our foreheads pressed together.

"*Thank you. Thank you for taking care of him all these months. For carrying him* and *Lore when I can not–*" his thoughts trail off and instead I'm flooded with warmth, with an emotion so strong I have to lean into him to stop myself wobbling backwards. Then he says; "I love you."

The world shifts a little on its axis, stars spinning in the darkness behind my closed eyes as I press my mouth to his for a second. I'd thought he might say it, *hoped* he might. Both of us holding on, just to be sure.

"I love you, too." I say. "And thank you. I did the best I could."

Ren leans forward to kiss me again, but is interrupted by a yawn from behind the half–open door.

"*Go on.*" I send to him. "*Take him to bed. Then the library. Spell.*"

He squeezes me close as if he can't bring himself to let me go, but then he runs his thumb along my cheek and releases, disappearing into the hallway. I steady myself for a minute, closing my eyes, unable to stop the smile spreading across my face.

"You're looking very pleased about something."

I squeal as Asher's voice booms into the room. I open my eyes to find her grinning at me like a Cheshire cat. Talking of. The new addition to our family is crouched on the bed, bright eyes wide and looking for trouble, claws already out.

"*Don't worry. Asher does that. You'll get used to it.*"

Aila raises her head, glancing between us, assessing. Then she jumps down off the bed, padding her way towards Asher, sniffing at her ankles. Smiling, Asher bends over and scoops her up, accepting two quick licks to the cheek before settling the kitten in the crook of her arm.

"Is everything ready?" I ask.

"Yes. And you're sure about it, so soon?"

I turn to look at her more closely. It's difficult to tell how Asher's truly feeling sometimes. She has such a deep well of resilience inside her, a well that seemingly has no bottom. You'd never know she's worried or scared. Even so, there are dark circles under her eyes and her cheeks look thin. "I don't know what else to do."

"I don't have any ideas either, if it makes you feel any better. Actually, no one does. Not even Joth, and he's done this before." Asher smiles, banishing the shadows on her face. She tickles Aila under the chin with her forefinger. "Let's see what this little monster can do."

The full moon streams through the enormous glass windows of the library as we enter to find the gang already assembled. Mona's there too, dressed in black trousers and a thick cream jumper, her blonde hair pulled back in an unruly ponytail, eyes like chips of ice. Willow is rummaging through a basket of herbs to find exactly the right ones. I'm lucky she's as smart as she is and as resourceful. After Joth's announcement, I told her what I needed, giving her my book of notes and the spell I've chosen. Even though she didn't like it, she agreed immediately. In the hour that's passed since then, she and Mona have collected mugwort, mint and lavender from the greenhouse, a tall white candle, and a small bottle of frankincense from who knows where.

"It's not everything, and not exactly how we'd do it if we had more time." Willow rubs her hand across her mouth. "But, good enough for government work, as they say."

"Who says?" Ren asks as he joins us.

BETRAYED

"*Lux okay?*"

"*Better.*" He nods and loops his arm around my waist, dropping a kiss on my temple.

"It's time." Mona says. "Almos't witchin' 'our."

I take a deep, calming breath. I can do this. I have enough magic, enough determination. Aila and my friends are with me.

Asher lets my familiar out of her arms as I straighten my back and move to the centre of the room. There's a circle of crystals placed around a cushion, the space big enough for me to lie down. When I'm settled, I call Aila to me, pulling her into my lap and bringing my nose to hers.

"*I know you just got here, that you're small and you might not understand what's going on. I wish I could explain. But you know what's in my heart and I need everything you've got. Every ounce of magic you can spare me. I need this to work. Will you help me?*"

Aila licks my nose in response. I hope that means yes.

For this spell, there are no words. Instead, I'll use intention to navigate through my lost dreams. My four companions will sit around the circle like the points of a compass, focusing their minds on the task at hand. I shouldn't need to draw power from them, but I will need them as anchors. Solid points of contact to pull me back should I go too far.

Once I'm lying flat on my back, Aila resting on my stomach, her head at my heart, Willow places a bowl of dried herbs above my head and the white candle at my feet.

"Remember, we need to keep our breathing in sync, in for five, hold for five, out for five. I'll count you on my fingers. If you're under for over five minutes, I'll blow out the candle and bring you back. It's not up for discussion." Willow says as the frown flashes across my face. "This is risky enough as it is. If you're not there in five, you never will be."

54

"Wha'ever worries yev go', wha'ever reservations. Cast um outer yer mind now." Mona's voice sounds into the quiet. "Magic needs focus an' belief t' work. No doubts."

I close my eyes and listen to the final shuffling movements of my friends as they get into position. I didn't know magic could be such a collaborative effort, that even though the power runs in my veins, my friends can taste it, *feel* it in theirs. It's possible to do it alone, but who would choose that over this?

"On my count." Willow says. And then: "in, two, three, four, five. Hold, two, three, four, five. Out, two, three, four, five."

As their breathing falls into a rhythm, I will myself to be still. My last action before letting go is to set the candle and the herbs alight. Breathing in the smoke, the freshness of the mint and the bitterness of the mugwort, the room around me slips away. I focus hard on Lore, on the cold, on the woman's laugh. Everything I can remember from my dreams. Then I allow my mind to fall into the abyss.

I open my eyes to Asher's laugh ringing in my ears. I push myself into a sitting position, my head brushing against something, the action sending tiny static shocks down my spine.

God, it's hot in here. Where am I?

I take stock of my surroundings, and I appear to be in a tent. It's dark outside although there's the twinkling of torch lights. Kicking off my sleeping bag, I move to the entrance, reaching for the zip. It's okay. This is it, the vision, it must be.

The wind whistles past my face as I open the flap, freezing cold and full of snowflakes. A stark contrast to the warmth of the tent.

"Finally! I never thought you'd wake up. We've got to get

BETRAYED

going, Sunbeam!" Asher grins at me. She's holding a sausage on a fork, twirling it over a stove.

I look down at my hands, and then out into the dark. From here I can make out the dark shadows of rock towering around us. Mountains. This is so strange, so real, as if I'm being flipped inside out. "Where am I?"

"What do you mean?" Owen wrinkles his nose at me.

Owen Lamorak? I'm so surprised I nearly fall back into the tent. Owen's here, of all people. *Why would I be in a tent with Asher and Owen? This doesn't make any sense.*

"Where are we?" I ask again.

"We're in France." Asher's dark skin furrowing between her eyebrows. She's also cottoned on to the fact that something's not right here. "On the way to the cave. Are you all right?"

"Yes, I'm fine. What cave—?"

Merle...

A low voice from far away.

Merle, wake up.

"The cave with the witch in it?" Asher starts to get up. "Are you sure you're–?"

Before she can finish her sentence, I feel a yank in my midsection, the anchor pulling me back to the present. I go tumbling into the darkness.

When I open my eyes again, I'm in the library, Aila's soft, warm body still snuggled with my own. I stroke the back of her head, alerting her to the fact I'm about to move, and then I sit up. "What happened?"

"You first." Ren says. "Did you get it?"

"France." I say, turning my attention to Asher. "Now, do you wanna tell me why we were in France, on a mountain, with *Owen Lamorak?*"

"I can say with one hundred percent certainty that I don't

56

know what you're talking about."

"I guess you could be on your way to the Templar," Ren muses. "There is one in France. And didn't Shelby say... I mean, didn't Morgwese say something about her son being in France...?"

"Oh my god." I stand still. The idea blooms in my mind like the perfect petals of the passion flower, the pieces sliding together all at once, like I'm being pulled apart and stitched back together in a matter of seconds. The path is clear, the beacons lit. "That's it, that's exactly it!"

"If you don't start talking sense, I'm going to strangle you." Asher smiles at me sweetly. It does little to hide the sharp edge of her words.

"Ren's right. Shelby told me she'd lost touch with her family and that they lived in France."

"We've been over this though, Merle." Willow interjects. "I can't find Methuse anywhere."

"I'm not talking about *Methuse,* I'm talking about *Maureen.*"

"There wasn't any *Maureen* either!"

Willow's right. I told her everything I could remember about mine and Shelby's conversations and we couldn't find Maureen. But I was blind then. "Shelby told me a lot of half truths, but never outright lies. Just like Elizabeth is Elaine, Maureen," I take in a deep breath, jittering with excitement. "Maureen is Morgana Le Fae."

Willow's eyes go wide, Asher jolts, Ren and Mona straightening their backs. Aila starts to purr.

"And you told me," I point at Ren, "that she's *so* powerful she might be able to bring people back from the dead. If she can do that, she can fix Lore."

"I also told you," the tone of Ren's voice doesn't match my excitement, "that she's had nothing to do with the Templar

BETRAYED

for hundreds of years—"

"Hence the trip *to* France." Asher says.

"She's the answer." In my heart I know it's true, it has to be. "We have to get Morgana."

Ren considers me for a moment. His mind running through the hundreds of questions he wants to ask. It's fair to say he's the most stubborn– '*level headed*'he calls it– but if he says *no,* we'll go back to the drawing board. I glance across at Asher, who is already raising her hand for a high five. Willow's beaming, her cheeks flushed pink, Mona's signature grin stamped on her face.

"Okay." He finally nods. "Let's run it by Joth in the morning."

7

"Absolutely out of the question." Joth says once the last of his chuckles have died away.

Earlier this morning, we hurried down to his office as fast as we could, piling up toast croissants and coffee on a tray. It's still early, the kids asleep, the birds only just beginning to call.

"What do you mean 'absolutely out of the question'?" I ask and throw myself into the chair opposite him, grabbing a croissant. Aila jumps into my lap, snuggling against my side. She's my constant shadow, the bond between us already twisting together.

"Morgana Le Fae won't help you." He has a smile on his face, but his eyes are stern. I've seen this look before. It's the face he was wearing when he told me it was '*absolutely out of the question*' to enter the catacombs.

"How can you know that?"

"Do you know her legend?"

BETRAYED

"I know what Ren told me. She banished Morgwese and then she left—"

"Partly accurate." Joth raises an eyebrow, Ren's palms clench on my shoulders. He's standing like a statue behind me, already expecting Joth's 'no'. "I'll tell you. It might surprise you to learn I'm somewhat older than I look."

"Unlikely," Ren whispers under his breath, gaining a scathing look from Joth,

"While I have no magic myself, as Templar guardian, I've been charged with overseeing the happenings here for well over three hundred years. I age slowly, about one year to your five."

"Why?" I ask.

Joth chuckles, "As you can imagine, it was a knight's rogue deal with a sorceress that did it. My great–great–grandfather Robert couldn't stomach the thought of dying, so he exchanged a life of service for time. As long as he served the Templar and the monarch with a pure heart, he would stay alive. We all got the curse, my grandfather, my own father, me."

"But you don't have an heir."

"No. But I don't need one. Now we have Lux and Lore. They will be the ones to serve when my time is over. Regardless, I was here when Morgana banished her sister. She was..." his eyes glass over a little. "Magnificent. She and Elaine... in fact, Merle, will you project?"

I nod and offer him my hand. 'Projecting' is the term Joth uses when he needs me to show us something. We do it almost exactly like we did the first time, everyone reaching out to touch my arm or shoulder. Contact is essential, but aside from that all Joth needs to do is summon the memory.

Going into other people's heads is strange. We agreed I wouldn't do it without asking, and I haven't. As a precaution,

60

everyone's learnt to throw up a shield, a door I have to knock on to be granted entry.

Joth's door is an exact replica of the one to his office. It's brown panels guarding a shimmering light. The hinges swing open and I reach for the memory, as if I can grasp it with my hands. Then we're in.

Morgana is standing on the grassy hill looking into the distance. She is beautiful. Her face is a mask of steel, emphasised by her high, sharp cheekbones and straight nose. Rain pounds around her and she uses the flat of her hand to shield her eyes from it. The dying sun casting shadows like blood. The huge stones of the circle she's chosen to banish her sister painted crimson. Her deep auburn hair blows in the wind, tawny eyes transfixed on something far in the distance.

"Get up Elaine. It's time."

The other woman stands beside her. The sisterly resemblance is hard to miss.

A whiplash of lightning forks over their heads and splits the stone behind where they're standing. It blisters the sky with red and yellow.

"To the other side, quickly." Morgana snaps. "You know what you have to do."

Elaine fades out of sight as Morgana turns. She goes to her belt and pulls out a sharp, almost translucent blade. Then she slices it across her palms.

"Et sanguinem meum, Hanc ego conteram recta, et sanguis meus, projiciam vos a facie mea."

With this blood, I break this line, with this blood, I cast you out.

The red river runs from her palms and is sucked into the grass. The line of fire spreads, racing to meet Elaine's blood, forming a circle. The ground shakes and splits. Morgana is

BETRAYED

*yelling the same words over and over. She turns her head to
the sky, her eyes black, reflecting the flashing light. Morgwese
appears in the stone circle, thrashing and gnashing her teeth.
She screams words we can't hear over the storm of wind and
dust. Morgana staggers backwards.*

"Keep chanting Elaine." *Morgana sends.*

*"It's over, Sister. You asked too much! Tried to take
things that aren't yours! You left us no choice!"*

"You aren't strong enough!" Morgwese hisses.

*"Our coven banishes you to the depths!" Morgana
screams. "We pray you rot there!"*

*The circle of blood now a circle of spinning, white light.
It is so loud that blood dribbles from Morgana's ears, her nose.
Morgwese shrieks one last time. Then she's gone.*

I open my eyes and see Asher leant forward with her head
between her knees. Projection always gives her nausea,
especially when the visions are strong. Ren's weight is leaning
wholly on the chair now too. I peer at Joth.

"That wasn't your memory."

"No." He shakes his head again. He has a wistful look on
his face, one that doesn't quite fit with the horrific scene we've
just witnessed.

"It's hers."

"Yes. The reason I know Morgana won't help you is
because I *know* Morgana. She denounced us, and everything
we stand for." He sighs. "She won't see you, or anybody
associated with the Templar."

"Why?"

"Because the Templar promised that if she and Elaine rid
them of Morgwese, they would disband. They would allow the
heirs to have lives, without us. To be free of the 'archaic
shackles' binding them." Joth steeples his fingers in front of

him.

"And they obviously didn't." Asher says from her place on the floor.

"She was already suspicious of us, of our order. Going back on that promise made her *so* angry. In the end, she couldn't trust us and wanted no part in anything we did."

"She left us with a promise of no further aid. No refuge, nothing. She will not help us." Joth's voice is quiet and lost.

"We have to try. I think I can bargain with her if I have to. We have nothing to lose."

"Merle..." There's something he's not telling me, and I have an inkling of what it might be. I saw *more* in his head. I saw whispering on staircases, dancing in candlelight, their tears. *Love.*

"Put aside your..." I choose my words carefully, "previous dealings with her. Let me ask for her help, with your blessing."

Joth leans back. He's not a stupid man. He knows what I've seen.

"Okay then, Merlin's Heir." He smiles. "You can make your case when we meet with the knights."

"I thought there were no more votes?" Asher says, wrinkling her nose.

"There aren't." Joth says, smirking. "You'll be making your request to the king and queen."

Willow and I wait outside the Knight's Hall after lunch, watching the knights file in. It's taken them hours to arrive and get settled. Enough time for me to get a shower and brush out my hair. It's grown long, and is even more unruly than before.

I left Aila dozing in the spring sunshine, curled up on my bed. Bringing her inside might be too much for the little cat right now. Everyone is sombre, a reaction to the terrible news of Oliver's death, and they're still yet to hear of the *Animus*

BETRAYED

Nostras Salvari that's about to be enacted.

"Did you see Amalie Percival? Wasn't she striking?" Willow whispers, cutting through the quiet.

"Yes. She was."

It's true. She's a newcomer to the table, taking the place usually held by her uncle, who is currently at Lydia's estate in Scotland. Amalie came to see us before she was whisked away, much more polite than some of the others. Her red hair hung in a plait down her back, long legs making her tower above both me and Willow. She looks exactly as I imagine Mary Queen of Scots looked: regal and beautiful.

"Asher used to date her."

"Huh. Girls got good taste."

Willow opens her mouth to speak again, when the great doors swing open. Joth stands, smiling at us, and we go to greet him. Before we enter, he gently brushes my elbow.

"I'll announce the enactment of the *Animus Nostrus Salvari*, and then hand the floor to you. Are you ready?"

"I'm ready." I say, and then follow him into the hall.

Ren sits in the Du Lac seat. On his right is Asher, then Bedivere, Sir Andrew Kay, Edward Pelleas and Peter Lucan. Across from them sit the remaining six. Amalie in Sir Percival's seat, Matthew Gawain, Greg Tristen, Johnathan Alymere and the Lamorak's. Lawrence sitting in the seat, with Owen standing dutifully behind him.

The others have squires, too Gawain has with him his oldest son Andrew, and John Alymere is flanked by his nephew, Thomas. The others don't have squires yet. They're either waiting for younger relatives to come of age— like Eyrie who will squire for Asher when she's thirteen— or don't have anyone to fill the spot. I take my place opposite Ren, at the monarch's right hand. He gives me a reassuring grin and then nods at Willow, who's taken up the position on my right.

64

"All rise," Joth says, not a second after everyone has finally stopped shuffling. "For the king and queen."

Twelve chairs scrape along the hardwood in unison as we stand. Only Lydia's seat unmoved.

Lux and Lore enter through the doors, held wide by a steely faced Mona and smiling Etta. The twins are bathed in soft winter light as they enter, both of them wearing the blue shirts Willow just shoved them into. Both of them were reluctant to come, wary of the older, sterner men at the table. It's the usual suspects, Sir Kay, John Alymere and Lamorak Senior, who refuse to fall in line. It's ironic how they choose to follow protocol to the letter when they want more land, but can't seem to understand simple instructions in the presence of their sovereigns.

When the twins are seated and Joth has made it to the end of the table, he motions for us to sit. "We gather today in the shadow of terrible news. Oliver Campbell has been slain in the line of duty, serving his Templar and his king and queen." Joth bows his head for a moment, steadying himself, taking a breath. "And I must deliver yet more bad news. This morning, I dispatched messengers to each of the Templar Guardians advising them of the decision to invoke the ancient law of *Animus Nostras Salvari–*"

A hiss runs around the room as the knights suck in a harsh breath. Most of their faces are slack, eyes wide. Only Amalie is wearing a triumphant smirk. She's so unlike Percival and it's not entirely surprising to say she and her twin sister, Aurora, aren't related to him biologically. Before Monty was 'found', he was a very successful car salesman and married to a man named Derek Astor. They adopted the Percival twins shortly before Monty was offered his seat. Amalie and Aurora are the orphaned daughters of Derek's sister, raised in France. That's where they live now, defending the French territories

BETRAYED

they grew up in. Derek died of a heart attack six years ago, and according to Joth, Monty's never been the same.

"That's quite the overreaction, don't you think?" John Alymere eventually rumbles.

"*Overreaction?*" I push back my seat, searching the faces until I find his. "Oliver is dead. *Murdered,* Sir John. On our watch—"

"Merle's right." Joth says, his voice commanding the attention of the room. His gaze lands on me, willing me to stand down.

"*Softly, softly.*" He sends.

I take in a deep breath and let it go.

"I don't take this decision lightly, but it's time to act. For years, you have been kept by this Templar. We have upheld every part of the terms you were promised. You all swore to serve, and that oath is binding."

The hush that falls is dense, settling like a blanket of snow. It's not often that Joth exerts the full extent of his power, but it's an impressive thing to witness. When there's no way for them to weasel out of their duty.

"We'll send further aid to Scotland as soon as we adjourn." Joth's eyes scan the room until they land on Ren. "Ren will go."

"Desperate times call for desperate measures." Lawrence mutters under his breath.

I'm out of my seat again in a flash. The only thing stopping me from incinerating Lamorak where he sits are Willow's nails digging into my shoulders as she tries to hold me down.

Before I can say anything, Joth stands, although much more slowly. His eyes are narrow, anger creasing the lines of his face, patches of colour blooming on his cheeks. He towers over Lawrence, who cringes under his icy stare. "Ren Du Lac has done more for this Templar in an afternoon than you've ever achieved in your sorry fifty years of service."

"He isn't even knighted." Lawrence stammers.

If it's possible, Joth's face gets even redder. He turns on his heel and storms towards the doors. "Wait here, all of you."

"Joth..." Ren starts.

"All of you!" He roars and disappears.

It takes a long while for him to come back, and the whole time we sit in silence. When he returns, his face is still flushed, and he's carrying a long roll of leather and velvet. Lux's face brightens when he sees it, and he nudges Lore with his elbow.

Joth unties the leather binding and then unrolls the bundle to reveal a great sword. Its hilt is bronze and encrusted with white gems, opals like my old ring. The end of the handle is carved in the shape of a lion. Joth manoeuvres the blade with ease and skill, even though it must be almost a metre long.

"You can't be serious!" Lamorak huffs.

"*Serious about what?*" I send to my friends.

"*You'll see!*" Asher's face is glowing with excitement.

"Desperate times, Sir Lawrence, call for desperate measures." Joth spits back.

"Joth, this really isn't necessary." Ren says.

"Too long have your services to this Templar been overlooked. Not only is it necessary, but you have wiped clean the debt of your ancestors a thousand times over. Your loyalty deserves title and respect."

"He hasn't even taken the tests!"

Joth turns back to Lawrence, his hands shake slightly. "I'm not only guardian of this Templar, but *all* Templars. In all things, until the Pendragons come of age, my word is *final.* As you well know, I can punish insubordination. If you like your land, your titles, you'll kindly keep your mouth shut for the rest of the proceedings."

BETRAYED

Lawrence's face turns scarlet, and he closes his mouth with a snap.

"Ren Du Lac," Joth says, no anger in his voice now. "Kneel."

Ren gets up from his seat and takes two steps forward into the open, dropping to one knee, hanging his head to expose his broad shoulders.

"The sword Secace is blessed by blood, water and the Guardian of this Templar. And with it, in recognition of your unwavering sacrifice and service, I am proud to deliver you into knighthood." Joth's voice wobbles, and tears of pride prick at the back of my own eyes.

"*Sois chevalier, au nom de Dieu.*" Joth positions the blade first on Ren's right shoulder, then on his left. Then he places it in front of him, the point sticking into the floor. "Rise, Sir Ren."

Ren gets up, his eyes a little glazed, as if he can't quite believe what's happened.

"The sword I hold belonged to Lancelot, and now it belongs to you. Keep it well, and it shall keep you the same." Joth puts a hand on Ren's shoulder. "I'm proud of you."

Ren accepts the sword, the grin on his face wide. "Thank you, Sir Joth."

I can't believe it, my heart swelling with pride. He's worked hard all these long years, and sacrificed so much. To finally be recognised is more than he deserves.

Joth nods and then turns back to us all. "Now, assuming there are no further *ridiculous* objections, we have work to do. The Heir of Merlin requests the floor."

Showtime. I push back my chair again and step past Willow.

"Thank you all for agreeing to come. I know the last few months have been... difficult, but we have an idea. Something that might truly work." I swallow, my mouth suddenly dry. I know how crazy this will sound. I almost can't bring myself to speak. But the twins sit up in their seats, captivated. Hoping for a lifeline. "Morgana Le Fae." I whisper before I lose my nerve. "I induced a vision last night, and that vision showed me a party of knights travelling to France, to find the witch Morgana and have her restore the queen." Now I turn to Lore. "You've made such good progress, more than we could have hoped for. But I can't help you alone. I'm so sorry." I stop, my voice breaking. It's an apology long overdue. It's my job to bring her back, and so far my efforts have been entirely lacking. "I ask that you allow me to take a party to France, to find the cave and have Morgana break this spell that Elaine cast. I think she's our best hope. My magic isn't yet strong enough, maybe in time..." I trail off. "But we've wasted so much time already, and we aren't safe yet."

"Morgana Le Fae won't help us! She denounced us!" Greg Tristen says.

"No one's seen her face in hundreds of years!"

"She betrayed us! To go to her would be the end of us!"

So many shouts, one after the other. All of them screeching, slamming their palms on the table. I think Sir Kay is even about to get out of his seat.

"Quiet!" Joth orders, to no avail.

The king and queen are wearing equal masks of contemplation, Lux's face slightly more drawn than Lore's. He's tired, we're all tired. I can barely think over the bickering. I snap my fingers and wish for quiet. Immediately, silence descends. The knights who were shouting have their hands to their necks and their mouths. I've stolen the words from their throats, and I'm not sorry to have done it.

"You will remember," I say into the quiet, "in whose presence you currently sit. This is not your decision to make." I scan the room and am met with a dozen blazing eyes.

BETRAYED

"Morgana may refuse, but we have to *ask*. We are *desperate*!"
I snap my fingers again and release them from my magic.

"It's madness," Tristen says, although he uses a much more reasonable tone, making eye contact with Lore before continuing. "What of the details?"

"We'll work those out after," I whisper. *Don't make me steal your voice again. Don't test me.*

The twins sit quietly for a moment, obviously considering our request. Then Lux turns his piercing grey eyes to meet mine.

"I want my sister back." He says. His voice is high and clear. "Go to Morgana Le Fae."

Joth quickly calls an end to the meeting after that and I walk Lux back to his room. He's grown taller, standing only half a foot shorter than I do. His hair is also longer and falls in front of his eyes.

"Do you feel okay?" I ask.

"About what?" He looks up at me and wrinkles his nose.

"Making big decisions in front of the knights."

"I should be able to. They think they know everything because they're grownups, but they don't! They don't live here, they don't know what it's like." His cheeks flush red. "They want to keep everything the same, and pretend that none of this is happening."

"They're scared."

"Everybody is." He glances into my face as we come to a stop outside his new room. This one doesn't have any artwork on the front, no *'No Girls Allowed'* signs. I worry that he's growing up too fast. "They're not scared of the right things."

"What do you mean?"

He rolls his eyes, reminding me so much of his sister that my heart aches. "They're only afraid of losing the things they have. I've heard them talking when they think no one's there. They don't want to lose their houses or their money. They don't care about Lore."

"They've grown old, Lux. Sometimes old people get stuck in their ways."

He considers me with a frown. "Then maybe it's time they didn't have ways to be stuck in."

Before I can speak, he slips into his room and shuts the door.

I stroll back through the halls and to my room to collect Aila. It's a nice day, the sun streaming through the glass, casting rainbows on the carpet. It's the perfect time to assemble the team and head into the greenhouse. To plan away from the prying ears of those that might work against us

8

REN

I'm still trembling as we file out of the hall, the great sword *Secace* strapped to my back. It was Lancelot's, *actually* Lancelot's. And now I'm a proper knight. I can barely believe it, that finally all my hard work has paid off. The rest of the meeting went by in a blur. It didn't even matter whether the twins agreed to Merle's plan. I am a knight.

Speaking of, before I can get to Merle, she's leading Lux out of the hall, watching him like a hawk. He seemed better this morning at breakfast, his face less drawn. He even asked about the prophecy again. I bet he knows more about the history of the Templar and the knights quests than any of us, aside from Willow and Joth.

I couldn't believe my eyes when I opened the door and found him sobbing on the other side. I would never have guessed that he was feeling the weight of his responsibility so heavily.

"He's been trying to hold it all together because of Lore, and he knew I couldn't tell." Merle told me after, curled around me in bed, whispering into the crook of my neck. *"He didn't want to give anyone grounds to question them, to put more pressure on her. That's why he wanted to keep it a secret."*

"Congrats, Sir Ren." Asher nudges her elbow into my side. "Got a minute?"

"Yes." I try to keep the suspicion out of my voice. "Why?"

She grins and dangles a key off the end of a finger. It's a huge bronze thing that swings on a purple ribbon. "Joth gave me this. He says there's not much time before we need to get going, and there's some special seeing stones in the relics room we need."

"What do you mean 'we get going'?" I feel my face pulling into a frown.

Asher looks at me as if I'm entirely stupid. "What do *you* mean? You're going to Scotland, and Merle and I, and whoever we can muster, will go to France. You *were* just in that meeting, right?"

I stop for a moment. My slow brain finally putting all the pieces together. I knew I'd be going to Scotland, and that someone would go to France. Of course, it would be Merle. But I hadn't imagined us being separated for so long, or her going into such imminent danger without me.

"I'll take care of her, you know. I promise. On Eyrie's life, I won't let anything happen to her." Asher looks directly into my eyes as she speaks. I know that too, and I believe it with every fibre of my being. But her words don't do enough to untie the knot of worry tightening in my stomach.

As we turn the corner onto the top level of the Templar, a place that no one ever goes, Asher literally collides with Owen Lamorak. His presence on this floor does nothing to ease my anxiety. We could never take to each other, even

BETRAYED

though he was the only person close to me in age. I've long suspected it's because of Lawrence whispering in his ear, telling him about Lancelot's disgrace and how I can't be trusted. Owen's almost as tall as me now, but still quite gangly as teenagers are, all limbs and jolting movements.

"Lost are you?" Asher asks, raising her eyebrows.

"Yes." He doesn't stammer, doesn't blush. Something is still amis. "What are you doing up here?"

"Official business for the king and queen." I step out of the way so he can pass me, alarm bells ringing in my ears. He was part of Mer's vision of the mountain and will almost certainly be going with them. I narrow my eyes. "What are *you* doing up here?"

He pauses for a moment, thinking. Then he shrugs. "I really did get lost."

That's strange too. That pause. A shiver runs down my spine.

"This has been *lovely,* but we really must get going. Official business, like Ren said." Asher grabs hold of my forearm, pulling me along and away from Owen. I feel his eyes on my back until we round the corner.

"He shouldn't be up here," I say.

"Neither should we. What's your point?"

It's all bravado, that sentence. She knows something's wrong as well as I do.

"All right, fine. It *is* weird. But he might truly have—" the words die in her throat as we round the corner to find the door of the relics room ajar. Asher looks down at the key in her hand, then to me, then back to the key. There's only one. Only Joth has it, sometimes Willow if she pesters enough. "Huh."

"Huh indeed," I say, pushing through the open door to inspect what's behind.

The room is like a tiny museum. Everything too precious

74

to be kept in the library is in here. Glass cases of old daggers, scrolls of records. Lux and Lore's letter of authentication, Guinevere's death warrant. There's even a black suit of armour standing in the corner, its helmet equipped with iron wings and a red plumage. Mordred's armour, taken from his body after his death at Camlann. It smells dusty and old, usually undisturbed. Nothing seems to be out of place, nothing amiss.

"Third glass case along. Joth said that's where the seeing stones are." Asher says quietly.

"Why are you whispering?"

"I dunno. Just feel like I should be." She creeps forward towards the case and gently taps a painted nail on the glass. "That's them. The Hag Stones."

Hag Stones, if I remember rightly, are stones that form with a natural hole in the middle. When the user holds it up to their eye, they reveal the true nature of the land underneath, the magic of it. "And we can use these to talk to each other? Do they not have phones in France?"

"You know full well we won't be able to use a phone. Not for serious stuff." Asher turns back to me, her eyes unusually dark. "Has it not sunk in for you yet either, that there really might be a war? That we really might have to fight?"

"It's not that." I shake my head, stepping towards the cabinet. On the second shelf down are three triangle stones, all of them black, shiny obsidian. "I've never been to war. I don't know how to feel."

She's quiet for a moment, considering, then she lets out a breath and opens the cabinet, picking up the Hag Stones one by one and dropping them into my palm. "All right, let's go. This place gives me the creeps. And you're sure you can't see anything missing?"

I take one last look around, noticing nothing. Until my eyes find an empty spot in the last glass cabinet on the row.

BETRAYED

That one is always quite empty anyway, which is probably why I didn't notice it before. But one of the purple cushions that would usually hold something is now bare. That means Owen, or someone else, *took* something. I stride to the cabinet, sliding open the door.

'*Carnwennan*', the faded piece of card in front of the cushion, reads.

"Do you know what that is?" Asher asks.

"No. But it shouldn't be missing."

Asher snatches up the card and puts it in her pocket and grins at my sneer. "What? There's no point having a resident history expert if we're not going to use them, and there's *no way* I'll remember how to pronounce that."

She's right, Willow will know what relic was supposed to sit on that cushion and why it might have been stolen. On the way out of the room, I take the key from Ash and make sure the door is firmly locked behind us.

Merle and Willow are waiting in the greenhouse, plates of sandwiches laid out on the table along with cake and tea. As soon as I'm through the door, Merle is in my arms, cupping my cheeks with her palms and kissing me so hard I can feel her teeth.

"I am so proud of you. How do you feel?"

"Good. Great."

She steps back and squeezes my fingers, pulling me towards the beanbags. Her face is lovely, clear skin and soft angles. But it's her eyes that always get me. Those bright, burning embers. "Lunch first, then planning. Joth says you're leaving today." She pulls her bottom lip between her teeth.

"*It's fine.*"

"*It's too soon.*"

"And you'll be taking Lux with you." She finishes out

76

loud. "And Mona."

"I will?" I flop into a seat and accept the plate offered to me by Willow.

"Do you think it's a bad idea?" She raises a dark eyebrow, cocking her head to one side. Aila, waiting next to her mistress, does the same..

"Why am I taking them?"

"Lux needs a break from this, from *here*."

"And Mona?"

"Even I know that." Asher takes her place on Merle's left, Willow completing the circle between us. "Merle's convinced Mona is wasted here, that she should be a squire."

"Facts are facts." Mer's voice is cold, not a tone she usually directs towards Ash. She's taken quite a shine to Mona's direct, no nonsense persona, the sly cleverness hidden by her bird–like features. "She *is* wasted. Mona's quick and smart and loyal. She would lay down her life for those twins without hesitation. She goes, it's not up for discussion."

"Joth—"

"Will agree to the terms."

The girl who casts her eyes to each of us, assessing one by one, is not the Merle I met in the coffee shop. This girl is the Heir of Merlin, a powerful sorcerer who serves as the Monarch's right hand. While we're friends, always, tied by the invisible need of family, loss and love, it's easy to forget that we do in fact answer to her. That her duty to Lux and Lore comes before us. *Always.*

"Mona deserves it." Willow adds. "She was born to be a knight."

"It's a shame she can't come with *us,* actually. We could do with someone else to watch our backs. Seen as we've got a witch to find and all that." Asher smiles, easing the tension. "Do we have a plan?"

BETRAYED

"Not yet." Merle pushes away her plate and drags her hand through her hair. "We know she's in the mountains somewhere, obviously well guarded. We'll need to speak to Joth."

"Will he know?"

A small smile plays at the corner of her lips. "I reckon so. I think he knew her *pretty* well."

"How well?" Willow asks.

"Well, enough to be sharing memories." I answer, wiggling my eyebrows.

"I bet that's not all they were sharing—"

"Oh, please!" Willow swats at Asher's thigh, rolling her eyes. "Good news for us, though."

"So now for the question of who we'll be taking with us." Asher says, looking directly at Merle.

"You don't have to come. I know you have Eyrie here. I would never ask you to leave her behind."

"As if I'd ever let you go alone." Asher scoffs. "Eyrie will understand, and it's not like I'm leaving her with strangers. I don't like the idea of sending you out there alone without backup."

"Good. I didn't really want to leave you behind. What about you, Willow?"

She sighs and drops the crust of the sandwich she's been eating onto her plate. "I'd rather stay here. I don't like the cold, or snow, *or* walking... I just don't know how much use I'd be and..."

"It's okay, Willow." Mer gives her a reassuring smile.

"It's probably best. You want to stay, anyway. Joth would lose his mind without someone he can trust to speak to." I say. "And who would keep the twins in check?"

"So, who else makes the cut?"

"Unfortunately, Owen." Willow says, "he was in the vision."

Asher and I meet eyes, something that doesn't go unnoticed by Merle, although she doesn't comment on it.

"That's three then. How many people do you think we need to trek up some mountains?" Asher turns her gaze from mine.

"You make it sound so easy!" Willow huffs. "You're going to climb a mountain, and I bet none of you can climb! It's not quite spring yet, so there'll still be massive avalanche risks, *and* the cable car won't be running. You can't ask for a guide who isn't in the Templar. People get hurt doing things like this. It isn't a joke."

"Amalie can climb a little." Asher eventually offers. "She's from the French Templar. She and Rory grew up in the Alps."

"I think," I say, unable to stop the stupid grin spreading on my face. "That we should ask the knights to vote."

All three faces turn to me wearing equal masks of surprise, then we all burst out laughing in unison.

"It's not the worst idea actually," Merle says when she's finished wiping her eyes. "Let's see who volunteers. There must be someone willing to go."

"I guess I better start looking at some maps, then." Willow says, finally calmed.

She packs up the plates and when they're stacked; I get to my feet and take them from her. We walk back to the kitchen, more hopeful than we've been in months.

9

Before we decide which of the knights will join us on our mad quest, I need to speak to Joth. Privately. Well, Aila will be there. But seen as she's an extension of my flesh and blood, we count as one. She's even bigger today, her coat much more orange and dotted with spots. She slinks down the hallway, sometimes weaving between my feet. To Etta's dismay, she's mostly been in the kitchen begging for scraps.

I don't want to be separated from Ren on a day when he's got limited time. My heart squeezes in my chest as I think of him leaving so soon. It doesn't feel right, him not coming with us. We've always faced everything together, right from the start. Being separated now, for an undetermined amount of time, is more painful than it should be.

As always, I find Joth in his office, sitting behind his desk and shuffling papers. He looks up at me as I enter, smiling. His tired blue eyes glinting in the lamplight.

"I was wondering when you'd finally make it here."

"We need to discuss some things before I leave."

"And when will that be?"

I sigh, brushing my hand through Aila's soft coat. "Tomorrow? Two days? We don't have much of a plan. Did you speak to the French guardian?"

"Lady Cassandra is expecting you, yes. Amalie called straight after the meeting. She's excited to meet you."

"I wish it was under better circumstances."

"Don't we all?" Joth smiles and leans back in his chair.

The relationship between us has changed somewhat over the last few months. When I first got here, he didn't see me as an adult who could be trusted to make decisions. But that illusion quickly slipped away as the responsibilities piled up. Now I'm his peer, his friend, someone that he trusts above almost all others.

"Lux is to go with Ren to Scotland," I say. I'm expecting an argument, and from the widening of Joth's eyes I'm sure I'm about to get one, so I quickly add; "and Mona. She's standing in as Lydia's second until Lydia chooses someone else." *or chooses Mona.* I don't need to add out loud.

Joth pauses in what he was going to say, then "I'll hear your arguments for Lux. Mona is an adult and she can do as she pleases. If she *wants* to go to Scotland, then she goes."

"Good." I nod and lean forward in my seat. It's good because I've already told Mona to pack her things and ready herself for the journey. Not that Joth needs to know that. "Lux should go. He needs a break from this place, Joth. A break from the prying eyes. You know he's been struggling."

"Yes."

"A few days on an adventure with Ren, actually *helping*, rather than sitting around and worrying, will do him the world

BETRAYED

of good. And I *won't* be here, Joth. Lore and Eyrie will be fine with Willow. They can work on the prophecy with her. They *love* that. But Lux," I shake my head, trying to swallow the lump in my throat, to stop my voice from breaking. "He needs this. He needs something."

Joth steeples his fingers in front of him and closes his eyes, considering. He doesn't want to let Lux go when things are so uncertain and dangerous. But to have him stay might be even more deadly. "And I trust you've properly thought this through?"

"I have. And, it isn't far, not really. He could be home in a matter of hours if he wanted to be. But we have to show him that we trust him. In a few years' time, he's supposed to *rule*. They both are."

He eyes me again, searching for any doubt in my face. There isn't any. I truly believe it's the right thing to do, that it's worth the risk to Lux. It might be the only thing that saves him.

"All right. I'll call ahead to Rab McGavin, make sure he knows to prepare for the King's arrival."

"Thank you."

"Was there more?"

Now it's my turn to eye him. He knows full well what I'm here for, the information I want. "Morgana. I need to know what you know."

"Most of the information I have is centuries old, *centuries–*"

"Joth," I say gently. "I didn't mean to see those other memories. You know I wouldn't pry."

He sighs and rubs his hand across his brow. "It hurts to think of her, and I haven't in so long."

"Were you in love?"

The smile on his face falters a little as he considers the question. "Morgana was the great love of my life, *is.* I hate to remember the way we left things, and now we might reconcile..."

"That's good, isn't it?"

He chuckles. "Not her and I reconciling, Morgana and the Templar. I'm an old man now, Merle. Morgana won't have aged a day, I don't hold any hope of that."

"Well, I don't imagine there are many men in the Alps she could have fallen in love with."

At that, he snorts. "I don't suppose there is. I don't want to face her. It's not something I'm sure I can manage. I wasn't part of the plot to betray her. I never would have been trusted in that inner circle because of my relationship with her. But I didn't stop them."

"Why didn't you?" It's a question I've been wanting to ask since I got the full story. Joth's lied to me before, or covered things up, but he isn't a bad person.

"I don't have a good answer for you, Merle. As you well know, the Templar, the knights, they need guidance, not abolishment. We do important work, we have things to protect and preserve. I thought I could make a difference here, that I could be part of an institution that meant something again."

"You are." I say. "It does."

A small smile flickers on his face. "I can only hope. Go on, ask your questions, just keep them mission oriented."

That I can do. I've already seen and heard enough gossip today to satiate my appetite for personal information. "Where do you think she is? Which mountain?"

"No matter which mountain she's on, you won't find her unless she wants to be found."

"We don't have time to explore six summits, neither do we have the skill. How do I let her know I'm looking for her? If you were a gambling man, where would you go?"

"You'll have to call to her when you get to France," he

BETRAYED

muses. "Magically, of course. The French Templar is in Saint–Gervais–les–Bains, specifically there in case we ever could locate her. You'll be close enough for her to feel your magic, so you'll need to send her a message. Tell her you want to talk."

"Will she answer?"

Joth chuckles, "no. I doubt it. She might never answer. *But* if you get close enough, you will *intrigue* her." Now he leans forward in his chair. "She will want to know exactly who's on her mountain and why they've claimed Merlin's power. If you make her curious, she might, *might,* see you."

That's better news than I'd hoped for. And I suppose she *will* want to know who is brave (or stupid) enough to raise her from her slumber.

"Okay." I nod. "Now, the offer I intend to make. I wanted to run it by you."

"You know there's only one thing she wants, don't you?" The smirk falters. "The only thing she'll agree to, *if* she agrees at all, is disbanding the Templar. Is that what you intend to offer her?"

"Not exactly." I've thought about this for a long time. In truth, I side mostly with Morgana, but I don't necessarily want the Templar disbanded. The knights serve a great purpose, *when* they serve. "We shouldn't promise her we'll get rid of the Templar, that's a promise we can't keep, one I don't want to keep. But, we can promise her a... well, I guess you'd call it an audit."

"An audit?" Joth raises his eyebrows. "What do you mean?"

"Well, Lux and Lore are eleven now. They're only four years away from being of age, right? It would be wrong of us, and *her*, to dismantle their birthright."

"Yes."

"But it wouldn't be wrong to give them the facts, all the

Templar's good things, but also all its bad things. I know you aren't happy with the way things are, that some of the knights exist above their station. My promise to her would be this;" I make my eyes meet Joth's and put one hand on Aila's head for reassurance. An ebb of calm washes into me, her feline focus at my disposal. "When Lux and Lore turn fifteen, and have the power to do what they will, the Knights of the Templar will have to justify their position, their assets, their land. Morgana can oppose them if she wishes and present her own evidence to the twins. Then, *they* will decide, as the king and queen, whether the Templar stands, or whether..." I trail off and shrug my shoulders.

He considers me for a long moment. "Like a trial?"

"Exactly. If Arthur's true heirs decide the knights stay, then no promises have been broken, right?"

"It's a better idea than I've had." He sighs. "There's no guarantee she'll go for it."

"Then I better just hope she finds me interesting."

"You'd better hope with everything you've got." Joth smiles and pulls back the top drawer of his desk. When his hands reemerge, he's holding a yellowing envelope and a gold ring embedded with a ruby cut into the shape of a rose. "I also have something for you, something I'd like you to give to her if you find her."

"You asked her to help, too?"

He slides the letter across the desk and then places the ring on top. "I've asked her for a lot of things. I don't think it will do any good, but for Lore's sake, I had to try."

"I'll make sure she gets it."

He looks at the clock on the wall above my head. I'm sure it's late, and he looks tired. "Is there anything else you need?"

"Just one favour." I push my chair back, putting the letter carefully in my pocket. I'll string the ring on the rosary Mona

BETRAYED

gave me and never accepted back. My ring, the key to the cave, now lies broken in the Relics room. "Take care of Ren and Willow and the kids. Make sure that they're ready, just in case something happens to us."

Joth holds my stare, then he nods. He knows how dangerous the road is, and what we're risking. "I promise."

"I'm going to find Lux. Get him ready."

"And I'll call the knights to order, although informally, to see who's ready to face Morgana Le Fae. I'll be there to say goodbye."

I find Lux in the library, lounging by the fire with a book. He's much less tense now, the relief of sharing his burden with someone he truly loves is evident. Not that he doesn't like me, but Ren's his older brother, his favourite person in the world. There's no one better to chase away his nightmares. As soon as he sees Aila, he swings upright and opens his arms. The big cat bounds forward, placing her already huge paws on his knees and licking the end of his nose.

"She likes you."

"She thinks I'm her dinner."

I snort a laugh, "she wishes! I've got some news, good news, I think."

"What is it?"

I plonk myself down beside him and ruffle the soft fur between Aila's ears until she purrs.

You big softy, you're supposed to be a predator.

"Do you want to go to Scotland?"

"Really?" Lux jumps from his seat so fast Aila tumbles to the floor. "Like now, with Ren? *Really?*"

"Do you want to go?"

He claps his hands in front of him, beaming from ear to ear. "Do you swear you're not joking?"

86

"I swear that Ren's in your room right now packing you a bag, and Etta's made your favourite snacks for the road." I grin and open my arms to him. He isn't usually overly affectionate, aside from when he's disorientated and upset. But he looks so happy I can't help but want to hug him. He folds into my arms, trembling with excitement.

"Thank you, thank you, thank you."

"Don't thank me yet." I say, pushing him back, keeping my hands on his shoulders. "It isn't a holiday. You've got a job to do."

"I do?"

"Yes. Mona is going with you. She's learning to be a knight. You're going to have to teach her everything you know, keep an eye on her, make sure she's getting on okay. It's a big responsibility."

His face becomes pensive for a moment and it takes all my self–control not to laugh. He's such a serious boy, and he'll make a wise and thoughtful king. "I think I can handle it."

Now I do laugh despite my efforts, "of course you can handle it. We know that. Are you ready?"

"Wait." He says and pulls away from me. He picks up the book he was reading, shaking it by the spine until a chunky yellow envelope falls out. "I want you to take this for her. Morgana I mean."

With shaky fingers, he hands it over. '*To the Lady Morgana Le Fae*' is scrawled on the envelope in his best handwriting. The other side is sealed with red wax and a stamp.

"Eyrie helped me." He adds sheepishly.

"I'll give it to her, I promise." I tuck the letter next to Joth's in my pocket, beaming with pride. "Right, come on, before we really do get left behind."

The next stop on my list after I've handed Lux off to Willow, is to find Ren. He's in his room, still packing his things.

BETRAYED

"How was it, with Joth, Lux?" He asks as soon as I've thrown myself onto the bed.

"All agreed. All good. Don't go."

He smiles and raises an eyebrow, grabbing his backpack from the chair by his bed, rummaging for something.

"I was going to give you this earlier, but we ran out of time." He hands me a flat black stone, as smooth as cut glass. It has a hole in its centre. "It's said to be part of the rock from which Excalibur was pulled. A Hag Stone crafted by Morgana. Asher and I nicked them earlier."

"A Hag Stone? And nicked them from where?"

"Yep, there's three of them. One for you, one for us, one for Joth and Willow. Hag Stones can see the land as it really is when you hold it up to your eye." He demonstrates and then hands it to me. I stare through the hole, but everything looks the same. "Legend says that this particular stone was made for Guinevere to give to Arthur to take on his search for the grail. So that they might see each other even though they were thousands of miles apart." He closes my hand over it. "I don't know if it'll work."

"I'll make sure that it does."

He smiles and brushes a lock of hair behind my ear. "Be careful. And be careful about who you take with you. I know you saw Owen in your vision, but there's something wrong with him. I don't trust him. Be on your guard."

I nod, keeping my eyes on his. "You too. Get back here as quickly as possible, where it's safe."

He pulls me to him, pressing his lips to mine. I don't hesitate in wrapping my arms around his neck, or in tracing my tongue against his bottom lip until he shivers.

"I love you." I say.

"I love you too." He presses his forehead to mine, his eyes closed. "Please, please be careful. Morgana is a loose cannon, and that's if you find her."

"I'll be fine—"

"People die on mountains."

"I promise I'll be careful. You should be too."

He nods, then kisses the tip of my nose. "I will be."

We make our way downstairs, fingers twisted together. It only makes it a little easier for him to leave, knowing I'll be going on my own adventure soon enough. We stop in the entrance hall, which is already full of people. Lux is saying goodbye to Eyrie and Lore, Mona dutifully holding his backpack stuffed full of books.

Ren puts down his bag and offers his arms to me one last time. "It'll only feel like two minutes until we're back together."

"I know." I croak, trying to keep my voice steady, but my throat burns from holding back tears.

"You two are *so* cute!" Asher's arms wind their way around our middles, squeezing us so hard my back cracks. I get a mouth full of orange braids as she buries her head between us.

"Thanks, Ash." I disentangle myself and step back.

"Came to say goodbye to Sir Ren." She claps her hand on his shoulder. "Good luck. I hear Scotland's cold this time of year."

"Thanks. You too." He picks his bag back up and swings it over his shoulder. He gives me one last kiss on my temple, one that in no way matches what I want our goodbye to be. Then he shares a look with Asher. I don't understand its significance, but she must, because she nods.

We watch them to the door, Lux giving me an excited high five before he climbs into the black car waiting for them. Mona gives me a solemn nod. She's a woman of few words. Ren gives us one last smile and a wave before getting into the

BETRAYED

car after them.

"He'll be all right, you know." Asher says, putting her arm around my shoulders and squeezing.

"I know."

"Ah, young love. I remember what it was like to be so smitten, and so utterly stupid."

Her comment startles a laugh from me. As always, I'm glad for her seemingly endless ability to distract me from my emotions. I squeeze my arm around her waist. "Don't worry, Ash, you're definitely still one of those things."

10

It's late by the time we finally settle in one of the larger sitting rooms, Etta bringing tea and biscuits for the occasion. I find a seat between Willow and Asher, pulling a sleepy Aila into my lap. She's had a big few days, all things considered and has earned a nap.

"I assume you have a plan." Tristen huffs at me. "This was your ridiculous idea, after all."

"Well, I realise we've a lot of work to do. We need to agree on the team, map out the trail, and figure out if we have any idea where Morgana might be—"

"This is a fool's errand," John Alymere cuts me off. "Once you open the door to that witch, there's no knowing what horrors—"

"You *coward!*" Amalie Percival steals the words from my throat. Her red hair falls around her shoulders to her waist as she stands, her cream cheeks marked with stripes of pink. "'Ow

BETRAYED

long 'ave you known we're at war? 'Ow long do you want to go on pretending nothing's wrong? Oliver is *dead*. And you sit there and do *nothing*!"

"You're out of turn, Amalie." Alymere says, his watery blue eyes full of venom.

"And you are *old*."

Her words startle a laugh from me and Asher chokes on her tea.

"You forget your duty and your sworn oath! You made a promise to Arthur's line, and instead of keeping it, you sit in your finery and wait for death." She swings her hair over her shoulder, her eyes daring any of them to challenge her. Nobody does. "Obviously, I will go with you to France, because it is *my duty*, and I am glad to do it." Then, after a deep breath, she adds. "And I can take us to the Templar. It's been too long since I've seen Rory."

"Thank you, Amalie." Joth smiles in her direction. No one else says anything as Amalie sits. Asher gives her hand an appreciative squeeze. "It's not an expectation that any of you will join this party, but we could use someone with expedition experience, and we'll need to get across the channel."

"You'll be needing me then, I guess." Eddie Pelleas grins over the top of his teacup. He's close to fifty, with salt and pepper hair and a five o'clock shadow and one of the few knights I've actually grown to like. Apparently, he used to be in the army, special forces. That's where Joth found him. At least he'll understand how to organise a brigade.

"I was certainly hoping you'd volunteer, yes." Joth asks. "Anybody else?"

"I'd like to volunteer myself, too." Greg Tristen says. "I think I could be useful."

I can't stop the surprise showing on my face and I get a not so discreet elbow in the ribs from Asher. *"Bloody hell, someone's in a good mood."*

"Excellent." Joth says as silence falls.

No one else speaks until Willow says; "What about you, Owen?"

All eyes in the room swivel to Owen Lamorak, and his cheeks flush a dull pink. "Me? You, you want me there?"

"I saw you in my vision," I shrug. "There's a spot for you if you want it."

"I do." Owen says with no hesitation. Not even when Lawrence glares at him from across the room.

"And we'll pick up Rory on the other end, no?" Amalie offers. "She and Richard can climb the smaller summits."

"So as it stands, the party going to France are Asher, Amalie and her sister, Aurora's husband Richard Pike, Eddie, Sir Tristen, Owen, and you, Merle." Joth counts us off on his fingers.

I nod. It seems like a good party, in all truth. I had wondered if Gawain might offer his services, but he's sitting quietly beside Sir Kay. From the remaining knights, I expected nothing less.

"I'm sorry to put you on the spot straight away, Eddie, but as you're the only one with any real experience here, I'll defer to you. What happens now?"

"First, we need to get to France. We should go as soon as possible, travel light and re–supply when we arrive. I'm assuming that will be possible, Amalie?"

"Of course."

"Once we're there, we'll take some time to acclimatise..." and with that, Eddie takes full control of the mission ahead. It's amazing to see how quickly his brain works, how sure he is about the task, and he has no problem delegating responsibility. Asher, Amalie and Owen are to figure out rations and supplies. Sir Tristen is to be his second in command to help plot the routes we'll take, and prepare us for the altitude and the cold. Even Richard and Rory are assigned duties.

"What about me?" I say, my voice tight. He's come to the end of his list of jobs and I'm yet to be named.

"Well, surely that's obvious?" Eddie turns to me, still grinning. "You need to make sure you've got enough magic to keep us warm, to protect us from an avalanche, to warn us about danger. And I assume you're intending to make a deal with Morgana? To offer her some kind of reward?"

"Wow, he's good." Willow sends to me.

"I do."

"Then you need to make sure it's air tight. If we're going all that way and taking this enormous risk, she'd better accept."

"And what *do* you intend to offer her?" Kay asks, his voice sharp like broken glass.

Your head on a stick? I think to myself.

"If my history is correct, Morgana left without the permission of the Templar. That currently makes her a rogue, and our enemy." I meet his gaze. "Not only is it her duty to restore Lore, but I will offer her a pardon. She will be truly free from us, and we will never call on her again. Morgana, if she wishes, will be struck from even our history, untied from us forever."

"She'll never agree." He insists.

"She will. A war is coming, Sir Kay, whether or not you like it. I think she'd rather offer her services in this small matter than be called upon to battle with her sister."

"I agree." Joth interjects before anyone else can speak. He knows as well as I do that it's best to talk about it as little as possible, seen as we're being dishonest. "When do you leave?"

"In the morning." Eddie says. "As soon as we can."

"And are we all in agreement?"

All heads nod.

"Good." Then Joth smiles, his eyes sparkling. "For the first time in almost 1,000 years, the Templar has made a unanimous decision. Wonders never cease."

After staying up well into the night strategizing with Willow and Asher, and packing vials of herbs and oils with Eyrie and Lore, I practically fall into bed. I'm happy to get up when my alarm sounds at six am, ready for the adventure. Aila is not. She tries to snuggle back into the warmth of the covers as I get dressed and hisses at me when I pull her out and set her on the floor.

We're going on an adventure. You could be more pleased about it.

Her glare tells me she'd rather rip me to shreds.

When I get downstairs, the front doors are open, our belongings already being packed into the cars. A sliver of the waning moon still hangs in the sky, the ground littered with frosty pebbles. Joth is standing by one black sedan, talking to Tristen, who has the keys hanging from his fist. Tristen is not my biggest fan, but when he sees me, he smiles. Joth waves me over.

"Owen, Amalie, Eddie and Greg are taking this car. You and Asher will go together."

I blanch. It's only just hit me, somehow, that France is a different country, somewhere I probably need a passport to enter. That's something I don't have. "Joth, I don't have a passport."

Tristen laughs, but not unkindly. "I was wondering when you'd ask about that."

"So what do I do?" Panic grips my insides.

"Being a secret, well—connected organisation has its perks, Young Witch. It's all taken care of." Tristen looks over

BETRAYED

the top of my head, still grinning. "It looks like your ride's here."

I follow his gaze. A small orange car is making its way up the path. The passenger door is a different colour to the rest, a startling blue, so bright it could be a clown car in a circus. Asher pulls up next to the sleek, black sedan, and sticks her head out of the window.

There's laughter from the steps. I turn to see Amalie doubled over, clutching at her ribs. Even Owen is smiling.

"Come on, Merle! We've got a boat to catch!" Asher shouts and then ducks her head back in to beep the horn.

"*If we can make it there in that old thing.*" I send to her, rolling my eyes even though she can't see. Now I understand why Tristen was laughing and why I'm riding with Asher alone.

Joth is grinning from ear to ear. "So, you're all set?"

"Yes." I say, mentally checking things off my list. The letters are safely tucked into my pack, the ring is threaded onto the rosary, Aila waiting for me on the steps.

I grab Aila, ruffling her fur and kissing her nose. Then I take her to Willow who is standing by the doors, anxiously shuffling from foot to foot.

"You're to stop worrying right now," I pull her into a hug, careful not to squish the cat between us. "Everything will be okay. You'll have your hands full with those two." I cock my head to the sleepy girls trailing their way down the stairs. "And you've got a prophecy to solve."

"And I'll do my very best to solve it." She pushes me back, rubbing my elbow. "Now go on, you'll miss your boat."

I give her one last hug and kiss her cheek, then I turn to Lore. "All right?"

"Yes." Her grey eyes meet mine. Then she sends, "*are you going to get me out of here?*"

96

"The Templar?"

She shakes her head and then taps her temple. *"No. Here. Where I'm stuck."*

I drop to one knee so I can look straight into her eyes. *"I promise you, on my mum and dad, and my oath, I won't rest until you feel whole. I promise you I'll come back with help."*

"All right?" I finish out loud, my throat straining against tears.

"All right." She nods.

"I love you. Help Willow and please try not to drive Joth crazy." I get up, hiding my tears from her with a wipe of my sleeve. "We'll be back soon. Hold on a little longer."

Asher says goodbye to Eyrie, who keeps a stiff upper lip for the most part, and only really starts crying when Willow puts her arms around both of the girls. I settle Aila in the back seat of the car while waiting for Asher, who eventually gets in, wiping her own streaming eyes.

"Ready?" I ask.

"Ready."

"And you're sure this thing will make it?"

"And you're sure you wouldn't rather walk?" Asher gives me the side eye.

"Might get there faster."

Asher howls with laughter and starts the engine.

Later, after what seems like hours of being cooped up in Asher's glorified sardine can, we finally pull over at a service station so Aila can stretch her legs. The kitten, now almost the size of a springer spaniel, has been surprisingly good for the last three hours. She's snuggled against Asher's coat, occasionally glancing up to check I'm still here.

As Asher fills up the tank, I go inside and buy snacks but when I get back, she seems a little agitated. Less relaxed than

BETRAYED

when I left.

"Is everything all right?"

"Yes," she nods, not looking at me. I swear her hands tremble a little as she places them back on the wheel. Aila narrows her eyes at us before hopping into the back seat, also sensing something wrong.

"Ash?" I ask again.

"I'm okay, I promise. Just felt a little sick there for a moment." She flashes a grin at me, but I'm not entirely convinced.

It's another two hours to Dover and we arrive just as the sun reaches its highest point in the sky. The turquoise sea fades into the horizon, the pale yellow light of spring sparkling off the waves, fragmenting in rainbows. White cliffs rise from the water's surface, so stark and bright they make my eyes hurt. I lick my lips and taste salt. The air is so fresh, so different from the musty fumes of car exhausts, and the hollow, ancient dust of the Templar. I breathe in deep.

"You'd usually get the ferry from somewhere over there." Asher points out of the window. "But we're travelling in style, well, *secret*."

Asher parks the car in the space beside Tristen. The others are already out and unpacking the boot. Amalie has her head tipped back in the sun, long arms stretched skywards.

"Why are we unpacking?" I ask her when I've completed my own stretches. "Aren't we taking the cars?"

"No silly," she grins. "We go on the boat on foot. Rory is expecting us at the other end."

"And how long will it take?" I look out at the choppy sea. The rolling waves are enough to make me feel seasick already.

"A couple of 'ours, maybe? Less if Eddie can sail as well as 'e says." She tosses her hair over her shoulder and pulls it up into a perfect, high ponytail.

It takes all my efforts not to scowl at her. *I wish my hair would do that.*

"And when we get to France?"

"We should be there just after midnight."

"*Midnight?*" I splutter. "But it's only lunchtime now."

"Long drive." She shrugs. "We go first to Troyes, stop there to eat. Then we go to Saint–Gervais–les–Bains. Most people think it's a town with a small commune that keeps to themselves but," she shrugs. "It's really us, right out of the way."

I take the rucksack that Asher hands me and pull it onto my back, then I follow them down onto the dock. The ship stands tall against the sky; the bow carving a harsh diagonal line into the horizon. The underside is painted black with a red edge, and above is a square cabin that doesn't match the sleekness of the body.

"Not what you were expecting?" Tristen asks from beside me.

"I wasn't really expecting anything."

"Well, you're in good hands. Eddie has Captained a third of the trips *Prydwen* has taken."

"*Prydwen?*"

"After Arthur's very own ship. It's better than what your friend over there wanted to call it." Eddie, who has climbed his way down to stand beside Tristen, snorts.

"It was something ridiculous, right?"

"I'll have you know it was a *fantastic* suggestion." Asher calls from the top of the steps. I'm surprised she even heard us.

Eddie rolls his eyes. "She wanted to call it *The Codfather.*"

I can't help the laugh that bursts from my mouth.

"It would have been better than *Prydwen.*"

"For once I agree." Owen says.

BETRAYED

"Well, thankfully, common sense prevailed." Tristen cocks an eyebrow, still smiling.

"Come on, Merle." Amalie takes hold of my wrist. "I'll show you around."

She guides me up the steps and onto the boat itself. I follow her through the cabin, suspiciously eyeing the controls. I don't understand how Eddie will sail the thing with so many buttons and lights. We go down another set of stairs and into boat proper. On the inside, it looks a bit like a caravan. There are two bunks against one wall, and a small storage space against the other. Amalie dumps her pack, and then takes mine, shoving it up against the wall.

"Bathrooms through there." She points to the small door at the far end of the boat. "We only really come down here when it rains. It gets so stuffy."

"So where will we go?"

"Up on deck It's sunny enough, and we brought sandwiches. Although," she stands on her tiptoes and rummages around in the cupboard, then hands me a worn, tartan blanket, its edges hanging with frayed tassels."It might get chilly with the wind."

The engine roars to life as we climb back up the stairs, and when we get to the top, Aila launches herself into my arms, almost knocking me backwards. I can feel the wariness radiating off her, that she isn't a big fan of the water, that I shouldn't have gone below deck without her.

"*I'm sorry,*" I send. "*It won't happen again. I promise you're perfectly safe.*"

"You're to put this on." Sir Tristen hands me a life jacket. "I don't have one for the cat."

"Do they make life jackets for cats?" Asher says, already strapped into her red vest.

I shrug and hand Aila over for a moment while I secure my straps. Then we're ushered into our seats by the older knights, and I find myself squished between Owen and Amalie as Pelleas steers the boat out into open sea.

100

11

When everyone is as comfortable as they can get on the cramped deck, and all the sandwiches have gone, there's finally time to pick the others' brains about Morgana. Amalie doesn't know much, only her legend. Tristen's ears prick up, though. I see his back straighten from where I'm sitting.

"Greg?" I ask, "What about you?"

"I've never met a witch, well, aside from you. But all the stories I've heard paint Morgana as a formidable adversary. When she left the Templar, it was *explosive.*"

I tip my head to one side and wait for him to continue. After a moment's silence, he does.

"According to the story my father told me, after she banished her sister, the knights asked for time to make everything ready to disband. They said it couldn't happen overnight because they had so much land and wealth. So, she also agreed to that, gave them a full year to sort themselves

BETRAYED

out, but as time went on and nothing changed," He shrugs. "She realised she'd been had and almost burnt the whole thing to the ground. They saved the Templar building, lost a lot of records, and then Morgana vanished. Never to be seen again. Well, until now, but I have a horrible feeling that we're wasting our time, and potentially our lives, for this mission."

"Why did you agree to it, then?"

Tristen's face softens, his eyes turning outwards to gaze over the sea. "Because Lila would have volunteered in an instant."

"I'm sorry."

He shakes his head, taking a moment to steady his words. "When you first got here, I doubted whether you'd be any help to us at all. I was wrong. Your tenacity, refusal to give up, your willingness to lay down your life for our cause without even really understanding it. I was so strongly reminded of her, and of how much she would have liked you, I had to come."

"I'm sure I would have liked her, too."

Now he smiles. "Yes, I'm sure you would have been thick as thieves. She was growing restless, as if she could feel a storm coming. So were some of the others, Amalie being one. What she said about us being cowards was right. We've been idle too long." He crushes his fist into his open palm. "And the cost has been more than I could have ever imagined. I won't sit about and wait any longer. We swore an oath. It's high time we got off our backsides and fulfilled it."

With that, I can't argue. I might have doubted Tristen's motive's before this, but now I don't. "Where do you think Morgana is?"

"I don't know, Little Witch. But if anyone can find her, I bet it's you."

I'm stopped in my response by Eddie shouting, "land ho!"

Everyone bolts up the stairs and looks out onto the

horizon. In the distance, there's a wobbly, dark shape across the sky.

Amalie claps her hands in front of her, eyes shining. "I'm so excited to see Rory!"

"Well, we've made good time." Pelleas smiles. "Hopefully, they'll be there to greet us when we arrive."

We pull into the dock twenty minutes later. The sun is still shining, although the wind is cooler, biting at my cheeks. I'm glad for the blanket Amalie gave me, which I pull tightly around my shoulders. Tristen goes below deck with Owen, and they hand our packs up one by one. Amalie is buzzing with excitement, hopping from foot to foot.

When the boat is finally secured, she leaps over the side, her boots thudding on the wood of the dock, dust rising from the impact.

"*Ma moitié.*" She cries, scrambling forwards.

Aurora Percival is waiting to embrace her with arms outstretched. Rory looks almost exactly like her sister. She has the same red hair, although hers is chopped into a bob, and sea–green eyes. Her jawline is also more square, her face oval compared to Amalie's heart shape. Aurora wraps her arms around her sister's middle and squeezes tightly. There's a man standing behind her, grinning. He has stubble on his cheeks, black flicks of hair around face and horn–rimmed glasses balancing on the end of his long, thin nose. He looks more like an IT consultant than a Templar knight.

"I know you're not really into PDA. I mean, neither am I... but just endure it, won't you?" Asher whispers in my ear.

I'm about to ask her what she means, but before I can, I'm pulled into a hug by Aurora. She grips my face with both her hands and then kisses my cheeks.

"*Salut* Merle! We've 'eard so much about you!" Her smile glows.

BETRAYED

"I've heard a lot about you, too." I say as my cheeks flame.

Thankfully, the man only offers me his hand. I shake it, his grip dry and strong.

"Richard Pike," he says. "Rory's husband. Good trip so far?" He takes the pack from my shoulders and swings it over his own.

"Yes, thanks. It didn't take as long as I thought."

"First time across, eh?" He smiles. The action changes his entire face, the tightening of his jaw muscles emphasising the strong lines of his features. "Good job it wasn't too choppy, then. I'll put your stuff in the car. You'll be coming with us – Amalie's special request."

"She got stuck with the boys on the way over."

He snorts. "That explains it, then. We also stopped for coffee. You take it black, don't you?"

"Um... yes." I take the paper cup from him, a little startled by his knowledge. Maybe Amalie forewarned him?

"No, I have a touch of Sight. Not magic, but I can pick up on things."

"Really?"

"Oh yes! Comes in handy when I'm buying my wife's birthday presents." He grins again and then takes another paper cup and offers it to Asher who has smudges of lipstick on her cheeks. There are clouds gathering in the sky as if it's going to rain. I wish Ren were here.

"A penny for your thoughts, Young Witch?" Eddie asks from beside me.

"I was thinking about the rain." As if I've summoned it with my words, tiny flecks of water start to tickle my face.

"Come on," Eddie swings his arms around my shoulders. "It's time to go. Now you've mastered the ability to change the weather."

"You're in the middle, short stuff." Asher grins.

104

"I'm like an inch shorter than you!" I say, but reluctantly slide over, squishing up against Amalie.

"An inch can sometimes make all the difference." Asher grins wickedly at me as she climbs into the seat. I narrow my eyes at her, my cheeks flushing with heat. Amalie howls with laughter.

"Are we all ready to go, kids?" Richard turns to us. I do feel like a child, about to embark on a family holiday. Although, this will be like no holiday I've ever experienced.

As we drive, the sea fades, giving way to green fields and then to a more boring stretch of road. My eyes begin to slide closed, my head falling forward onto my chin. As if she can sense it, Rory turns around in her seat.

"You can sleep. Lei already is."

Lei must be her nickname for Amalie. I smile and lay my head on Asher's shoulder. She shifts a little, then leans her cheek on the top of my head. Usually I struggle to sleep on car journeys, but we were up early, and this time I'm out like a light.

The next time I open my eyes, the light has changed, and the car is pulling to a stop. A dull orange glow surrounds the fading sun. Streaks of pink, yellow, and blue rush across the sky. I open my eyes fully. "Are we here?"

"Ha!" Asher laughs. "You sound like Eyrie! *Ash, are we there yet?*"

"It's a valid question." Amalie shifts, the bones of her spine popping. "But no. I told you the journey was long. It's time to eat."

I stretch up to the sky as we clamber out of the back seat, Aila arching her back and letting out a huge yawn. A sweet ache runs through my limbs, tingles flooding my foot where it's gone to sleep.

BETRAYED

I feel Aila's intention in my mind, the request to go into the trees nearby and hunt her own meal. She looks at me with her glowing turquoise stare, waiting for my answer.

"Go." I send. *"Be safe. Be quick."*

She growls her agreement before pacing into the shadows.

I hobble behind Rory and Richard and into the cafe. The boys are already there. Eddie is munching on bread, Tristen and Owen are pouring over a map. I drop into the seat beside them.

"I told them to wait until we've eaten." Eddie casts his brown eyes up to mine, then to Rory. There are crumbs on his chin. "But they wouldn't. Owen's *convinced* she's hiding in the Aguille Verte but who knows?"

Ash rolls her eyes and turns to me. "What are you having, Merle?"

"Pizza." I eventually shoot at her.

"And salad."

"Salad?" I stare at her and wrinkle my nose. *"Since when do we eat salad?"*

"You're gonna miss that green stuff when we're a thousand feet up. Fine, we'll do pizza, pasta, salad, and split it?"

I nod my approval.

When I look up, there are six faces staring at us with confused expressions. I spend so much of my time with my three closest friends; I forget that not everyone knows we sometimes talk like this.

"Um... sorry. Wait, let me..."

I send out feelers with my mind for each of them. I find the twins and Richard easily, along with Eddie and Greg. When I get to Owen, though, I'm met with a strong, black wall. Odd that he'd know how to shield. *How* does *he know?*

106

"We were just deciding what to eat. We do this sometimes. I didn't mean to be rude." I send to the group, not wanting to alert them to anything wrong.

Rory claps her hands with delight. Even Tristen is smirking a little.

"I'd heard rumours about your telepathy." He says. "It's a little different in reality, isn't it?"

"Weird." Owen says.

I frown at him. I know he didn't hear it. There's no way. Surely he knows that? So why is he mimicking their responses?

"She can send pictures too, and memories. It's kind of like a film." Asher answers.

"How interesting!" Richard slides into the seat opposite. "Just your memories or other peoples?"

"Other peoples." I turn my attention from Owen, filing the information away for later. "Do you wanna see?"

"Me too!" Rory sits down, her eyes lighting up.

"You're not prone to seasickness, are you?" Asher cocks an eyebrow, looking a little green. "Watching those things makes me want to throw up!"

I explain to the others how projection works, and then offer my hands to them. Owen shakes his head and decides instead to help Asher order the food.

"Now close your eyes."

I dig down deep into my memories and pull up the one of Merlin. In my experience, it's the biggest crowd pleaser. I also like to hear him read the prophecy. When his words fade, and he's traced the lines of the mark on my arm, I open my eyes.

"You really got to see him?" Eddie whispers. "That was really Merlin? I knew you'd been given the message, but I had no idea you actually *saw* him."

"It really was." I smile. "I saw him crack out of the rock."

BETRAYED

"And what of the prophecy?" Richard asks.

"We've spent the last six months trying to decipher it. Willow will continue while we're away."

"The shores of Avalon are supposed to be silver." Rory muses.

"Are they?" I ask. It's the first I've heard of it. "Have you ever been there?"

"No." She shakes her head. "It's too close to the borders of the fae realm. Too dangerous."

"Aren't Lux and Lore supposed to rule it?" My heartbeat quickens. We haven't spoken of it much, but Joth always makes Avalon sound pleasant, like a tropical island. I don't want to send the twins into danger.

"It hasn't always been, only since Morgwese made her move."

"And by the time we send them, there'll be peace." Tristen's eyes reassure me. Then they flick over my head and Asher plonks down in her seat.

"Won't be long. I hope you're all hungry! We got *loads*." She grins.

Ten minutes later, the staff bring over the food, and in the end, we all decide to share. I help myself to a mountain of pasta, pizza, and warm crusty bread slathered with butter. At Asher's insistence, I even eat a full bowl of greens.

When we've eaten enough for our bellies to be full and groaning, we trundle back out into the cold. I resume my place in the middle seat, and after a while, I feel Asher rest her head on my shoulder.

"Don't go to sleep, Ash. It's okay to pretend, but we've got to talk." I send to her.

She shifts a little, but doesn't open her eyes. *"About?"*

"Owen."

She lets out an audible sigh. *"I was wondering when*

you'd ask about that."

I'm not exactly sure what *she's* referring to, but her statement does nothing to ease my nerves. *"What are you talking about?"*

"Owen sneaking about in the Relic room? Ren didn't tell you?"

At the sound of his name, my heart floods with longing. *"He didn't. But we'll get to that later. I mean, Owen's shields."*

"What?" she starts, but then Amalie taps me on the arm.

"I want you to tell me more about when you got your magic! I can't believe I missed the most exciting thing that's happened in like 600 years!"

I sigh. *"To be continued Ash."*

Then I launch into the story of the cave.

12

REN

Lux starts moaning about how long the drive is almost as soon as we set off. Not even Mona asking him questions, which I'm sure she doesn't care about the answer of, is enough to stop him fidgeting after an hour. It *is* a long drive. Lydia's estate is high in the Cairngorms, just to the east in Ballater.

Each of the knights, once they're sworn, receives a plot of land and manor house in the part of Europe that Arthur once gifted their ancestors. My estate, now I'm truly a knight, will be in Tintagel, down south in Cornwall.

We drive through the night, only stopping a few times for coffee and snacks. Lux eventually dozes with his head on Mona's shoulder. She and I sit in a companionable silence, mostly looking out of the windows even though there's little to see. I've known Mona almost all of my life. I remember meeting her on the first day I arrived at the Templar, fifteen years old to my seven. No one has ever cracked her iron facade, nobody other than Merle. Mona practically worships the ground Mer walks on.

I wake Lux up when we're passing Balmoral, so he can see the castle in the orange sunrise, grass glittering with frost. The further into the wild we go, the thicker the snow gets, heavy mists blocking the beauty of the surrounding park. Visibility is so bad we almost miss the turning to the small castle.

"Are we here?" Lux asks, staring out of the window.

"Yes." I say as the car pulls to a stop. "Listen, I know you know Oliver has died, and I know you know what that means."

A small nod from Lux.

"Lydia is inside, so is Rab McGavin. Do you remember him?"

"Yes."

"They're going to be sad, okay? Because Oliver was their friend, and this has been a terrible shock. I just want you to prepare yourself."

Lux gives me another one of his steely nods. I know he understands. He's been dealing with grief all these long months himself. I squeeze his shoulders one more time, and then usher him out of the car. Rab is waiting for us, already helping Mona get the bags. The guardian of the Scottish lands is my height, dark red hair pulling back from his temples in a widow's peak. He also has a thick ginger beard threaded with white and grey. When he notices me, he puts down the case he's holding and comes to shake my hand. His grip is like iron.

"'Ey up, lad. I hear congratulations are in order."

"Hello Rab. Thank you, and my condolences. I'm sorry we're not here under better circumstances." I wave to Lux to come forward and introduce himself. As he does so, the morning light illuminates his golden hair in the image of a

BETRAYED

shining crown.

"I don' suppose you'll remember me, young Pendragon. Yev grown almost a foot since I last saw ye!"

"Hello Mr McGavin."

"No one's called me tha' in a long time. Ye can come again." Rab winks at Lux, who grins apprehensively. I'm not sure he understood more than two words in the whole sentence. "Cin ye help me wi' the bags?" Without waiting for an answer, Rab puts a rucksack in his hands and then steers him towards the doors. "Lydia's in the sitting room. She's taking tea, waitin' for ye. I assume Joth sent word of a plan?"

"Yes."

"Then I'll ge' the king settled and show Mona to her rooms before I join ye."

Lux's cheeks flush red. He knows when he's being dismissed, but I just grin at him. "It's okay, Rab, they're part of it. We'll wait until everyone's ready."

"All righ', sui' yourselves." Rab shrugs and continues towards the house. Lux's face is set with confidence, something I've not seen there for a while.

"He's goin' t'be a grea' king one day," Mona says quietly from beside me, having snuck up on me like a shadow. "And yer t' le' me go into Lady Geraint first. I'd like to gi' 'er the option of turning down Merle's request wi' out other people watchin'."

"She'd be lucky to have you as a squire."

"She would." Mona's usual feral grin spreads across her face. "Bu' she's t' 'ave the choice. Tha' was Merle's only condition. That Lydia agrees wi' ou' pressure."

"All right. Well, I'll get the rest of the bags. See you in there."

I give Mona five minutes before following her into the sitting room. I find her beside Lydia, who is pale faced and red

112

eyed, but nodding in agreement.

"Thank you for coming." She gets up, pushing herself from the sofa with one hand, curling the other around her stomach. There's a round bump there, hidden under layers of woollen jumpers.

"I'm sorry–"

"Yes, I know. All I've heard are condolences, and I appreciate yours, but–" Lydia sighs. "Nobody really knows what to say. There isn't anything to say."

"Then you'll be glad to know we've come with something to *do*."

"Something to do, Sir Ren, is what I've been waiting for." Lydia smiles. It looks a little odd on her too white face, her dark eyes showing she hasn't slept a wink in days, but at least it's a start. She eases herself back onto the sofa and motions for me to take a seat opposite. I pour the tea while Mona plumps up a cushion behind Lydia's back. A few minutes later, the door cracks open again as Lux and Rab join us. Monty left last night as did we. There was no point him staying up here with us on the way, and he'll be more useful elsewhere.

When we're all settled, I reach into my rucksack and pull out a letter written on heavy parchment in Mona's hand and give it to Rab.

"Two days ago, Joth announced the immediate effect of the *Animus Nostras Salvari*. That's the declaration."

Rab breaks the seal on the envelope, scans the page, whistling with awe. "Merry said as much, bu' I wanted t' see it for myself. Wha' does the old man wan' us to do?"

"We're to pack up the estates–"

"An' leave 'em unguarded?"

"No." I shake my head, reaching back into my rucksack and pulling out a glass vial of black liquid. "This is a potion called *Letum de Mors*. It kills everything magic that it touches.

BETRAYED

Drains the power right out of any spell, enchantment, witch, wizard, or faery. Which is why we didn't send it with the other mixtures. When we tried it on one of the smaller faery rings at home, it decimated the earth. Nothing will grow there for at least a hundred years, but it closed the ring. For good."

"And you want to pour it into the rings before we leave? Burn them?" Lydia asks.

"Yes. As many rings as we can find. Then we'll close the outposts, bring everyone closer to the heart. We need to be a united front, ready for what comes next."

"Which is wha'?" Rab again. "Do any of ye truly have any idea?"

I take in a deep breath and let it out through my nose. In some situations, it might be best to reassure him, but I've known Rab forever, he's a straight shooter and always has been. "I can tell you what I believe, but no. No, we don't know. We've never faced anything like this before, not for hundreds of years—"

"What about Merle? Where is she?" Lydia turns her deep blue eyes to mine.

"She's gone to France, to help Lore." Lux answers before I can.

"You better sit down, Rab," I say. "This might take a while."

It takes me half an hour to explain the decisions made this last week, how Merle has taken a party to find the legendary Morgana Le Fae and request her aid. They listen in stunned silence, but when I'm finally finished, Rab chuckles.

"Aye, it's abou' time someone came to shake us up a bi'. I be' old John Alymere's face wer a picture!"

"And will she help? Will they find her?" Lydia asks.

"We don't know. We hope so."

"She'll help if she exists." Lux says. The surety in his voice quietens us all. "If she ever swore an oath to Arthur, she will."

"An' wha' makes ye so sure?"

"Because oaths are binding, even when you don't want them to be." Lux turns his grey eyes to mine. He knew what he was doing when he went to Merle about his nightmares, how to work the magic between them.

"He's go' a point." Rab grins. "And besides, once she hears wha' great com'nay ye all are, I be' she comes runnin'."

"Let's hope." I say. "We'll need a map of the known faery rings if you have one, so we can figure out how long it'll take to close them."

"Tha's easy enough te find. I cin take ye to the rings day afta tomorrow—"

"Oliver's funeral is in the morning." Lydia says. "His parents still live up here, and they wanted it done quickly. I also offered them the remaining staff, if they'll go. They might need protection and I—" Lydia stated everything so matter–of–factly up to this point, but now her voice wobbles. "I want to stay at the Templar, the main one, with all of you. It'll be safer there when the baby comes."

Mona reaches across the space between them, offering her hand, which Lydia takes. "Joth's already 'ad a room med up for ye. Yer to stay wi us for as long as ye'd like, forever if ye wan'."

Lydia nods, her bottom lip trembling.

"All righ' then." Rab says. "I cin ge' ye tha' map by the end o' the day. We'll attend the service tomorrow and then ge' to work."

Rab shows Lux and me to our shared bedroom on the second floor. The decor is old, faded floral wallpaper peeling at the edges. It's a little like Merle's old room and I turn away from Lux to hide the stupid smile on my face. It isn't ideal for us to be separated like this, but—

BETRAYED

"It is our duty." Mer's voice echoes inside my mind, finishing my thought. We've talked about it before, whether our hearts can withstand our oaths. We have sworn to serve, and everything else comes second. Even us.

I'm planning on staying here no longer than five days, three if I can find Abrasax without raising too much suspicion. It's my intention to ask Lydia about it later tonight. Well, it's my intention to ask her if there are any parts of the old stronghold that house ancient relics, and whether I might see them. I'm not sure what to tell Lux. Bringing him here was dangerous enough. But there's another voice inside me insisting I trust him with it, the secret. That what it'll do for his self–esteem outweighs the negative consequences.

I peer out over the grounds, most of the Highlands covered in dense, white mist. I'm hoping it clears up enough that I'll see some of the picturesque landscape I've heard so much about. Asher's lands are up this way, but not as far out in the sticks as Lydia's estate. She says Inveraray is the most beautiful place she's ever been. If it hadn't been for Merle calling us into action, she never would have left.

"Lux, there's something I need to tell you." I say, turning away from the window. He looks up from where he's unpacking his bag, a wad of hair flopping in his face. He's long overdue a haircut, it seems.

"Yeah?"

"I need your help with something else, a secret mission. We really are here to destroy the rings and bring Lydia back with us, but there's more."

Lux raises his eyebrows, waiting for me to go on.

I explain to him what Joth told me about Abrasax and why we need to find it. "As far as I know, we're looking for a stick, a stick carved out of some special wood that looks like a tiger's eye gemstone. It'll be lots of different brown colours.

And you might feel its magic."

"I know about Abrasax." Lux says. "I've read about it. And you really think it's here?"

"Joth does."

"What will you tell the others?"

"That we're looking for old iron weapons. We're collecting them in case we need to use them in the fight, if it gets to that—"

"It's going to get to that." Lux turns his icy grey eyes on me. They're shining like beacons. "It's in the prophecy Merle brought back. '*The mad will rule in the court of the dead... the kingdom burns by the will of the damned...*' It has to be talking about Morgwese. She's mad."

"In every way imaginable." I agree. "But prophecies are confusing."

"This one isn't." Lux shrugs. "You're just not listening."

I grumble at him and lay down on the hard, single bed, nothing compared to the comfort of back home. "You should tell Willow when we get back. She'll have something to say about it."

"Eyrie will beat me to it. She said so. And it was her idea, really. She's smarter than me." Colour blooms across his face, pride.

"She's smarter than everyone, I hear. Maybe even Willow." I say, laying back on the bed and crossing my arms behind my head. "I'm going to sleep until dinner. We're going to have a long few days."

I don't really sleep now at night. None of us do. Like Lux, I dream of Lore, floating in the dark, eyes white, lips bloodless, ashen hair glowing around her like a halo. Sometimes, I hear her screaming.

I don't know what plagues the rest of them.

I always sleep better with Merle, when I can concentrate

BETRAYED

on the soft rise and fall of her breath rather than the silence of the dark. I know she thinks she's a burden to me at night, tossing and turning, thin sleep and nightmares. But it's better. Anything is better than this.

Lux wakes me with a shake several hours later. It's dark again outside, the curtains drawn against the silvery moon.

There are five who sit at the table for dinner, but barely any of us eat the stew we've been served. It's too sombre, too quiet, the house too full of grief. Rab bids us goodnight at half past seven, Mona follows at eight. Ten minutes after, I give Lux a pointed glare. He rolls his eyes but pushes his seat back from the table, leaving Lydia and me alone.

"Lydia," I start, but she holds up her hand.

"You can stop with that tone right now. I know Oliver is gone and I don't need to be constantly reminded by everyone's pity. I'm a knight of the Templar, not a princess. We knew the risks. I still do. Did Joth just send you to check up on me? To fuss?"

I stare at her grave face, her lips quivering with anger. I debate going ahead with my plan, the lie I've decided to tell, but I don't think I can. It's true, she is a Knight of the Templar and she has been the twins' loyal supporter from day one. She also respects Merle's position here and has fought in her corner all these months. She deserves better than dishonesty. "Joth didn't send me to check up on you. He sent me to look for something. Something ancient and powerful that might help us win this war. I can't tell you what it is. I swore to Joth I wouldn't. But I want your permission to search for it, and I want to know of anywhere on this estate that an ancient relic might hide. Can you help me?"

Lydia considers me for a moment, no doubt assessing the truth of my words. Then she nods. "I'll help you. Tomorrow, after the funeral and in the daylight, I'll show you where."

13

It's almost midnight by the time we reach the French Templar. It's much grander than the Templar I now call home. Ebony turrets pierce the skyline, swirls and spikes of stone silhouettes against the starry backdrop. Asher helps me out of the car and gives me a backpack.

"It's quite something, isn't it?" She whispers.

I nod. All around us, crooked headstones poke from the damp grass. Aila winds her way between my feet as we walk up the path. She's enjoying the chance to stretch her legs so thoroughly that she's not even curious about where she is.

The door has huge stone pillars on either side. Carved into them, just above my head, are the life–size images of saints. A man in a robe stares down at me with bulging vacant eyes. The stone monstrosity beside him is missing a head. I shiver.

"It's always a bit daunting the first time." Amalie slips her hand into the crook of my elbow. "It's much less imposing in

BETRAYED

the day."

It *is* imposing, but it's also beautiful.

"It isn't as big as Joth's Templar, and it's not as modern... converted in the 18th century, you know." Richard says from behind us.

I dread to think what it's like inside if he considers my home Templar *modern*. Rory ushers us into a small entrance hall. The white stone is a stark contrast to the gritty rock outside. We go through a set of double doors and into the sitting room, where there's a fire burning in the grate. Above the mantel is a picture of Arthur. He's wearing a glittering crown and standing next to a woman in a gold and white gown. Guinevere smiles demurely out at the world, her green eyes seemingly alive, golden braids hanging to her knees. In one hand she holds a bouquet of lilies, the other is clasped in Arthurs.

"Lovely isn't it?" A sweet soft voice sounds from behind us and Aila twitches in my arms. I turn slowly to find a woman emerging from the gloom. She's a little shorter than I am, with a halo of silver hair braided around her head and flowing over her shoulder. She looks to be around Joth's age with fine lines painting her cheeks. I set Aila down as the woman comes closer, first greeting her knights with kisses, then clasping my hand in both of her own, which are warm and dry. She smells of jasmine and magic.

"I'm Lady Cassandra, guardian of the Templar. It's a pleasure to finally meet you." She has a thick French accent, much thicker than either of the Percival twins.

"Merle." I squeeze her fingers. "Thank you for having us."

She stares at me again, as if she can see into my soul, then she turns back to the room. "I know who you are, young witch. You've 'ad a long journey, and must be tired. We've set up the guest room, although you'll be sharing."

"Sharing's fine." Asher smiles.

"Go on then, off to bed with you." Cassandra waves her hands in front of her. "I'll see you for breakfast in the morning."

"I'll show you where!" Amalie grabs my hand.

On my way out of the room, I feel Cassandra's gaze on me again. *"We've a lot to discuss you and I. I look forward to it."*

I look over my shoulder and meet Cassandra's eyes, grinning. I've never met anyone else with proper magic before, other than the evil fae queen, and I can't wait to find out all about Cassandra's abilities.

Amalie takes Asher and I up two flights of stairs and into an attic room with a sloping roof. There are two single beds with a nightstand between them, and a door against the back room that Amalie tells us is the bathroom. Above the beds hangs another picture of Guinevere. This time, though, she's in a tower, waving a delicate white hand at the knight below.

"You're big Guinevere fans over here, huh?" I ask, mostly as a joke, but Amalie nods her head eagerly.

"Well, this is her Templar. Not all of them have such grand dedications, but yours is Arthurs, this is hers. The Welsh Templar is Myrddin's, or Merlin's, as you call him. I don't remember the rest." She shrugs.

Amalie hugs us both goodnight and leaves for her own room. A yawn slips up my throat, and I excuse myself to get changed for bed. I don't know whether now is the time to discuss what happened in the restaurant, that Owen blocked my magic. I also want to know what Lamorak was doing near the relic room.

Once again, I wish Ren was here. Every time I think of him, the sweet ache of longing pounds in my chest. We won't be apart for long, two weeks at the most. Even so, it feels like an endless stretch of time. I sigh, wash my face with warm

BETRAYED

water and plait my hair down my front. It's probably best to tell Asher everything, to see what she knows in return and then figure it out from there.

I push my way back through the bathroom door, wondering how to start, but I needn't have worried. Asher is already asleep. She has the covers pulled up to her chin and is snoring softly. I can't help but smile at her peaceful face.

"Come on, you." I whisper to Aila, who bounces up onto the clean white sheets of my bed, arching her back in a stretch, extending her long sharp claws as she does so. "Let's get some rest."

I sleep a little after the big cat has finally settled beside me, but it's restless and unsatisfying. I keep dreaming of Owen and Asher on the mountain. Flashes of snow and ice, and tumbling rocks. It's only Aila's warmth and calming energy that helps me get any sleep at all.

When I finally call it quits and decide to get up, the light behind the curtains tells me it's only just morning. I slide off the heavy covers and hunt around for a jumper, which I find stuffed in the bottom of my backpack. When it's over my head and my boots firmly pulled on my feet, I make my way downstairs.

The unfamiliar halls are full of eerie shadows. Stone gargoyles loom from the walls in odd places, grinning down with their open mouths. I stop to study a particularly gruesome one, so gruesome that Aila hisses at it, the hackles on her back raising in alarm. It leans out of the wall, claw–like fingers reaching down, tongue lolling out of its head, as if it's laughing.

"Not very pretty, is 'e?" a soft voice sounds from behind and I jump. When I turn, I find Cassandra smiling at me. She's dressed in a long, cobalt robe that brings out the colour of her eyes. They're dark blue like sapphires, almost purple.

"No, he's not."

"Are you always an early riser?"

"I couldn't sleep. Bad dreams."

She nods as if she completely understands. Maybe she does. "Tea is excellent for soothing an anxious mind, no? Will you join me?"

"Sure." I follow her downstairs and into the sitting room. There's already a teapot and two cups on the table, as if she was expecting me. "Joth didn't mention you had magic."

"You'd 'ardly call what little gift I've got magic, Chère." She pours tea into one of the awaiting cups, a small, wry smile playing at the corner of her mouth. "My gift is watered down through 'undreds of generations. I can send messages over a short distance, mix a few potions, and will live an 'undred years yet, maybe more, but that's it."

"Are you an heir, too?"

"We traced my ancestors back to Vivianne. Joth's father, Ammeus, thought I might 'old some real power, but—" she shrugs.

"Vivianne, as in the Lady of the Lake? The one who fostered Lancelot?"

"Very well remembered." Her eyes sparkle. "'Ow is my boy doing over there in England?"

For a second, I don't know whose she's referring to. Then it hits me that she must mean Ren. He's the only Du Lac heir I know of. "Ren never said he had family here."

"I wouldn't really call us family. It's unlikely 'e's even made the connection between us. But as you know, some of us are bound in peculiar ways. I keep my eye on 'im, as Vivianne kept 'ers on Lancelot. Not that 'e's ever needed anything."

"Well, he just got his knighthood." The thought still fills me with pride, and it must show on my face because Cassandra beams.

BETRAYED

"It's 'igh time. Joth's worked the boy for too long with none of the perks. Although, those are few and far between nowadays."

Perks? I didn't even think about that. The other knights have land of their own and duties. Does that mean Ren has land too? If so, where is it? Will he have to move? Will I be able to go with him, or do I stay with Lux and Lore?

Cassandra eyes me carefully, and even if she hasn't read my mind, she must be able to sense what I'm thinking. "I didn't realise you two were involved."

"Well, yeah." Heat warms my cheeks. "Although it isn't really big news."

"At least you've chosen a good one, some of these knights," she rolls her eyes. "You'd do better to stay alone forever."

I snort. She's probably right.

"Tell me about this trip you're embarking on." She refills my teacup and then pats my knee. Blue veins show through her thin skin, an orange gemstone glittering on one finger. "I got Joth's letters, but it's never the same as 'earing it in person."

"Where would you like me to start?"

"Where all stories start?" she grins. "At the beginning."

By the time I'm finished recounting the events of the last six months, the rest of the party has joined us.

"We need to find Morgana, because I can't help Lore on my own." I finish. The statement doesn't fill me with dread now, as it once did, and I'm glad the weight has lifted from my shoulders.

"And do you truly expect to find 'er?" Cassandra hits me with a pointed glare, then she sends. "*Do you really expect 'er to 'elp you if you do?*"

"She definitely won't help if we don't ask." I say. "And Lore didn't betray her personally. She might be persuaded to

124

help an innocent."

"Maybe." Cassandra muses. "She's been up in those mountains for at least two 'undred years. Solitude can do strange things to people."

"She might be glad of the company." Richard chimes in. I admire his optimistic spirit.

"And I'm going to send her a warning, tell her we're coming somehow, what we want."

"Not until after breakfast, you aren't." Asher says.

"Lady Gaheris is right." Cassandra gets up, smoothing her hands down her front.

"And we've got some planning to do," Eddie jumps in. "I'd like to brief you all before we do anything else. Make sure you know what we're getting into."

Cassandra ushers us into the dining room where I eat an excellent breakfast of eggs, toast, and croissants. In fact, I pack away more than the rest of the party put together. By the time I'm swallowing my last mouthful of jam covered pastry, Pelleas is looking at me with mild surprise and concern.

"Hollow legs." I reassure him as I chase it down with hot coffee.

After, Molly, Cassandra's housemaid, takes us back through to the sitting room where we all squish onto various sofas and armchairs. Eddie stands at the front waiting for us to give him our full attention.

"Right," he begins, rubbing his hand through greying hair. "We've still got a few days here before we need to start climbing. I know you're eager to get off," Eddie sends a pointed look my way, "but it's important we do this properly."

People die on mountains. Ren's words echo through my mind. I want to fix Lore, more than anything, but I'd not endanger the party. Not for the sake of a few more days.

BETRAYED

"It's about an hour's drive to the mountain from here. We'll start the climb on foot from Chamonix, hike the Mer de Glace and spend at least one night camping at the Refuge du Couvercle...' Eddie trails off as he realises everyone is staring back at him with blank expressions, everyone except Owen.

"See, I told you she was in the Aiguille Verte. That's what we're climbing, isn't it?"

"How can you be so sure?" Greg asks.

"My grandad stayed here for a long time, climbed the mountains. He heard rumours. He used to tell me stories about the adventures he went on. They used to do stuff like this back then, explore, find glory." Owen smiles, the first genuine expression I've seen him make this entire trip.

"I remember your grandfather," Cassandra says. "And 'e did believe that *something* powerful was 'iding in the mountains."

"He thought it was the Holy Grail." Owen says and then chuckles at the eight shocked faces that now swivel to him. "What? He *did* believe that! He thought Morgana was a myth to cover up the Grail's hiding place... but they never found anything, and then Grandma had Dad so—" he shrugs.

"And it does just so happen," Eddie says, taking back command of the conversation, "that the Aiguille Verte would be *my* best guess. According to the albeit very limited accounts we have of various expeditions and the fact that it's difficult to climb, it would be the best bet for a hiding spot."

Everyone seems to have been put at ease by Owen's story. *I* have been. It's so simple and innocent. But alarm bells are still ringing inside my skull. If that's the reason he's so sure, then why is his brain locked down like Fort Knox? Why was he in the relic room? And *why* did he lie about being able to hear me?

Maybe he's leading us astray? A wicked little voice

126

whispers in my ear.

Maybe. But I don't think so though. I think he really means to help us get to her. There was no lie in him when he told us about his grandad.

"How would you know?" Shelby's voice cackles in my head. "*You never noticed* my *lies."*

I bite down on my lips so hard I taste blood and Aila tenses on my lap, her claws extending and digging into my thigh.

"Sorry," I send her way. *"It's okay. Everything's okay."*

It *is* true though, and I'm still ashamed of that. Although then I was dealing with the best of the best, and she never actually *lied.* Full faeries *can't* lie, I learned after many hours of study with Willow. Shelby/Morgwese though was not quite full fae, her human half giving her some leeway with the truth. But maybe she's right. Maybe I wouldn't know.

The toe of Asher's boot clips my shin and I sit upright, startled. She flicks a glance to her left, Eddie asking me a question.

"Sorry Eddie..."

He smiles and waves my apology away, "what do you think? As the leader of this party, what do you want to do?"

For the first time, I feel a jolt of nerves in my stomach. I've never climbed a small mountain, never mind a big one.

"Don't worry, Little Witch, we've got a good team. Everything will be okay." Greg smiles.

"All right then." I say. "Let's climb the Aiguille Verte."

14

Lady Cassandra disperses the knights as soon as Eddie has finished talking.

"Amalie, Rory, Owen, you will go to town to collect whatever supplies you need," from one of the folds in her robe, she pulls out a shiny black card. "Spare no expense. And no arguments." She glares at the twins with her strange blue eyes. She's obviously been using that same look to keep them in check for years. Then she turns to Greg, Eddie and Asher. She stares at Asher a little too long. I know telepathy when I see it. "You three will plot this route you intend to climb, every inch of it."

"What about me?" Richard asks.

"You and I are going to assist Merle with her spell. We have magic in our blood. We can help." Cassandra takes in a deep breath, letting it out in a sigh as she takes one last look around the room, ensuring everyone is assigned a task. She runs this Templar like a tight ship. I wonder how much we might have achieved at home under her strict rule. Then she claps her hands together, two short whip cracks in the quiet. "Excellent! Dinner will be served at seven pm sharp. We'll see you all again, then."

After everyone has left to undertake their respective duty, Aila and I follow Cassandra through to the Library. For a second, I expect to see Willow poring over a book, raising her head to greet me with whatever interesting fact she's been discovering. But she isn't there and disappointment twinges through my heart. Being away from my Templar is strange and unknown. I can't wait to get back.

Aila, sensing my distress, rubs her side against my shin. She's still growing and more rapidly than I've ever seen anything grow. From what I know of Lynxes, they usually get to about two feet tall when they're an adult, and what they lack in size they make up for with their speed and agility. But Aila is already that big and shows no sign of slowing down. Her coat is so thick now I can barely see my fingers through the fur.

"*We're going to do some magic.*" I send to her, scratching the spot behind her ears

"*Get ready.*"

The big cat turns her lovely turquoise eyes to me, the waves of contentment rolling from her. I swear she even smiles.

"Did you ever have a familiar?" I ask Cassandra, who is watching our exchange with her own smile.

"No. I don't have enough magic for that. They're difficult to summon. Only the most gifted among us are able." She reaches across the space between us and squeezes my wrist. "Now, what are we looking for?"

"I'm not exactly sure," I say, stepping closer to the ancient bookshelves. "We could try to locate her somehow, then my

BETRAYED

message will be more direct? I can send out a pulse of magic. She might recognise it as Merlin's."

"When I was a girl, I had a tutor named Marilyn. She was as strict as they come, but she knew about magic." Cassandra smiles wistfully at the memory. "She knew I didn't have much, and that I'd never wield true power. But I could channel what I did have with *focus.* She would make me stand with my eyes closed and ask me to concentrate on what I wanted, to trust that my spark would shine on its own. Would you try it?"

I look down at Aila, who's peering at me expectantly.

"I don't have a better idea, so it's worth a shot. Ready, Aila?"

The big cat nods her head and then settles herself between my feet. I take a deep breath and close my eyes.

If I were a witch hiding on a mountain, what would get my attention?

A deep, almost unsettling quiet descends on the room as I gather all of my focus. Into it, I channel my want to help Lore, the urgency with which we need Morgana's help, the insistence that she answer when I call.

There's a shuffling sound, something freeing itself from its long forgotten position on a shelf. I open my eyes to find a huge volume whizzing towards me and I snap out my arm to catch it in my palm. When I look back at Richard and Cassandra, they're both smiling.

"It seems we've found our book," Cassandra says. "Let's do some magic."

To find the spell itself, we move to the living room. The book in my arms is heavy enough that it makes a dense thudding sound on the table when I put it down. On its cover is a crescent moon and a seven pronged star, a title in an ancient script that isn't quite Merlin's, but it's close. Under the wave of

GABBY SKELDON

my hand, the bronze clasp pops open and I'm met with a yellowing page full of twisting blue ink.

"Here," I say, pushing the book towards Cassandra. "It's in French. Can you translate?"

Lady Cassandra nods and pulls the huge volume closer to her, scanning the words, her thin lips moving slowly. When she gets to the bottom of the third page, she stops. "This might work. It claims to be some kind of summoning spell, or location spell. The language is old, so I'm not sure of the exact translation. It says we need some herbs, candles, jasmine, a goblet full of water..."

Fifteen minutes later, we have our instructions and our ingredients and it's time to get to work. Richard pushes back the furniture so there's space for us to sit and we do so with our legs crossed and our knees touching. Aila, who can't sit cross–legged, places herself between Richard and me, completing the circle.

I carefully slide a bowl of water into the space between us, placing four tall white candles around it as if they're the points of a compass. Cassandra grinds the sage with the salt until it's crushed into fine crystals. She pours it in a circle, from candle to candle, and as soon as the last gap is closed, the air in the space changes. It's almost like stepping into the fae rings, hot and sweet smelling. Cassandra is grinning. Even if she has very little magic, I know she must feel the pull of it, power begging to be let loose. I'm only so sure because I can feel the pull of my own.

I unhook the rosary from around my neck and pull free the ring Joth gave me. The spell says the name of the person will do, but an item belonging to them would be even better. I pick up the scrap of paper on which I've hastily scribbled *Morgana Le Fae* in Merlin's script, and then I drop it into the bowl. The ring follows it in, creating circular ripples in the

131

BETRAYED

water's surface.

"In a moment," I say. "I'm going to close my eyes and call your magic to me. I've never done it before other than with Aila. I don't know what it'll be like for you. But once we're in, we can't break or the spell won't work. And I'll need someone to light the candles."

Richard holds up a lighter, stolen from its place beside the hearth.

"Okay then. Let's do it."

I stare at the bowl for a moment, settling myself, and then I close my eyes. In the dark, I search for their auras. I find Aila's magic immediately, and the pulses of it are bright and white, the same shade as mine. On my left, I find the glow of Cassandra's gift, blue and purple, the same colour as her mysterious eyes. Directly opposite, there's a splash of orange winking on and off. Richard. I pull at its thread, coaxing it to me as one might coax embers into flame. Once I'm sure the web is as strong as it can be, I add an influx of my magic, a steady stream of power, lighting us up like a beacon.

"Inveniet." I say, as clearly as I can. And with those words, I channel all of my energy, every ounce of concentration I can muster, and I focus it all on Morgana. *Find her. Find Morgana Le Fae.*

As the word leaves my lips, the ground begins to shake, and I open my eyes to find the water in the bowl shuddering. It rises into a sphere. In the air before us, it transforms into a range of rolling peaks. One sticks out high above the rest. A red light glows from within it like a burning heart.

"*I'm coming.*" I send into that light with all the strength I have. "*I'm the Heir of Merlin, and I'm coming. Be ready to answer my call. Be ready to do your duty.*"

As the water swirls again, losing its shape, a pulse radiates from our circle like a strong wind, rippling through the

Templar, sending an aftershock into the world beyond. Ten seconds later, the water falls back into the bowl with a splash. Droplets flick into my face and hair. The air loses its warmth, the magic web around us spent.

"Well, *something* happened." I say, grinning at them both. I pull Aila from her place beside me and rub her ears, kissing the top of her head. *"Good job."*

"I've never felt anything like that before." Cassandra whispers. "Never."

"It can be a bit of a shock," I say lamely, although I don't wholly agree. The first time I did proper magic, it was exhilarating, feeling the power flow from my core to the tips of my fingers. Being able to create something from thin air.

"It was bloody brilliant!" Richard says. "Can we do it again?"

Cassandra chuckles, a slow trickle of joy, then Richard joins in and soon I can't help myself. Five minutes later when Asher pokes her head around the door, we're all wiping tears from our eyes.

"Everything okay?" She cocks an eyebrow.

"Fine." I answer. "We did the spell."

"I know. I felt it," Asher says. "*Everyone* felt it." Then: "If you're done, can I borrow you Merle?"

"Sure." I grab the ring from the bowl. I don't think either of my companions would take it, but it's better to be safe than sorry. I help Cassandra to her feet and start to tidy, but she waves away my hands.

"Richard will clean up."

"Charming," Richard says. He's still grinning from ear to ear, cheeks flushed. "Go on, attend to whatever important heir business you've got going on."

I give him a thumbs up and motion for Aila to follow. When we're outside, Asher hands me my coat and my boots.

BETRAYED

"Are we going somewhere?"

"We need to talk." Her face is graver than the tone of her voice. "I couldn't think of how else we might get some alone time."

"My favourite kind of time." I wiggle my eyebrows at her. She cracks a little smile, but she's distracted. I pull on my outdoor wear as quickly as possible and follow her into the cold.

As we step into the grounds, wonky gravestones poke out of the earth like decaying teeth, and an icy wind immediately whips my hair from my face. I tuck my hands into my pockets, wishing I'd brought gloves.

"If you trip, you'll fall flat on your face." Asher muses, seemingly some of her good humour returned. "That's what my grandad always used to say."

"A very wise man." I pull one hand out and immediately regret it. "What's with the cloak and dagger routine?"

"I'd hardly call it that. Now seems like the best time to talk, while everyone's distracted."

I agree. We're due to go up the mountain in a few days, and we need to have everything sorted before then.

"There's something wrong with Owen," Asher says. "And I feel like I put my foot in it with Ren. You meant something different when you said there was a problem. You didn't know about the relic room."

"I didn't."

"We went to get the Hag Stones." She flicks a sideways glance at me and opens the wrought–iron gate at the bottom of the path. I hope she knows where she's going, as I have no idea. Aila doesn't seem to be bothered either way. She looks to me for permission to hunt, and then bounds into the snow, rolling around and burying her head in the huge drifts. "Joth told us to get them. We don't know what it's going to be like

134

up there. There might be no other way for us to communicate with the Templar if something happens." She scrubs her fingers through her hair, the tips red with cold.

"Okay. And you saw Owen there?"

"We bumped into him on the stairs, and when we got to the room, the door was open, something was missing. Carnwennan."

"Sorry, what?"

She rolls her eyes. "Carn–wen–an."

"I still have absolutely no idea what that means, Ash." We've walked far enough up the rough dirt track so I can only see the back of the gothic church. There's a bench a few metres away, which I motion to.

"It's a dagger. In fact, it's Arthur's dagger. The legend says there's some magic in it, although I don't know enough to say what kind." She looks out into the middle distance. The view is stunning: rolling hills, slender trees with tiny blooming leaves. In the distance, the iron peaks of the mountains. "Willow would know."

"Doesn't she know everything?" I can tell from the pang in her voice that she misses Willow. Hell, *I* miss Willow and it's only been a day. "Cassandra might know something about it. She's got some magic, you know?"

"I didn't."

"Apparently she's descended from Lady Vivienne, of the lake. She doesn't have strong magic, but enough to make casting that spell easy."

"Can we trust her?"

"I don't see a reason not to."

Asher nods slowly. "What do you know about Owen? What happened that spooked you?"

"Last night in the restaurant when I projected for the group, I had to feel out for everyone, but Owen was shielding.

BETRAYED

And not just your regular shield, it was like a hard black wall."

"But he said he heard you. He was talking about it at the counter like he *heard* you." Asher's brow is furrowed, the lines around her nose and eyes deepening.

"I *know* he did. That's what made it strange. But there's no way. There's no way he heard me. There wasn't a *single* crack in that wall. It's the strongest barrier I've ever seen, not that that's saying much."

"Did he put it there himself?"

"What?"

"Did he put it there himself?" She says again. "Or do you think he had some help?"

"From who?" To my knowledge, there aren't any other witches in the Templar.

"Hmm, let me think for a moment. Who might want to enlist an inside man to help further their evil plot?" Ash brings her hand to her face, stroking an imaginary beard until I nudge her with my elbow.

"All right, point taken." It's a possibility I hadn't considered before, that someone might have put a block in his mind to stop me from fishing for information. "Would he truly betray us, though? After his family has served for so long? I know he's a bit... but he's still young! Being strange doesn't automatically make you a traitor."

"No, it doesn't." Asher says. Then, she holds up her hand to count on her fingers. "But, he stole a magic dagger from the relic room, he blocked you out of his mind and lied about it, he knew about Morgana being in the Aiguille Verte." Asher grips my wrist tightly and I flinch at her sharp nails. "How would he know a thing like that? Unless you bought his crappy story, too?"

"You didn't?"

"Please." Asher rolls her eyes. "It's a bit too perfect, isn't it? And on its own, it might not be concerning, but with everything else we know?"

"Why would he agree to come here, then? If he was working against us?"

She gives me a dark and brooding look. "Maybe he has his own plans for Morgana?"

I pause for a moment, thinking about her words. We both know things aren't exactly as they should be within the Templar, that there's a poisonous vein running at its heart. While Owen sometimes acts oddly, his behaviour doesn't suggest he's covering up the level of deception we suspect him of. It's like he's two people, one dark and angry, the other an innocent seventeen–year–old trying to help his friends. I wish for the thousandth time that *our* friends were here to help. "Let's see what the others think. We need to check in with them anyway, and test out the Hag Stone. It'd be just our luck to get up the mountain and not be able to use it."

The rest of the afternoon is uneventful and I spend my time with Asher, practising conjuring weightlessness spells and heat bubbles. None of us are experienced climbers after all, and while we'll have ropes and be able to learn some basics, lightening our load will certainly help in the long run.

After dinner, which is at seven pm sharp exactly as Cassandra promised, Asher and I make our excuses and head off upstairs. Just before we escape, Cassandra pulls me into a hug, kissing both of my cheeks.

"Goodnight, Sweetheart." She whispers in my ear. "I'll see you in the morning for tea."

Once we're in our room with the door firmly locked, I fish the Seeing Stone out from my backpack and place it between the three of us. Asher is casually sprawled across her bed. Aila, who is now almost as long, is snuggled into her side.

BETRAYED

"She knows a better offer when she sees it, don't you, Aila?" Asher says, sticking her tongue out at me and rubbing the cat's tummy.

"She'll come crawling back." I say, positioning myself at the end of the bed. It's time to call. I don't know if Joth and Ren will be ready, but hopefully they can stop to answer. Once we're ready, I take a deep breath and wave my palm over the stone, whispering, "*Audite*."

At first, nothing happens. Then the stone vibrates on the sheets, filling with silver liquid. After a second, I can hear muffled sounds emanating from the mercury–like pool. "Hello?"

"Merle?" It's Joth's voice, a little crackly, as if we've got a faulty connection. I home in, focusing my energy on making it clear. "Merle, is that you?"

"And me!" Asher says. "Is it working?"

"It's working! I'm here!" Willow's excited shout blares through the stone.

"Me too." Ren adds. At the sound of his voice, a warm shiver runs through me.

"Sir Ren." Asher grins even though he can't see. "Sir Joth, Lady Willow. How is everything?"

Willow laughs, the notes airy and full of joy. "Everything's fine on our end. Eyrie misses you."

"How's Lydia?" I ask before anyone else can talk. I'm anxious to know her and the baby. For a few seconds, no one speaks, and cold panic trickles through my core.

"Lydia and the baby are fine." Ren says slowly. "This morning we attended Oliver's funeral and tomorrow we'll start closing the other rings with the *Letum de Mors*. We should be heading home straight after."

"And how is the situation in France?" Joth asks.

Asher and I meet eyes over the stone, a shared grimace. I

explain as quickly as I can about the impenetrable shield Owen built around his thoughts, how he lied to us and how he insisted he knew Morgana's location based on the stories he was told as a child.

"I told you he was up to something." Ren growls when I've finished.

"I don't know what, though." My aching head can't make sense of it, and I'm in no state to convey my mixed feelings. Asher touches my wrist and raises her eyebrows in question. She can see I'm waning.

"We're gonna have to wrap it up." She orders. "Merle's tired."

"All right." Joth agrees, even though he doesn't sound pleased.

"It's been a pleasure, folks." Asher says. "That's us, over and out."

I don't wait for a response before I let the connection go. As soon as the strain is gone, I feel better. I collect up the stone and put it back in my rucksack. Then I turn back to Asher. "That wasn't too bad."

"Took a lot of power though, right?"

I nod.

"So we'll save it for emergencies only. That's okay. We shouldn't be on the mountain for more than a few days."

"Do you really think we'll find her?" It's a question I've not asked her yet, one I've been scared to hear the answer to.

"I think," Asher says, smiling. "That six months ago, people doubted Morgwese's existence, and you proved them wrong. So if Morgana Le Fae *does* exist, you'll be the one to find her. If she's there, she'll help. She won't be able to say no to you. You've been so sure up to this point. That's one of the best things about you. You make a plan and you stick to it, no matter how crazy or how much of a long shot it is. You see it

BETRAYED

through, right to the end. Don't doubt yourself now."

"Okay." I say. "Thank you. I'm glad you're here."

"Gross." Asher grins. "I don't know about you, but I'm actually knackered. We should get an early night, especially if Cass wants to see us in the morning. We can ask her about that dagger."

15

I wake to the sound of Amalie calling my name.

"Merle? 'Ere, sit 'er down, get me some water." Her gloved hands brush at my face.

"I'm all right—" I say, gripping her wrist.

From metres above us there's a god awful crack, a mighty twig snapping. The ground shakes, rumbling around us.

"Lei, look out!" Rory screams from somewhere above, her voice piercing the air.

Amalie's eyes go wide as she looks over my head, the cloud of falling snow and rock quickly descending, running down the mountainside, a river with no intention of stopping.

I shove Amalie away from me as hard as I can and she stumbles backwards. A hand reaches for her, pulling her to shelter behind a huge rock sticking from the cliff face. I gather all of my strength, locating the others' auras and throwing up whatever shields I can around them.

"Aila!" I shriek into the night with my mind. *"Aila run!"*

BETRAYED

The last thing I see before I throw myself behind another rock, curling up into a ball and covering my head with my arms, is Tristen's horrified face.

I sit bolt upright in bed, the sheets pooled around my waist. I'm sweating even though the room is cool, my breath coming in uneven gasps. Aila is already by my side, checking me over, licking the tears from my cheeks. I look around for Asher, but her bed is unmade and the bathroom door is closed. The light tells me it's early morning. Powdery snow rests on the window sill, casting strange shadows on the floor.

"You all right?" Asher pulls open the door, her toothbrush sticking from her mouth. "Heard a noise."

"I was dreaming. What time is it?"

She shrugs. "Like seven? I reckon it's time to get up."

She's right, even though I'm still tired. We need to see Cassandra before the rest of the Templar wakes, and we have a busy day ahead. I tie my hair in a messy bun and get changed into leggings and a fluffy jumper. When Asher's ready, we make our way downstairs, the temperature slowly dropping until I'm shivering despite my layers. Thankfully, there's already a fire burning in the grate of the sitting room, and Cassandra is waiting for us, sipping daintily from a teacup.

"Bonjour mes Chéris." She says in greeting, motioning to the empty chairs.

Asher goes to the sofa, but I position myself by the fire, grateful for the warmth. After the tea is poured, or in my case coffee, and we're settled again, Cassandra looks at me expectantly. "I felt magic last night."

"Yes, we were using a seeing stone."

"And what is it you were trying to see?" A small smile lifts the corner of her mouth.

"We wanted to check we could get in contact with

142

Joth and the others, in case we need to, on the mountain."

"And 'ow did you fare?"

"It worked, even if it was a little draining."

"I 'ad Molly prepare us an early breakfast." Cassandra raises an eyebrow. "She'll be through any second now."

"Thank you." I smile. Asher nods her head in appreciation, but says nothing.

As promised, Molly bustles in a few moments later with a tray of toast and various condiments. She grins at me as she sets it down, showing me a small black hole where one of her canines should be. A hank of dirty blonde hair hangs in her face, and she speaks not a word of English. Cassandra thanks her in French and she looks happy enough. I eat more than my fair share of toast while Cassandra eats nothing and Asher only nibbles at the corners of a slice.

"And what about this morning? Even though it was only small, I felt a shift in the air." Cassandra says.

I chew my mouthful slowly, giving myself a moment. It's becoming apparent that Lady Cassandra has more power than she initially led me to believe. The vision, while strong, only lasted a few moments. She was waiting for something or she's unusually perceptive.

"I was dreaming." Tristen's horrified expression crosses my memory, the rumbling sound of crumbling snow. I shiver involuntarily and pull Aila closer to my side. "But only for thirty seconds at the most—"

"There are faery circles less than 'alf a mile away. If I'm well rested enough, and the air is still, I can sometimes feel out there, looking for disturbances."

"Not a bad trick, considering all the attacks." Asher says, and I wince as the colour drains from Cassandra's face.

"I knew the fae were getting stronger, that this time would come. It's sometimes as if I can 'ear them calling me."

BETRAYED

The far away look in her eyes gives me a little cause for concern, but right now we've bigger things to worry about. "Do you know anything about Carnwennan, Arthur's dagger?"

"I know the legend." She settles back in her chair and sips at her tea again. "Why? Do you have an interest in Arthur's godly artefacts?"

"I do, if they can help us."

"Well, I'm not sure 'ow much truth there is to the story, but I'll tell you what I know." She looks at us expectantly, waiting for us to get comfy and settle in for the story. When she's satisfied she won't be interrupted by shuffling, she continues. "Carnwennan, along with the sword Excalibur, and the spear Rhongomyniad, are named as the weapons given to Arthur by God. Special sacred things. Evil too."

"Special how?" I ask simultaneously with Asher's, "*Evil how?*"

"Special because God made them." Cassandra smiles, pursing her lips against a chuckle. Well, I suppose we deserved that. It *was* obvious. "Also because King Arthur named them as the things 'e wouldn't give to 'is cousin, who 'e loved dearly. Arthur vowed 'e would share almost anything else, but not those items. They 'ad strange ideas back then, no? 'Ow well do you know your 'istory, Merlin's Heir?"

I glance up at her violet eyes. I know more than enough. Over the last six months, Willow has crammed so much history into my head that I've often thought it might fall off my shoulders. Mostly, though, I studied Morgwese and her legends, the rise of Camelot, Merlin's scripture's and books of magic. "Of Arthur and his quests, I know very little."

"Wonderful!" She claps her hands together, clasping her fingers on the last beat. "The twins used to entertain my story telling whims, although, by the time they got to nine or ten, they were sick of them. The only time I really remember

144

Carnwennan being mentioned is in the story of *Culhwch and Olwen.*" She raises her eyebrows. I've never heard of it. "It's a Welsh tale originally, a romance. Culhwch is the gallant hero of our tale, and as with all stories back then, our noble knight was in search of a fair princess after being cursed by a wicked queen. Much like 'is cousin Arthur, Culhwch was raised away from court until he came of age. When 'e arrived, he found his mother 'ad died and 'is father, the king, 'ad remarried. Culhwch's new stepmother, worried the king may cast 'er aside for a younger, prettier, maiden, decided to secure her succession to the throne by offering Culhwch 'er daughter's 'and in marriage."

"His *stepsister?*" Asher interjects.

"The very same. Culhwch refused the offer, which *greatly* offended the queen. So the queen cursed the 'andsome prince; if 'e wouldn't 'ave *'er* daughter, 'e would be destined to love the daughter of someone much more despicable. The curse dictated that Culhwch could only marry the beautiful Olwen, daughter of the Giant King. The prince became immediately infatuated by 'er and vowed to make 'er 'is wife. To do so, 'e called on 'is cousin Arthur—"

"And off they immediately went." I sigh.

"Yes, indeed." Cassandra gives me a wry smile. "When the party from Camelot found the Giant King and his people. Lovely Olwen agreed she would marry Culhwch, but the Giant King refused. For 'e 'imself had been cursed. An evil old witch cast a spell that promised death to the Giant King on the night of Olwen's wedding. As soon as she married, 'e would die."

"No wonder Arthur needed so many bloody knights around." Asher huffs. "He lost one every other day to one curse or another."

At that, Lady Cassandra bursts into a gale of musical laughter. "Quite right, Lady Gaheris. We could talk for a

BETRAYED

thousand years, maybe more, about the curses upon curses that befell Arthur's poor knights, siblings, and wizards." She wipes a tear away from her eye. "If you *do* find Morgana, you'll certainly 'ave to ask her if she really 'ad to spend a year with the nose of a pig!"

"I wouldn't if I were you," Asher says under her breath. "She might turn *you* into a pig."

After our laughter dies down, Cassandra continues. "In the spirit of fairness, the Giant King agreed to let Culhwch marry 'is daughter if 'e could complete about forty 'impossible' tasks." She raises her bony, wrinkled fingers in air quotes. "'Ere, the legend gets a little lost. There's been no record found that tells of all the quests, but as you only want to know of Carnwennan," she shrugs. "The Giant King tasked Culhwch with bottling the witch Orddu's blood so that 'e could use it to dress 'is beard. And don't ask!" she says quickly when she notices the horrified expression on my face. "I 'ave no *idea* why 'e'd want to do such a thing. Maybe it's because he's a giant? We'll never know! Anyway, off the knights went. They found Orddu, also known as The Very Black Witch, and 'er mother Orwen 'igh in the mountains—"

"Seems to be a common theme." Asher says.

"Long story short, Arthur used the dagger Carnwennan to cleave Orddu in two. It apparently cuts through magic, the power given to it by God stronger than any of the dark arts. It also supposedly covers its user in shadow, makes them 'arder to— is everything all right?"

I go rigid in my seat, the toast in my stomach turning to lead. It's obvious then why Owen has stolen Carnwennan, what he means to do...

"Lady Gaheris?" Cassandra croaks.

I whip my head around to look at Asher. I assumed Cassandra broke off because of *my* reaction, not because of

146

hers. But Asher is slumped in her seat, eyes scrunched up tight and hands clasped over her ears. Her usually soft face is drawn tight, lines scrawled around her lips as if she's trying to close everything out.

Rather than fear, anger sweeps through me. Asher has kept this secret from me long enough. Whatever she's hiding, I have to know. Right now. With a sweep of my hand, I close the sitting–room door and lock it. Cassandra is rising from her chair to assist my friend, but I wave her away too.

"Asher." I kneel in front of her, pulling at her arms. She starts to cry, resisting me. I pull harder, digging in my nails.

"Stop it, Merle!"

"Out with it, Ash. Out with it. Now."

She's still shaking, pushing vigorously against me. Rather than fight her anymore, I take in a deep breath and close my eyes. I search for her mind in the fog. Usually her door is made of solid chestnut, twisted with ivy and wrought iron bars. Today it's splintered and battered, wet with mould, the ivy brown and wilted.

"It's all right. Asher, it's all right." I send to her along with as much soothing energy as I can muster in my panicked state. *"I'm here. You can tell me."*

"I heard the death knock!" She squeals, thrusting me so violently from her head I fall backwards onto the carpet. "I heard it again!"

Then she bursts into floods of uncontrollable tears.

From my place on the floor, I look over at Lady Cassandra. I don't know what a 'death knock' is, but from the startled look on Cassandra's face, and the way she's slowly sinking back to her seat, it can't be good.

"'Ow many times?" The old woman says. When it doesn't look like Asher will answer, she rasps again; "Ow many times?"

"Three." Asher raises her head, her watery green eyes

BETRAYED

staring first at me, then at Cassandra. "I've heard the knock three times."

I rise to my feet and turn to Cassandra. Suddenly I feel cold all over, as if I've stepped out into the rain, or fallen into a snowdrift. Cassandra is staring at Asher with eyes as wide as saucers, blinking rapidly. Her hands are clasped at her chest, and she's squeezing them together so tightly there are patches of white at her fingertips where the circulation has been cut off. When she notices me gawping at her, she relaxes, breathing out audibly through her nose.

"Right," I say, with a lot more bravado than I feel. "You better start explaining what she means."

Cassandra clears her throat. Her voice is hoarse, as if she's been shouting for a long time. "Another legend among us, although one which isn't much believed, is the 'death knock'. One story says that the person who 'ears three knocks at the door and answers to find nobody there will lose a loved one. The knocks are supposedly the soul leaving the mortal plane."

My heart leaps into my throat. Asher loves many of the same people I do, and the thought of something happening to them is enough to almost send me spinning into my own floods of tears. But no. We spoke to Willow, Ren, and Joth last night. Eyrie was fine when Asher phoned yesterday afternoon. If something had happened, Joth would have told us.

"Another theory," Cassandra goes on. "Is that the 'earer of the knock is being warned of their own impending doom. The knocks serve to warn them that their time is coming, like a premonition. The person may change their fate after the first two knocks. But after the third..." she trails off and looks gloomily down at her hands.

"And you believe this?" I turn on Asher. "That you've heard these knocks and something's going to happen to you?"

148

"I didn't at first!" She raises her head to me, eyes still watery. Even so, she manages to glare. "I heard the first about a month ago, before we decided to come here. I thought there was something wrong with my hearing!"

"What did it sound like?" Cassandra asks, her voice taking on a strange, hollow quality. She's still staring at Asher, although this time instead of the shadow of fear, there's a strange hunger in her eyes. I don't like the way the question has been asked, but I *do* want to know the answer.

"Like all the sound has been sucked out of the room, then there's a great big knock, so *loud.* Have you ever heard someone bang two stones together? Well, like that, except it echoes *through* your head! And when you finally think you'll go deaf, it just stops," the words tumble out of Asher's mouth so fast I barely catch all of them. "I heard the second one when we were driving down here, when we got to the services. It's a good job really that we'd stopped."

I raise an eyebrow at her and she flushes. So that's why she'd been so shaken up.

"I asked Bedivere about it, seen as he used to be a doctor, but he'd never heard of anything like it. I was going to forget about it, but then I asked Willow—"

I snort and throw myself back down onto the sofa. As much as I love Willow, which I do, and admire her ridiculous talent for sorting and absorbing knowledge, asking her for information on a topic can be both a blessing and a curse. Not only will she find and deliver every available fact on the subject, but she'll do so without filtering the relevance of those facts.

"And I suppose she told you about the hundreds of knights that died after hearing three knocks nobody else heard?"

Now Asher scowls at me properly. "I'm not an idiot,

BETRAYED

Merle. I know how it sounds."

"Do you? I once asked Willow if she knew anything about stress headaches after a long session in the library, and by the end of that conversation, I could have had either an inoperable brain tumour, or been cursed by the evil eye!"

"It isn't the same!" Asher leaps to her feet and begins to pace. "At first, she was listing off all these knights that had heard the knock, and I knew it was ridiculous –I'd almost convinced myself! But then she was going on about Sir Gaheris, the *actual* Sir Gaheris, the first one, about how he'd supposedly heard them just before he died, and every single name I checked, every single one, Merle, they're in my line!"

I lean forward, pressing my elbows into the soft skin just above my knee and the tips of my fingers into my temple. Now I understand. If what she's saying is true, it's a very persuasive and strange coincidence.

Besides that, Asher is my best friend, and she's terrified. I owe it to her to take this seriously.

"Okay Ash, I get it. I mean, I'm a freaking witch, so none of us can claim it's bizarre that something like this could happen. But–" the little colour left in her face drains from it. "*But* there's no need to panic. You've heard a lot of stories, and come across a string of strange coincidences–"

"No need to panic?! I've heard the third one, Merle! That's the *last* one! And what about Eyrie..." at the mention of her sister, Asher's voice cracks.

"Look, we don't know how reliable the stories are, or if they can be trusted at all! So, *until* we know that, just calm down, okay? We can fix it."

"She's right, you know." Cassandra agrees. She's been quiet for so long I'd forgotten she was there. "All those ridiculous old myths, so much lost in translation! Or changed as they go, like Chinese whispers." She hauls herself up and goes to my friend, pulling her back towards the chair and pouring a fresh cup of tea. I see the minute tremors in her fingers as she pours. She pushes the cup into Asher's hands.

"For now, stay here. Go on, if you can, like nothing's happened all right?" With a flick of my wrist, I unlock the door, already striding towards it. Aila gets to her feet, but I shake my head at her. *"Not you. Stay with Asher. Cheer her up, okay?"* Then out loud I say: "I'll be back in an hour."

"Where are you going?" Asher asks, sniffling.

"To speak to Joth. Just sit tight, all right?" I give her what I hope is my most reassuring smile. "Everything will be fine. I promise."

Ten minutes later, I'm walking the path that Asher and I took yesterday afternoon. After I left her and Lady Cassandra to their tea, I sprinted upstairs for my coat and the seeing stone. Even though it might use a lot of energy, this matter is too sensitive to discuss over the phone.

The thought of Asher's death is terrifying, the heavy, led weight of it stuck in my throat. She's really the first friend I've ever had, someone I trust with everything. And Asher holds us up. Without her strength, we'd have fallen apart months ago.

When I get to the bench, I uncurl my fist, which has been tightly clenched around the stone. I roll it into my palm and close my eyes. Thinking clearly of Joth, the dark wood of his office, the smell of whisky, ink, and old paper, I whisper: "*Audite.*"

For a moment nothing happens, the stone laying flat and lifeless. Then its centre swirls with metallic silver liquid and I hear a crackle.

"Merle? Is that you?"

"Hello," I'm glad to hear his voice, even though it's been less than twenty–four hours since we last spoke.

BETRAYED

"Is everything all right?"

"No, Joth. Listen, I don't have long." As quickly as I can, I tell him Asher's story. It only takes me a few minutes, but by the time I'm finished, I'm out of breath and my stomach is growling uncomfortably. To my surprise and delight, Joth chuckles. "What's so funny?"

"I'm sorry," He splutters. "I shouldn't laugh at poor Asher's expense, but really, it's all nonsense. It's true that most of the Gaheris line died in strange ways, but that's because before Asher, they were mostly dare devils or idiots."

"And you're sure?"

"Oh yes. The other squires and I used to tease one another with those stories. We had Timothy Kay scared witless—"

"But she heard something, Joth." I cut him off. I'm more than willing to believe that the death knock stories are a joke, but Asher isn't making up the sound she heard.

"I think the most likely explanation for that is the one I've just given you. Someone's idea of a practical joke." From the tone of his voice, I can imagine the look on his face. The soft look he reserves for the twins when they've done something silly, and he's trying to convey sincerity to comfort them.

"And the names? The thing she checked?" I insist.

"Stories, Merle. All stories, I don't expect there's a lot of truth in them."

I stop arguing, but I'm not entirely satisfied.

"Tell Asher I'm sorry for the cruel ordeal she's been through. I'll call her later, reassure her if that's what's needed."

"Great." It's time to cut the line between us, the uncomfortable ache in my stomach now a painful gnawing. "Got to go, Joth."

The journey back to the Templar is much happier. I'm

152

glad it's good news I can deliver to Asher, even though I've got to make sure I do it without laughing as Joth did.

I find the rest of my party sitting at the breakfast table. Asher was waiting for me nervously at the door. I barely had time to knock the snow off my boots before she pounced.

"Joth says not to worry, Ash." I'd taken hold of her hand and sent the message telepathically. That way, she'd also had the benefit of being able to feel my intention, of being sure I wasn't lying. *"I'll tell you everything, but first I need to eat."*

Watching the worry drain from Asher's face and the weight fall from her shoulders is one of the best things I've ever seen. I knew she'd been worried, but I hadn't realised quite how catastrophic the situation was.

You need to be a better friend. I scold myself.

"Come on, eat up." I say with that in mind as I push a second helping of breakfast towards Asher. "We've got a mountain to climb."

"Don't mind if I do." Asher says with a huge smile on her face. "Don't want to waste away now I've got a long life ahead of me."

We spend the rest of the day preparing for our trip. Yesterday, Owen and the twins did an amazing job of gathering our supplies. I'm given a red snowsuit with yellow patches on the knees and elbows. It weighs a ton compared to my usual coat and I'm glad I've been practising my levitating magic. Not only do I get the suit, but Amalie also presents me with a hat, gloves, a fleece, thermal underwear and thick woollen socks. Then there's the boots, mountaineering ones that come with things called 'crampons', which are spikes that can be attached when the climb gets hard. There are all the other things they had to get, too: ropes, harnesses, helmets and camping gear. There's so much stuff that we have to shift it all into the library to organise. We dutifully make our packs,

BETRAYED

trying everything on and testing what we can.

When we're finished, I talk them through how I intend for the heat bubbles to work, and how I'll try my best to help us all move, whether that be by stabilising us or our things as we climb. Eddie goes next. He explains the route, how we'll be on foot from Chamonix, hike through the Mer de Glace and camp at the Refuge du Couvercle. The lodge itself won't be open, so we'll have to set up camp. According to Eddie, we're going to attempt the ascent of the Aiguille Verte in one day, following the Whymper Couloir as best as we can. We'll leave in the middle of the night and hopefully be with Morgana by the time the sun hits the rock face. We don't talk about coming back down, about what will happen if she isn't there.

At dinner, which is a wonderful spread of vegetable stew, dumplings, and potatoes, Eddie announces his intent to leave in the morning.

"There's no point in delaying anymore. The sooner we get up there, the sooner we can come back." He says, looking for our approval.

The rest of our party grumble with agreement.

I, for one, would like more time, but I can't tell whether it's because I still have things I need to figure out, or because I'm nervous. Even though I've known for some time we're going to climb the mountain– in fact, it was *my* idea– it's only really just dawned on me that it's actually going to happen. That tomorrow, I'm going to put on my snowsuit and head into the wintery terrain, intending to hunt a witch.

I'm exhausted when I finally drag myself upstairs. Aila's yawning too, her steps slow and heavy. However, when I get to my room I find Cassandra sitting on my bed. She's wearing red silk pyjamas, and a long matching robe. Her hair is unbound down her back, and falls almost to her knees.

"Ah, there you are." She gets up and comes to me. Her expression is serious and nerves jangle in my stomach.

"Is everything okay?"

"I wanted to say goodbye properly." She stares straight into my eyes. "I've enjoyed 'aving you 'ere, and as old as I am, I never thought I'd get to look upon the magic of Merlin with my own eyes."

"I'm glad to have met you, too."

She waves the comment away and kisses me on the cheek. "Good night then, Merle."

Cassandra makes her way to the door, and as she's about to pass through it, she turns back to me. "Oh, and I found something you might like. It took me all afternoon to figure out why you'd be interested in Carnwennan, and finally I realised it must be because you 'ave it and want to know its power, or someone else does. If it's the latter." She flicks a look back over her shoulder, those piercing sapphire eyes burning straight into my soul. "You should 'ave your own weapon of God to fight it with."

She dips her head towards my pillow and then steps out, closing the door behind her.

I turn to look, and waiting there is a battered bronze object. It's cold and heavy in my hands. The shape is a hollow cylinder at one side where it's supposed to be attached to a lance, and a lethal point at the other.

"*And God gave unto Arthur, Rhongomyniad,*" Lady Cassandra's voice echoes in my head. "*So that 'e might protect the weak in their darkest 'our. May you, Merlin's Heir, do the same.*"

16

REN

Oliver's funeral is as terrible as I expect it to be. Usually there would be more mourners, all of us making the trip to honour Oliver's service. Instead, there's only Lydia, Lux, Mona and I, Rab, Oliver's parents, his sister, and the household staff. We march dutifully across an acre of wet grass and heavy, looming trees, until we reach the small chapel nestled in the Scottish hillside. Oliver's coffin is made of dark wood and perched on the stone altar at the end of a thin row of pews.

Lux's face is grim as Rab McGavin gets up to say some words. Then Oliver's father stands. We hear about the squire as a boy, how much he loved Lydia and the baby about to be born, how he loved his position in the Templar. It's such a loss. When he's finished, pulled back to his seat by his wife, Lux gets up. I don't know what his plan is. He knows he's under no pressure to speak. He moves past me, walking down the narrow aisle until he's right at the front. He reaches out and lays his small hand on the coffin.

"Thank you for your service, Oliver Campbell." He says, then he walks back towards me as Lydia and Oliver's mum begin to cry again.

We file back outside and take Oliver to the cemetery where he's lowered into the ground. It's always a gut wrenching sight, seeing the coffin go down. I can only imagine how Mer felt at her mother's grave side. How could she stand it?

After the priest says their final words, it's back to the house. There is no wake. Instead, Lydia explains what's going to happen now, to Mr and Mrs Campbell. How she's coming to our Templar until the baby arrives, that she'll send any extra staff to them, that she'll visit as soon as she can. I know they're heartbroken, not only from the loss of Oliver, but now the baby. It'll be born so far away. But there's nothing they can do about it. It's safer to be with us.

Mona insists we all eat lunch despite our lack of appetite, and after we've finished, Lydia turns to me. "With the weather so bad, we can hike out to the rings tomorrow. I can't take you, not today."

"All right."

"But I'll take you to the basement and the attic. If whatever you're looking for is here, it'll be there."

Lydia makes Lux and I put on jumpers before allowing us to set foot under the floor. She says it's bitterly cold down there in the winter and probably damp. As we descend and the thick musty smell gets stronger and stronger, I begin to dread the task ahead.

"Here," she says after leading us through a weaving tunnel and pulling on a weathered old string to turn on the light. "There are a few old trunks. We've never opened them,

BETRAYED

not since we moved here." She doesn't falter as she says 'we'. It doesn't seem to even register. "There's more in the attic. You'll probably have better luck up there. But it'll be getting dark soon, and it's awful down here at night."

"Thank you." I say.

"I'll wait in the kitchen." With a small smile, she makes her way back upstairs, leaving Lux and me to divide up the search.

"It's not here." Lux says after an hour of trawling through debris.

I rock back on my heels, pulling my arms out of a dusty box. He's right. These trunks are full of nothing but junk. Old papers, bills from the house, it's not old enough.

"It might be at the bottom. Make sure you look everywhere." For the first time in my life, I hear Willow's voice. It's just like her to be thorough. God, I must be tired.

"Pass me the last trunk, then. I'll check it."

Lux rolls his eyes, but he drags the chest closer, leaving lines on the dirty floor, and then flops down beside me. "We'd feel it if it's as powerful as you said."

"Yes. But I'll always be wondering if we missed something if I don't look." I pop the clasps and find the trunk full of old books. I take out the volumes one by one, shaking them at the spine to see if anything falls out. Nothing.

"What's this?" Lux says, scrabbling around at the bottom of the box. When he shows me his palm, he's holding a heavy silver ring with a jet black stone. The ring is carved with what looks like lions, twisting around the band. It looks ancient.

"Just looks like a ring to me." I say, stacking the books back into the trunk.

"Can I keep it?"

"You'll have to ask Lydia. It's her house."

158

Lux nods, then tries to slip the ring on his finger, but it's too big, so he puts it in his pocket. We stack everything back as we found it and then head upstairs.

"No luck?" Lydia asks as we re–emerge.

"Nope, but I found this cool ring," Lux says, straight to the point. "Can I keep it?"

"If it was in one of those old boxes, they aren't mine. They've been here since well before me." She looks to me for confirmation and when I give her a nod, she gives Lux a thumbs up. "Let's try the attic, then."

We follow her through the halls and up three flights of stairs. On the last landing, she stops at a portrait on the wall. It's a watercolour of the house. The garden is in bloom and there's a family pictured, an older man surrounded by seven boys.

"Legend says," Lydia starts, "that the old Laird of Knock Castle haunts these halls."

"What legend?" Lux asks.

"Well, Oliver told me," she says, then she stops. I don't know if she's going to carry on, if she can stop her voice from shaking enough to speak. Then: "the Highland clans used to fight all the time. And Old Laird Gordon had an ongoing feud with the Forbes clan. Their land was just over the hill. One day, the seven Gordon boys, *all* of Laird Gordon's sons, went onto the moors to dig pete, but they accidentally stepped over into the Forbes land. They all fought, and the Gordon boys were killed, their heads spiked onto the ends of their spades." Lydia wiggles her eyebrows. "The Old Laird was so overcome, he tumbled down the stairs and that was the end of him, too."

"Is that true?" Lux asks, unconvinced.

"You'll know the answer if you find a ghost up there." We've reached the end of the hallway, and Lydia points to a hatch directly above our heads. "Ladders are over there, and

BETRAYED

you'll forgive me if I don't go up." She pats her stomach. "Be careful. Dinner's at six."

"Thank you." I call to her retreating back. Then I turn to Lux. "Let's go find this wand."

The attic is stifling compared to the basement, and up here it smells like sawdust and mice instead of mould. I send Lux to the far end of the room to start on the wardrobes while I take the boxes.

After the first yields nothing, my mind begins to wander to the place it always goes. To Merle. She should be in France by now, settling into the Templar and figuring out a plan for the climb. A hollow pang reverberates through my midsection. I hate that I'm not with her. I know she can look after herself, and she has Asher and the Percival twins, all three of which will be her fierce protectors, and that's before I get to Tristen and Pelleas. Sir Tristen has always been a bit stern, even more so since Lila died, but he's a good knight. And I actually *like* Eddie. It's Owen Lamorak who's the problem.

At the thought of him, my anxiety spikes again. There's definitely something off about him. I've seen him staring at Merle when he thinks no one's looking. His eyes are always heavy with anger, as if he means to do her some harm. I don't know if I could live with myself if something happened to her because of Owen. The thought alone is enough to make me sick. At least I should get to speak to her today, test out the seeing stone to make sure they can contact us on the mountain if they need to.

"Found something!" Lux calls, snapping me out of my daze.

I push aside the leather suitcase I was about to snap open and find Lux, knee deep in papers. At the bottom of the wardrobe, hidden amongst the old shoes, is a long, thin black box. It wouldn't usually look out of place, it *doesn't*, but the

160

box, or whatever's inside it, definitely doesn't belong here. Lux is staring at it warily, as if it might bite.

"Can you feel it?" He asks.

"Yes, I can feel it." It's like a strong vibration, making my hair stand on end and my teeth rattle. It doesn't make a noise, but I imagine it would sound exactly like an electric fence. If said fence was set to fry. I don't want to take it in case my arm shatters, but Lux isn't going to, and I suppose it's my duty to protect the future king. Rolling my eyes, I reach for the box, and as soon as my fingers touch the cardboard, the vibration stops.

"Open it then." Lux whispers.

I do. Inside the box on a cushion of black satin is a beautiful, glittering wand. It's shaped exactly like the wands in every one of Willow's books, a long, slender stick that's pointed at one end, the other carved for the shape of a hand. There's a delicate twist just below where the palm would sit and it's set with a turquoise stone shaped like a teardrop. The gem is beautiful, streaked with blue and green and gold, but it's nothing compared to the wood. The tip of the wand is dark chestnut, which swirls into chocolate, honey and caramel as it moves towards the stone. Delicate shades of orange and yellow thread through its varnished surface and it seems to glow with its own inner light.

"Woah." Lux says.

"Woah indeed." I agree. "I think we've found it."

Finally, something is going our way.

Lux nods. "Then let's get out of here."

I package the box back up, wrapping it in an old scarf before taking it down and hiding it in my suitcase. It's too good to be true and I can't risk anything happening to it. Lydia narrows her eyes at me when I tell her the search was unsuccessful, but she doesn't question it. Until I can get

BETRAYED

Abrasax to Joth and actually confirm it *is* Abrasax, I don't want anyone else knowing about it.

After dinner, I head back upstairs to speak to Merle and test out the seeing stone. I ask Lux if he wants to join me, but he pulls a face and shakes his head. Boring, he says.

We don't talk for long, only enough time to trade the most basic of information. My gut tightens when Merle and Asher tell us about Owen and his strange behaviour. The alarm bells ringing in my skull louder than ever. I should be there with them, making sure Mer is safe.

I don't tell them about Abrasax, and what Lux and I have found. Merle knows we were looking for it, which means Asher might as well, but I don't want to get their hopes up or have the information fall into Owen's hands.

After, when the silver liquid in the stone's eye has faded away, there's a tap on the door and Lux lets himself in. "Was it boring?"

"Everyone got to France safe, if that's what you mean?" I say, smiling.

"Good, I'm—" he starts, but then cuts off as his gaze travels to the window. "There's someone out there."

"What?" I fly to the window to check, but see no one. The fog is still thick, hanging on the branches of every tree. There shouldn't be anyone roaming around at this time. "Are you sure?"

"I saw a woman..."

"Mona?"

"No." He shakes his head. "No. I didn't recognise her."

I put my hand on his shoulder, squeezing firmly. He could be seeing things. It *is* dark, but it isn't worth the risk. If he *did* see someone, they could be here to hurt him. It could be faeries back to finish what they started. "Wanna go check it out?"

His shoulder tenses under my palm. "What? You want me to go with you?"

"If there is someone out there, I would rather it be two against one. It's okay if—"

"No! No." He cuts me off, already reaching for his coat. "I want to go."

"Come on, then." From my backpack, I pull out my old iron dagger and hand it over to him, hilt first. "Not sharp. Doesn't matter though. You know how to use it."

"This is *so cool*." Lux says.

"Be careful. We go out there, scout the perimeter. If there's nothing, we come straight back inside. Deal?"

"Deal." He gives me a quick nod.

With that, I zip up my coat and head down to the front doors. We make it unseen until we get to the foyer.

"Goin' somewhere?" Mona asks, smirking, raising one thin blonde eyebrow.

"Lux saw something."

"Lady Lydia wen' tout to chapel. Said she wanted to be alone."

"It wasn't Lydia," Lux shakes his head. "She wasn't pregnant."

"An' wha' did she look like?"

"Long reddish brown hair, but she had her hood pulled up. I could only see the ends."

Mona must see the worry on my face because she straightens her back. There's nothing to say it wasn't one of Lydia's staff, running across the grounds to give her mistress a message, but something is telling me it isn't. An ugly snake of doubt and fear raises its head in my chest. I know of someone who might sneak after the Lady of the house and wish to do her harm. To finish what was started here only a few days ago. I turn to Mona.

BETRAYED

"Go and get anything made of iron you can find, and alert Rab. There might be something wrong. Maybe it's nothing but..."

"I'll be righ' back." Mona says, understanding dawning in her pale eyes.

"Lux–"

"You said I could go!"

"And you still can." I say. He's going to be king soon, after all. He can't stay wrapped up in cotton wool forever. "But this might be more dangerous than I thought. Make sure you're ready to act if you have to, but you'll need to stay behind me. At least until I know exactly what we're dealing with."

"Who do you think it was?"

I grit my teeth and shake my head. It's not something I want to say out loud. I'm saved from having to explain myself by Mona, who returns with a long iron poker and a kitchen knife. She hands me the poker and keeps the knife for herself. I've seen her practising throwing daggers, over and over again. She's even been teaching Lore. And she's good.

Without another word, we head into the gardens. I lead the way, with Mona bringing up the rear. Lux paces us between us, wide eyed, hands trembling on the hilt of his own knife. Even so, I don't insult him by asking if he wants to go back.

The chapel materialises out of the gloom, creepier now than it was in the light. I wish Merle was here.

"Move, go on. Something's wrong." Her voice whispers in my ear as if I've conjured her into being. *"Quickly."*

I take a deep breath, trying to control the panic blooming in my stomach. I don't check behind me as I pull open the double doors, trusting that Mona will take Lux and run at any hint of real danger.

For a moment, I can't see anything as my eyes adjust to the changing light, but as the picture in front of me becomes clearer, my blood turns to ice in my veins. Lydia is crouched in one of the pews, her hands covering her stomach. Someone else is standing at the altar, slowly lowering her hood as she turns.

"Hello, Sir Ren." Elaine of Garlois drawls, grinning so wide I can see three rows of her needle–like teeth. "Did you miss me?"

17

L eaving the next morning is much less dramatic than I thought it would be.

We wake up early on Tristen and Eddie's orders and it's as black as ink outside as we eat the breakfast prepared for us. Aila munches a plateful of raw sausages and sardines, while I cram as much in my stomach as physically possible, starting with two jam loaded croissants and finishing with a hot coffee and a bowl of cereal.

Asher's also piling the food in, now she's not scared she's been doomed by strange noises. I'm glad she's back to her normal self. Although something isn't right with that. I don't believe she's heard the coming of her own death, but she *heard* something. Joth says it's a practical joke and even Asher is happy to forget all about it. But how would Owen, if it was *him*, be able to make a knocking sound that only she could hear? It doesn't make sense.

There's no time to figure it out now. We're already

pulling on our thermals and giving our rucksacks one last check. I've done my best to enchant the weight of them, to make them as light as possible, but I'm not sure how long it'll last as we climb and I get colder and weaker. I will be able to draw some power from Aila as a last resort, but she'll need her strength for the climb too. For a fleeting moment, I considered leaving her in Cassandra's care but really I couldn't face being separated from her. She nuzzles my cheek as I crouch to tie my boots, as if she heard my thoughts.

We say our cold goodbyes on the steps, climbing into the car one by one. Cassandra gives me a squeeze, kissing both of my cheeks, reminding me with her soul searching stare of the weight of Rhongomyniad in my backpack. Or '*Old Rhongo'* as Asher has taken to calling it.

Eddie says we'll drive as far as Chamonix, then we'll be on foot, making camp for the night at the Couvercle Hut.

"Which is fine by us." Eddie says. "We need to begin the ascent of the Whymper Couloir by one am, much past that, and it's too dangerous. The risk of falling stones and avalanches is too great."

The real trek begins when we've dumped the car. It's freezing cold and our gear is still heavy, even with my magic. Asher and I walk together, occasionally Amalie links arms with me, chattering in my ear like a bird in spring. As the day unfurls in front of us, the mountain looms in the distance. The rock forces itself from the snow in jagged grey edges, towering around us on either side. I've never seen anything like it, something so immense. I can't even begin to take in the peak, lost in the clouds. The bright blue sky holds the sun above us, its pale rays fragmenting off the mountainside.

"You'll be there in two days." I think to myself and shiver.

"At least it's pretty." Asher muses as we emerge at the top of the glacier, taking in the glittering snow.

BETRAYED

"That'll be no consolation if we freeze to death," I say.

"Death's not on the cards for me anymore," she smiles, bumping my shoulder.

Before beginning the next part of the hike, we stop for lunch, tucking into sandwiches and tea. We're in good spirits for the rest of the day, especially when we see the Refuge on the horizon. We aren't staying in the building itself, even though we're unlikely to find many more parties looking to climb in the off season. It's safer to keep to ourselves.

By the time we reach the camp, I'm exhausted and can't wait to stop. Asher and Rory cook while I light the fires and help build the tents. It's two to a tent, Rory and Richard, me and Asher, Owen and Greg, and Eddie and Amalie.

I eat all of my food even though it's not a scratch on the meals we've been having at Cassandra's. There's a little talk, but it's cold and we have an early start. Only Owen sits alone, staring at his hands, twitching occasionally, as if he's going to get up. He never does.

My stomach turns uneasily as I try to sleep. Asher's snoring softly beside me and I finally have time to think about Lamorak, his strange behaviour, and his theft of the dagger. In Cassandra's story, Arthur used Carnwennan to kill a witch, and I'm sure now, with every fibre of my being, that Owen's intentions are the same. Ren was right. Owen is planning something, but I'm not the target. *Morgana* is. And when I save her life, she won't be able to refuse me.

I open my eyes to Asher's laugh ringing in my ears. I push myself into a sitting position, my head brushing against something, the action sending tiny static shocks down my spine.

God, it's hot in here. Where am I?

The wind whistles past my face as I open the flap,

168

freezing cold and full of snowflakes. A horrible contrast to the warmth of the tent.

"Finally! I never thought you'd wake up. We've got to get going, Sunbeam!" Asher grins at me. She's holding a sausage on a fork, twirling it over a stove.

"Where am I?"

"What do you mean?" Owen wrinkles his nose at me.

Owen Lamorak? I'm so surprised I nearly fall back into the tent. Owen's here, of all people. *Why would I be in a tent with Asher and Owen? This doesn't make any sense.*

"Where are we?" I ask again.

"We're in France." Asher's dark skin furrowing between her eyebrows. She's also cottoned on to the fact that something's not right here. "On the way to the cave. Are you all right?"

"Yes, I'm fine. What cave—?"

"The cave with the witch in it?" Asher starts to get up. "Are you sure you're all right?"

I lean back on my haunches, sighing with relief. Yes, it's all coming back now. I'm in France with the others, on a quest to find a witch. I try and give her my most reassuring nod.

"There's coffee," Amalie calls.

I take a deep breath and duck back into the tent. It's just another vision, the echo of the one I had in the Templar. I'm too tired and cold to think about it too much, and I still feel like I've been flipped inside out.

"Good?" Asher sends as she comes to retrieve her hat.

"Yes. This is where I came in the vision, do you remember? That was strange."

As we finish packing, Eddie stands in front of the group, calling us all to attention. We'll be leaving a couple of tents here in case we need to come back. We'll pack the rest with us, another contingency, in case we need to camp further up. It's

BETRAYED

not something that we want, but if the terrain is too treacherous, we'll have to stop.

"I know we've run over the plan once, but it's best we do it again before we start the ascent." He says. "We climb together, I'll lead, Gaheris and Lamorak in the middle, Tristen bringing up the rear. Everyone will need to wear their crampons when climbing the ice. Do you all know how to use them?" We nod. "We're still in the off season, no people but huge avalanche risks, we've also got to watch out for the rock falls." As if to annunciate his point, a huge *cracking* noise thunders through the sky. It's like nothing I've ever heard, shaking me to my bones. I crouch to Aila's side, hugging her close. She's done well so far, born for the snowy conditions. But she's still a baby, not even a month old.

"You're not the only one who got thrown in at the deep end." I soothe her. I know she understands a bit of what I say and I hope it's reassuring for her to have me near.

"We'll be careful, Eddie." Rory promises. "And Merle's been practising her spells."

I have. Heating spells, blocking spells, freezing spells. I might not be strong enough to stop a whole avalanche, but I should be able to protect us from small threats.

"I know. But the climb is going to be tough and cold. If you need a break, you say. If you want to go back, you say. There's no shame in it. Does everybody understand?" We all nod our agreement, Owen looking a little green. Then Eddie says; "Right, come on team, let's shuffle."

The first two hours go without a hitch, even though we're climbing in the dark. Eddie is patient and kind, helping me slide the rope through my harness and position my ice axe correctly when I'm scared I'll slip. Tristen makes us stop on a wide ledge, and Asher and I hand out granola bars and warming potions. It isn't until we begin the ascent again that I start to feel faint. It's manageable at first, just seconds where my brain feels as if it's floating away somewhere before it snaps back. Asher's walking in front of me, close on the heels of Rory, who's helping Richard and Owen move their packs over a rough patch of ice.

My vision starts to run. I have a sense of déjà vu that's so strong it almost makes me sick. I've been here before, I've *seen* this. If only I could remember what happens next—

"Merle? Merle, are you all right?" A soft French accent calls behind me.

I can't answer, my legs seizing, body rolling forwards.

"Merle? 'Ere, sit 'er down, get me some water." Amalie's gloved hands brush at my face.

"I'm all right," I say, gripping her wrist. There's only a second to think before I act. Now I know what's coming.

From metres above us there's another one of those god awful cracks, this one making the other sound like a twig snapping. The ground shakes, rumbling around us.

"Amalie, look out!" Rory screams from somewhere above us, her voice piercing the air.

Amalie's eyes go wide as she looks over my head, the cloud of falling snow and rock quickly descending, running down the mountainside, a river with no intention of stopping.

I shove Amalie away from me as hard as I can and she stumbles backwards. A hand reaches for her, pulling her to shelter behind a huge rock sticking from the cliff face. I gather all of my strength, locating the others' auras and throwing up whatever shields I can around them.

"Aila!" I shriek into the night with my mind. *"Aila run! Hide!"*

The last thing I see before I throw myself behind another rock, curling up into a ball and covering my head with my

BETRAYED

arms, is Tristen's horrified face.

Eventually, the rumbling stops over my head, and though I'm physically okay, I'm buried.

The only thing stopping me from complete panic is my muscle memory, which immediately sparks into action. I imagine my body radiating heat, lighting a coal at my centre, pushing its blaze outwards. The snow above me starts to melt and, using my now burning hands, I dig my way out. I'm disorientated as I break the surface, taking huge gasps of the cold, clean air. I scan the landscape, looking for anyone, any sign of movement. There's a loud growl above and to my left. Aila.

"Are you hurt?" I send to her.

She's not. I feel her stretching her limbs and padding out into the snow. The image of Asher flickers in her mind.

"Yes. Find her. I'll look for the others." I get to my feet, spinning in a circle. There's no sign of them, but there is a huge river of snow and ice running down the path we just climbed. They have to be on the other side. I threw up the shields, just like I practised, and I saw Tristen grab Amalie.

"Hello?!" I scream out with my mind. *"Is everyone okay?"*

"Eddie, Amalie, Greg." Comes straight from Tristen. *"All fine, back on top, but not on the same side as you."*

"Merle!" Owen calls from fifty feet above, waving his arms.

"Don't move." I send back to Greg. *"I'll check back in two minutes."*

I race up the hill and find Asher and Aila with Richard and Owen. Rory is sitting on the floor, grimacing while gripping her arm.

"We've got trouble." I send to Greg.

"It's broken!" Rory squeals as I get closer. "Oh, my god it's broken!"

172

"It's all right," I say, placing my hands around either side of her arm. At first she's reluctant to let me, but her eyes fill with relief when I send a wave of numbing magic her way. Aila goes to her too, rubbing her soft fur against Rory's cheek.

"I don't have the skills to heal this," I whisper to Richard. "You'll have to get back down, take her to a hospital."

"The others?" He asks.

Rory whimpers at the thought of her sister.

"They're all fine. I promise."

"What now, chief?" Asher stares at me over the tops of their heads.

"Do you know the way?"

She gives a tentative nod.

"Owen," I say, knowing full well he can't hear me any other way. "Me and Asher are going to carry on while the others help Rory back down."

"But—" Richard protests.

"Do you see another way?"

No response. There isn't one to give. She has to go down, and he has to take her. The others are already on the other side. They can go for help. If we were to go with them, we'd have to start again. There just isn't time for that. No, we need to go forward.

"I'll come with you." Owen says.

Asher and I meet eyes. We could risk it alone, send him back, and half of me wants to. But he's been studying the map with Eddie. He knows what to do on the mountain. He believes in Morgana's existence, and even if his motives are dangerous, he categorically knows the way.

We divide up the provisions and walk the others back down the mountain to Eddie and Greg, who are trying to make their way through the snow. While I can relay information between the groups, once I'm gone, they won't be able to

BETRAYED

communicate with anyone, not even each other. I reluctantly dig the Hag Stone out of my pack. I'm loath to give it to them, but Richard's tiny spark of magic might be enough to make it work and Rory needs to get back down.

"Can you use this?" I ask, placing the stone in his hands.

"What do I do?"

I tell him the words and how to make it work, how to answer if someone calls. "If they haven't dug through to you in an hour, contact Joth. He can let Cassandra know to send someone."

"What will you do, won't you need it?"

"We'll be fine," I say. There's nothing to do but hope I'm right.

When I get back to Asher, Aila, and Owen, they're ready to climb again.

"The sooner we get off this damn mountain, the better." Asher says, staring up at the huge white wall of ice in front of us, her mouth set in a grim, determined line.

18

After another hour of climbing, it becomes obvious we aren't going to make the rest of the ascent today. Chunks of ice keep tumbling past us, followed by ribbons of snow and small rocks.

"The warmer the day gets, the more unstable the climb. That's why we're leaving in the middle of the night. Once the sun is up, it's too late." Eddie told us an age ago. He wouldn't want us to go on any further, especially not without him.

We set up two tents on a small alcove and I use my magic to hold them into the ground, casting a protective, heated net over them to give us a better chance at making it through the evening. As we're rolling out our sleeping matts, I tell Asher that I had to give up the Hag Stone. Her face creases with anxiety. Now there's no way to contact anyone if we get stuck. Nowhere to go but up.

"Don't let him know," she tells me. *"We can't trust him."*

I agree wholeheartedly. Owen doesn't really make any

BETRAYED

fuss as we split the duties of putting up the tent and cooking rations. We sit huddled together around a small flame, one that I can barely keep going in the cold. I wonder if the others made it back, if they somehow dug through the snow, or if Cassandra sent someone to help them. I sorely wish I'd not given up the stone so I could check somehow.

They might've died without it, I remind myself. *And you've still got Ash.*

The knight in question pats me on the knee. "I'm going to turn in. We've got a long way to climb tomorrow."

"I'll be in in a moment." I send to her.

Asher brings her eyes to mine, searching my face, then they go to the big cat lounging at my feet. She looks docile right now, but she's not. One sound, one *thought* and she'll pounce into action.

After Asher's crawled into the tent, I turn my attention to Owen. He's fidgeting in his seat, dark circles under his eyes. It's so strange, how he seems to always be warring with himself. The emotions flicker on his face in tandem with the flames from the campfire. Anger, determination, and sometimes, fear. I can't make sense of it and I can't get in his head to check. I haven't tried since we stopped for food when we arrived. Maybe...

Owen hisses something under his breath.

"What was that?" I snap.

He glares at me, a thin haze of red across his cheeks and the bridge of his nose. For a second, I don't think he's going to answer and then, "Are you sure we shouldn't have gone back with the others?"

"I'm sure. You know the way, don't you?"

He nods slowly. "I think so."

I stare at him, the swampy green eyes and wisps of blonde poking from underneath his hat. He looks young, certainly too young to be on a knight's quest on the side of a dangerous mountain. Certainly too young to have planned a mutiny against the Templar alone. But it's exactly Morgwese's style, isn't it? To infiltrate the inner circle. The longer he looks at me, the more agitated he seems to become. For a wild second I think I might get it out of him, whatever plan he's got.

"Is there something you need to tell me, Owen?" I make sure the question doesn't come out of my mouth too harshly. Like it's a question I might ask anyone.

His face creases for a moment, his eyes going so dark they reflect the glittering stars. He opens his mouth, and I really think he's going to say something. There's another war on his face. Two sides ripping at each other. Then his jaw snaps shut.

"Goodnight then, I guess." I say when I'm sure he's not going to speak.

I leave him in the snow and clamber into the tent, stripping off my coat and getting into the sleeping bag. Asher is already snoring softly and Aila stretches out between us before she settles, nuzzling her huge head against my cheek as a goodnight before closing her eyes. The last thing I do is check our packs, moving them to the front of the tent so they're easy to collect. Getting ready in the dark is already difficult enough, no need to make it worse.

I think of Lore before I sleep, of Ren and Lux in Scotland, of the witch I hope to find. I can't exactly *feel* her, but we must be close. For the last hour, there's been another presence with us, a whisper on the wind. It's subtle, barely there, but still something. The only other person with magic up here is Morgana Le Fae.

At some point in the night, I hear shuffling and the grating of the zip being unfastened, a cold burst of air as Asher leaves. I'm too tired to think much of it and there are too few hours left in the night to force myself properly awake.

BETRAYED

Eventually I sleep again, but it's thin, plagued with nightmares. Lore's slack face and Lux's broken sobs. They're so horrific that it takes me a moment to register that Asher's gut wrenching scream is real.

I snap my eyes open, immediately throwing off my sleeping bag and pulling on my unwieldy thick trousers and boots. Then, the ground begins to shake again and a deafening boom rocks the mountain. I immediately throw out the net of my magic, searching for my friend who apparently didn't return. I find her bright blue light racing through the dark, flashing with red and black. I don't know where Owen is.

I bolt out into the snow to another one of those thunderous claps splitting the sky. It's so black I can't see my hand in front of my face. Aila growls low in her throat beside me, her eyes already adjusted to the dark.

"Asher?!" I shout into the abyss. I can't see her. I can't see anything. I only know which direction to start in because of her aura burning like a beacon behind my eyes.

"*You're a goddamn witch! Do some magic!*" Willow roars in my head. Of course it would be her, the only one of us who has really got any sense. I conjure a stuttering ball of light into my palm. In front of me is a jagged sea of ice and stone, the other tent that was pitched, washed away by the wave. I can't see Asher or Owen, but I didn't imagine that scream. I launch myself into the snow, wading forward, and just over the lip of stone to my left, I see Owen on his knees.

"Owen?!" I shout, my voice whipped away by the icy wind. He doesn't turn. Maybe he didn't hear me. What is he doing?

Aila growls again from beside me, tensing her hind legs to launch forward.

Owen's on his knees, but he's not only that, he's leaning

over the chasm, hanging onto something.

With a descending horror that robs the breath from my lungs, I realise he must be holding onto Asher. She was swept away in the avalanche, thrown over the side. Now the only thing standing between Asher and death is Owen.

My limbs turn to lead, frozen to the spot.

"*Move!*" Ren's voice. "*Get her! Move!*"

Aila reacts faster than I do, leaping towards Owen, her claws outstretched to swipe. When Owen sees her, the big cat ready to kill, the malice drains from his face, replaced by fear. Crying out, he shoves backwards, throwing himself into the snow. And he lets go of Asher's hand.

She does not scream as she falls.

I scream, though. Loud and long. I force my limbs to move, even though I know it's already too late. I'll never be quick enough to get to her, neither is my exhausted magic quick enough to race over the edge to catch her. I slam to my knees at the edge of the cliff in time to hear the wet crunch of her bones as she hits the floor.

I feel it; the impact cracking through my body. The thud echoing through my brain like a siren.

The entire world stops as her little blue light stutters once, twice, and then winks out entirely.

No. No, it can't be. I try to take a breath, but I can't. My throat locked, heart frozen in my chest. Asher is not, can not, that sound *was* not –

I shriek into the night, my voice slicing through the quiet, so piercing and full of rage that the ground shakes.

You're going to cause another avalanche.

Aila skids to a stop beside me, nuzzling me to get up, her canines digging into the soft flesh of my forearm as she tugs.

"*Hurry, hurry, hurry.*" Those nagging teeth say.

No. I can't go. I can't leave her, I can't –

BETRAYED

"There's no time for this now." Merlin's voice cuts through the black spots in my vision. *"Lamorak means to kill you, too. Run."*

Aila is still ragging on my sleeve, dragging me back from the edge.

I'm sorry. I'm sorry. I'm so sorry. I think to my friend, whose aura no longer twinkles next to mine. *No. No. No.*

"Get up!" Another voice demands, a seemingly invisible hand wrenching me to my feet. *"Get up and run. Do something."* It's not a voice I recognise, but one that can only be the witch's. *She's here. She's really here.*

Aila lets go of my sleeve to growl. Over the brow of the hill is a dark shadow, stumbling towards us. While I can only make out his silhouette, I can tell he's holding a knife.

Carnwennan. Witch Killer. The only blade on earth my magic can't save me from.

I scramble to my feet, racing as fast as I can to my tent. There's only one thing to do: find my gear, get the spear head and try to beat him to the top of the mountain. I spin to take note of where Owen is, still a way behind me, and I send a bolt of lightning over my shoulder. It misses him by a fair way.

"You could kill him." A voice I recognise but can't immediately place slithers around my mind like a serpent's tongue. *"He deserves it."*

That might be true, he might deserve it. He killed my friend. My heartbeat flickers in my chest as I relive that blue light being doused, fire blistering through my blood. I could do it, one shot and it would be over.

Is that truly who I hope to be?

Aila stops in the snow, squaring her shoulders.

"No, we need to run, come on!"

She glowers at me and stands her ground. Her intention for me to flee pierces my heart like an arrow.

"Aila! *No!*"

"*MOVE!*" Wind whips around my shoulders, whether it's the cat or the witch I don't know. The remains of my heart shred as I turn away. I have to leave her behind.

A memory flickers to life in the depths of the dark as I climb, a shining little blonde girl twirling on her toes in the catacombs, spraying cake crumbs across the kitchen as she can't hold in her laugh.

Asher is my heart, Aila the very bones of me. But Lore is my queen. It doesn't matter that I want to deal with Owen myself. I would ruin this mountain, reduce it to rubble in vengeance, if it wasn't for her. To fail in my mission, to risk death before finding Morgana would doom Lore.

There will be time after to take revenge.

Not if you die on this cursed mountain side.

I make it to the tent, pulling on my coat and grabbing my crampons and rucksack. There's no time for anything else, only time to run.

I keep those pictures of Lore in the forefront of my mind.

Don't stop. Don't look back.

I do stop long enough, however, to pull Rhongomyniad out of the front pocket of my pack.

I've made a good head start up the ice when an awful yowl of pain echoes across the rock face and a gash opens up across my calf. I yelp, sliding backwards and losing some of the ground I've just made. Owen must have got Aila. Not too bad, not fatally, but if I don't do something, he'll kill her too.

"*Leave him to me.*" I command across the space, yanking on the thread of magic between us, the line that can't be broken. "*Hide.*"

The big cat roars in displeasure, but I feel her retreat. Now Owen's focus will be on me as I hobble up the cliff. It can't be far, and even though my magic is depleted, I can still

BETRAYED

outrun him. I just need to get close enough for Morgana to—

There's a sharp grunt from about ten metres behind me, much closer than I thought.

Move, move, move!

I slam my ice pick into the snow, pulling myself up the almost vertical wall of ice, up and up until my arms and legs burn. I'm running on empty and I throw one last bolt over my shoulder. It fizzles into a snowbank but illuminates Owen's form. He's close, too close.

A way in the distance, perhaps 100 metres, is a shining light. At first I think I'm imagining it, but I can't be. It has to be something, the white glow turning to pink and orange. The ground levels out and I clamber to my feet. That has to be it, the door to the cave and if I can just—

A gloved hand clamps around my ankle, yanking hard, throwing me off balance. I tumble to the ground, rolling onto my back, snow clouds my vision, freezing clumps of ice falling onto my face. I throw what's left of my magical reserves into a shield when I feel Owen's knee slam into my chest, knocking the wind from me. He recoils for a moment, stunned.

There's a horrible expression on his face. His mouth is twisted in a desperate sneer, his eyes bloodshot and forced wide. He doesn't know who I am, and I don't recognise the person staring back at me. Owen sweeps his arm towards me and I raise the spearhead, the blades sparking off each other, screeching into the night. He uses his free hand to grab my wrist, bashing it against the floor until I let go of the spear head. Then he lunges again.

A lance of pain screams across my cheek, the dagger slicing straight through my magic. I cry out and try to scrabble out from under him, raising my arms to cover my face.

"Morgana! Morgana, help me, help—"

Then the cold silver blade of the Witch Killer slides into

my chest.

I choke from the shock of it, the pain greater than anything I've ever felt, cleaving the muscle of my heart in two. A river of flame shoots from the wound, enveloping my whole body in agony. I can't draw breath, I can't move, my vision running black and grey. I definitely lose consciousness as he slides the blade out, raising his arms above his head to deliver the final blow...

Suddenly his weight is gone from my chest, forced off me, tumbling back with a cry of anguish. I feel those magical hands again as I fall in and out of life, dragging me up the slope, rushing me to the summit.

I have time to think of Lore before my eyes slide shut.

"*I'm sorry.*" I wail to her across the darkness. "*I'm so sorry.*"

I'm cold all over, and tired, so tired.

I have a moment to think of Ren before the darkness takes me.

19

REN

I make my face feign shock to give Laina, *Elaine*, the reaction she wants. She looks different from when I saw her last, the day she tried to kill me. Older and more worn out. My stomach rolls, not with fear about what will happen now, but at the memory of what happened *then*.

"*I don't know why I'd be with her all night, instead of you.*" That's what I'd said to Merle, the morning after, when she'd had that blank, cold look on her face.

"*You don't owe me anything.*" She'd said back. But I did, I *do*.

I still don't remember the night. The last thing I can recall is Merle being led through the crowd by Joth, beautiful, radiating power and magic even then, every head turning to stare. Then the evening floats away like a balloon, the string of memory cut.

"Don't worry, this is a social call, not an act of war." Elaine keeps her grin in place, but her eyes move from mine and settle on Lux.

Shit. Shit. Shit.

"What do you want?"

"First, my sister thought to send her condolences–"

There's a high whirring sound and a thud as Mona's knife spins end over end, close enough to my cheek that I feel the breeze it leaves behind, and slams into the wooden beam to the faery's right. I don't turn to look at Mona, it's an obvious miss. If she wanted Elaine's eye, she'd have it.

"Last warning." Mona says quietly.

"Hmm. Yes." Elaine chirps, wafting her hand as if she's batting away a fly. "I've been sent on an errand, Mags left something of hers here, something very powerful. One of a kind. You wouldn't be looking for it too, would you? Wouldn't happen to have found it?"

I keep my face straight but can't stop Lux from taking a breath in surprise. I've trained for years, not only in combat and how to defend myself against faery charms, but also in how to talk, how to keep my emotions covered up regardless of what I'm actually feeling. Lux will one day know all those things, but not today.

"Tha's wha' ye wer lookin' for when I caught ye snoopin' in the Templar." Mona says, trying to distract her. Mer was right, she's been wasted all these years in service.

"I was looking in the wrong place though, wasn't I?" Elaine draws herself up to her full height, peering down at us. "Because I smell magic."

This time, even I don't manage a neutral expression, my nose screwing up in a scowl. No, that can't be right. Abrasax is inside, not here. Maybe it's so powerful it's left a residue on

BETRAYED

Lux and I?

"I don't know what you're talking about." I say.

"Hmm. That's a pity. What about you, *Nephew*, what do you know?" Elaine turns her glowing amber stare onto the king. "Because I think *you're* the one who's got what I want."

What? What does she mean...? My mind whirs. What could Lux possibly have that Morgwese wants? Other than royal blood. Behind the faery, the back door to the chapel cracks open. That should be Rab McGavin, back up just in time.

"What did you do to my sister?" Lux asks.

"Poor Lore," Elaine whines, sticking out her bottom lip. But she takes a step forward, a crucial distance, a crucial distraction. "I hear she's still under the weather."

"I want you to undo it."

"Can't do that, I'm afraid." She glides forward another two steps. I move onto the balls of my feet, ready to attack. "Now, Nephew, what have you got in your pocket?"

In his pocket?

Lux says nothing, standing his ground. Rab enters my field of vision as he creeps inside. In his hands, he's holding two small glass bottles full of black liquid. *Letum de Mors.*

"Give it to me." Elaine demands as the room hums with static. The feral beauty of her face melts, skin turning blue at her nose and around her lips. She raises her hand, fingers stretched, nails like claws.

"I'll give ye exac'ly five seconds to disappear from this place." Rab says from behind her, causing her to jump. His voice is calm, no edge of panic or fear. As he talks, he uncorks the bottle. "As I understand it, if what's in this wee bottle was to fall on ye, it'll ea' ye alive. A punishmen' yer rightly due, if ye ask me."

Elaine turns her head towards Rab, which gives me time

186

to move in front of Lux. The only thing in his pocket is that old silver ring. I've got no idea what it is, or what they want it for. But over my dead body, are they going to take it.

When Elaine sees the potion in Rab's hands, she hisses, baring her teeth. "Fools! Fools to even make such a monstrous thing–!"

"Five." Rab says. "Four."

Elaine screams, eyes darting between Lux and Rab, weighing up whether she can risk the grab.

"Three. Two."

With a hollow shriek, she transforms completely through her fae form and into a whirlwind of ash and dust, twisting past Rab and out into the night, rocking the wooden door on its hinges.

We all stare at each other for a moment. The only sound is our collective breathing. Then Rab corks the potion bottle and brings his eyes to meet mine.

"Firs' thing tomorrow, we'd better close those rings."

Mona gets to Lydia first, hauling her to her feet, gripping her elbow and helping her back through the pews, muttering something about tea. I find Lux with a confused expression on his face, grey eyes like gathering thunder clouds. Not for the first time, I wish I was telepathic, like Merle, so Lux could understand me.

Say nothing. Don't mention the ring at all.

Instead, I have to settle for putting my hand on his shoulder and steering him out of the doors behind Lydia and Mona. Rab comes out last, locking the chapel behind us.

"We'll go at daybreak to close the rings." He says.

"It was good thinking, to get the potion."

He shrugs. "I want'd something tha' would kill it."

I don't get to talk to Lux about the ring in his pocket until

BETRAYED

much later that evening. First we debrief, check on Lydia and make new plans to head back to the Templar tomorrow. There's no time to waste, not now we've got what we came for and apparently, some other powerful object we didn't.

"So what do you think it is?" Lux asks me. We're both sitting cross–legged on my bed, the ornate silver ring placed on a book between us.

"Tha's a dispelling ring." Mona says from the door. She was so quiet I didn't hear her approach, and she's obviously got the eyesight of an eagle.

"What's that?" I ask.

"D'ye not know yer own histry, Sir Ren du Lac?" She raises an eyebrow.

"I apparently do not."

She flashes a wolfish grin. Mona has forgotten more about the Templar and our history than I will ever know. She might even know more than Willow in terms of strange stories and myths. "Legend says it's a ring tha' can uncover or lif' any enchantmen'. It wa' given to Lancelot by Lady Vivienne when he lef' for Arthur's cour'."

"And does it work?"

"There are stories of 'im usin' it. An' *she* wanted it."

That's true, Elaine *did* want it. I wonder what for? Why would Elaine want something that could break an enchantment? They're already magic. Thank god she didn't seem to know about Abrasax. That would be the last thing on earth we need.

"You should have it." Lux says, pressing it into my palm. "It's technically yours."

"But you–"

He shakes his head. "It's yours."

"All right." I curl my fingers closed around the ring. "Thank you."

Rab comes for us early in the morning, well before the sun comes up. The four of us trapes across the moors, the heather thick and full of spikes, slowing our progress to a crawl. By the time we reach the rings– a cluster of ten bright red toadstools that are out of place in the highlands– my jeans are soaked to the knee and Lux is shivering. I hand a bottle of the *Letum de Mors* to each of them.

"Each ring will only need a drop." I say, remembering the devastating effects the potion had on the ring when Merle tested it. And there's Elaine's reaction to it to consider.

Fools to even make such a monstrous thing!

She's right, it *is* monstrous. A magic killing weapon, it's only intent to destroy.

We go about our duty silently. As each ring closes, the ground shakes, sometimes bubbling up thick yellow liquid and foul smelling sludge. Lux closes the last one, by far the biggest, and as a black droplet falls into the circle, it screams with agony.

"It's for the best," I say, clapping my hand on his shoulder. "I promise."

"T'wasn't always this way." Mona says. "In Arthur's time, everyone lived together, in *peace.* I' coul' bi tha' way again."

When you and Lore are in charge. She doesn't need to add.

We file back to the house now that horrible job is done. The cars are already waiting on the gravel driveway, Lydia directing the staff loading them up. She keeps looking back at the house with longing. Only a week ago everything was different. Now her whole life is upside down.

"You'll be back in no time." Rab says, gripping her into a rough hug before ushering her into the back seat of the car. "I'll stay a few days, make sure everythin's locked up tight, then I'll make the rounds on the other estates. Will ye send aid?"

BETRAYED

"Everyone we can spare when they're back." I say, shaking his warm, calloused hand. "Thank you."

"Good luck." Rab smiles and then turns to Lux. "It's been a pleasure, yer Highness."

Lux's cheeks flush crimson at the title, something he'll have to get used to. It must be strange though, he can't feel like a king when he's helping Etta scrape leftovers off plates and running round changing sheets with Mona. It's all part of Joth's grand plan, though, to raise them to be good and hardworking people, so that when the luxuries of ruling present themselves, the twins will understand how to be kind.

With the final goodbyes over, and Abrasax and Lancelot's ring tucked safely in my backpack, I get into the black sedan with the others. I can't wait to get home. I can't wait to speak to Merle and make sure she's okay. They'll be gone for another week at least, but just to hear her voice will be enough.

We make good time back to the Templar, arriving mid afternoon. Joth doesn't make a scene asking if I've found anything, but I know from the long look he gives me that he expects to see me in his office later. I'll also have to tell him about Elaine and the ring. Christ, how has Merle managed duties like this for months? Endless problem solving and change.

It's after dinner when I finally have a chance to gather the artefacts we found and take them to Joth. He's waiting, as always, with a crystal glass of his finest whiskey, one poured out for me.

"Welcome home." He says, giving me a brief hug before sitting back down. "Now I want to hear all about it. Did you–"

Joth's words are cut off by a huge clattering smash somewhere in the hall. It sounds as if the ceilings fallen in or one of the great chandeliers has come crashing down.

190

Then Willow screams.

I'm up on my feet in seconds, racing through the door and down the hall. It can't be an attack. Not here, not now. Not when we're so tired and unready to defend. I skid to a stop in the foyer, drawing my iron dagger. I always carry it now, it's too dangerous not too. But what I find there doesn't require it. My eyes aren't even really able to take in what I'm seeing.

"Get some help!" Willow screams at me from the floor where she's cradling something, *someone,* although I can't tell who. "Run!"

20

I wake to the sound of a woman humming. It's hot, wherever I am, and it smells like cinnamon and spice. Before opening my eyes, I try to get my bearings. The last thing I remember is Owen's weight pressing me into the snow and a sharp icy pain sliding up my ribs. I can see his swamp green eyes glaring into mine, every speck of dirt on his awful pale face. Then there's Aila to think about, and Asher –

I squeeze my eyes tightly shut, locking my throat against a cry. Asher, my poor, lovely Asher, lost in a mountain of snow. Fallen. Gone.

It can't be. It can't truly be. My voice wails inside my head. *She can't be gone. She can't be–*

I don't even let myself think it. The pain is too great to even consider. Tears creep from under my lashes, sliding down my cheeks.

"Oh come on now, Darling. There's no need for that." The woman's voice is soft, and exactly as her melodious hum suggested it would be. Then I feel her hands on me, pulling me into a sitting position. "Look, have a drink of tea, that's it."

I slowly blink open, my eyelashes gummy with salt. As my eyes adjust to the candlelight, I find a cup being pushed towards me, forced into my hands and towards my mouth. The tea tastes like lavender and valerian. A sleeping draught. I try to pull my head away. A sharp flare of agony twists through my cheek, but the woman insists.

"You were hurt very badly by that knight. The healing isn't done."

"Aila?" I choke out.

"Stop it! She's right beside you. Be careful with your face. Don't talk."

What does she mean about my face? I reach towards the side of the bed with my fingers outstretched. Aila's huge head meets my palm, her wet, pink nose brushing against my skin, then her tongue drags its way across my wrist. Fresh tears burst from my eyes. *Hurt badly?*

"Now drink this—"

"Poison—"

All the air drains from the room. I'm flung back into my pillows by invisible hands, my head turning against my will to see the woman proper.

Morgana Le Fae stands at my bedside, whisky coloured eyes glowing like the embers of a fire. She is as beautiful as the sunrise, her cheekbones sharp, soft, delicate lips turned down in a scowl. She looks feral in the half light, the shadows of flickering flames from the candles dancing across her skin. *Morgana Le Fae.* It's really her. She is really here. And a second too late, I realise that the look on her face might mean she wants to kill me.

Then she takes a deep breath, closes her eyes, and lets the air out in a whoosh. "I'll blame that on the awful ordeal you've

BETRAYED

just been through. If I wanted you dead, I'd have let Owen Lamorak carve out your heart to take back to my sister. But, seen as I've spent all this time *and magic* keeping you in one piece, I intend to at least hear what you've got to say. To know why Merlin's Heir comes knocking at my door."

I swallow. She knows everything. Maybe she's been keeping tabs on us. Not so disinterested in the Templar, then?

"I don't know why you're smiling." She says, low and viscous. "I still might decide to eat you yet."

Now my smile spreads fully on my face, stopped by a sharp pain as whatever wound I have in my cheek pulls taught. Then I think of Asher. How pleased she would be, how she'd roll her eyes at Morgana's dramatics. The smile falls right off my face and my hands begin to shake. That horrible ice cold lance shoves its way back up between my ribs, my lungs aching with every breath.

"Right, that's quite enough. If you want to make it back to your friends, you'll do exactly as I say. Drink the tea." She forces the liquid down my throat and then pushes me back into the pillows, using her magic to pull the covers up to my chin. She goes to the end of the bed and whirls with her hands on her hips. "I'll come back when—"

"Stay."

She tips her head to one side, long auburn hair trailing to her waist in soft curls. Then her eyes soften and she says, "Do you like stories, Merle?"

"Yes," I slowly move myself down the bed, patting the space beside me, so Aila jumps up. I can feel the valerian working already, I'm going to sleep, there's no two ways about it. I might as well be comfortable.

"Telling them or hearing them?"

I snort. "I never was much of a storyteller, I always get too excited and ruin the twists. My dad used to tell them."

"So did mine until Uther Pendragon killed him." She spits, flashing a snarl my way. Any sense of peace I've just gained evaporates. "But Merlin, Merlin told me many *great* tales. You've his love of storytelling to thank for your life quite frankly, and that your magic smells so much like home."

I say nothing, too tired to form words, my eyes sliding closed.

"How about I tell you the story of how my dear, dear friend Lancelot saved his beloved Guinevere from certain death." From the sound of her voice, I can tell she's moved to sit beside me. "I was there that day, you know. I'd've helped the stupid bastard too if he'd asked. Always was a hothead, though!" Morgana runs the pads of her fingers across my eyebrow. "Go to sleep, heal, and I shall weave the tale into your dreams."

Sleep takes me, tumbles onto me like a huge unending wave. And while my body relaxes, my consciousness doesn't fade. Instead, there's a buzzing white light opening in front of me. It's so bright I have to cover my eyes. When the glow fades, I lower my hands to find myself in a grand hall. The walls are white stone, swirling with caramel, cream, and pink. It's part of the marble from Merlin's cave, I'm sure of it. The ceiling towers above me in a cavernous arc, and as I follow its line, I find myself staring into the eyes of Merlin.

My heart skips a beat and I can't help the smile spreading across my face. He looks younger, long brown hair pulled back in a ponytail. He's standing at the far end of the hall next to a wooden throne. Its back rises almost seven feet, and Merlin is just as tall. While I'm staring at him, a knight in a red vest comes running right towards me. Before I can move, he charges straight through my midsection. There's a strange sensation of an ice cube melting in my stomach, then it's gone.

BETRAYED

He streaks around the corner and disappears.

"To me, Little One." Merlin's voice whistles around my head.

I rush across the hall, almost tumbling over the blood red rug, and only just tucking myself into the alcove beside him before shouting starts outside.

"You can see me?"

"You're my blood." He shrugs as if that explains everything, a half smile playing on his lips. *"Now stay back. There's trouble."*

I'm about to ask him to elaborate, but the shouting outside has spilled into the hall along with about fifty knights. At the front of the stream is a tall man with shoulder length golden hair, streaked with red and burnt orange. He's handsome enough, with a wide flat nose, a square jaw and the same piercing grey eyes as Lux and Lore. As soon as I see him, goosebumps race down my arms, the aura around him so bright it's almost blinding.

Arthur Pendragon, King of Camelot, strides towards the throne. The gold crown he wears, encrusted with rubies, sits askew on his head. For a moment, I'm star—struck. I'm seeing the man who set my destiny in motion, the greatest king who ever existed, someone who most believe to be a fable.

"Magnificent, isn't he?" Merlin sends.

I swallow, unable to find words.

Arthur throws himself into the king's seat, the wood grating against the stone floor with the force. The other knights circle around him, all of them babbling. They're so similar to the knights at home, arguing and squabbling, that I have to physically resist the urge to snap my fingers and make them fall quiet. I'm sure I hear Merlin chuckles under his breath.

"Silence!" Arthur shouts, and for a wonder, everyone is

immediately quiet. I wonder if Lux will command so much respect when he is king. Will Lore when she is queen?

"Problems, Arthur?" Merlin leans forward to whisper in the king's ear.

I can't see his face, but the stiffness in Arthur's back tells me something's wrong. "They say Guinevere's deceived me."

"Who says?"

The crowd of knights part like the red sea. Making his way to the front is a boy of about eighteen, with shoulder length caramel coloured curls and pale, sallow skin. His eyes are almost the same colour as Morgana's, like whiskey and honey. They sit above a slightly long hooked nose, and below thick bushy eyebrows. His clothes are all black, and he's got a grim look about him. Trouble stamped over his every movement.

"Sir Mordred, my liege."

My stomach flips. Mordred Pendragon, the bastard child of Arthur and Morgwese, the one who tumbled Camelot almost single–handedly. That means Morgwese won't be far away. Dread uncoils in my stomach.

"She isn't here." Merlin sends to me. *"And besides, this is just a dream."*

"And what business do you have, Sir Mordred?" Arthur's voice is full of thunder. I know from my history lessons that the prince was a constant thorn in Arthur's side. The king never accepted Mordred, vehemently denying siring him.

"In your absence, your queen has taken a lover, supposedly one of your most loyal knights." A sly grin spreads over Mordred's face. He looks like the cat that's got the cream.

"And what proof have you?"

Mordred sweeps his arm behind him, giving way to a troop of armed guards and two women. I recognise one as Morgana. Her beautiful face is twisted in rage, long curls

BETRAYED

bound down her back in a plait.

The other must be Guinevere. If Morgana is beautiful, Guinevere is radiant. She has the face of an angel, unblemished skin and perfectly symmetrical cheek bones. Her lips are the colour of pink rose petals, bowed in the middle. As she stalks forward, her sea–green eyes survey the spectacle in front of her and she tips her slightly pointed nose into the air like she's above it all. I've never seen a ruling queen in real life before, but this is the elegance I've always imagined they'd exude. She shakes her hair free over her shoulder, not golden like in most pictures, but an intoxicating shade of strawberry blonde.

"Why, she admits it, *Sire.*" Mordred says. The mocking note in his voice makes me wish I could put my fist through his teeth. "And you know the punishment for treason."

A volcano of noise erupts from the left, whether for or against the queen, I can't tell.

"Guinevere?" Arthur asks. He knows it's true. His voice says he's known for a while, but he'd never have outed her on his own.

"You've been gone for ten years, Arthur." She says, staring straight into his eyes. There's no shame in her expression, just serene acceptance of what's coming. "You never loved me."

The entire hall erupts into shouting again. Mordred is grinning from ear to ear, the unrest he wanted coming to life beyond his wildest dreams. Morgana is shoving her way to the front of the crowd, elbowing through those trying to hinder her passage.

"Will you stand for it, my king? Or will you do what your very own laws dictate?" Mordred howls over the crowd. This is what he really came for, to make a stand against his father, to take the throne if he smells weakness.

"Tread carefully, Arthur." Merlin whispers.

198

"What would you have me do?" The king bites back.

"Silence, you runt." Morgana's eyes are blazing, tendrils of magic snapping loose around her, a force to be reckoned with. "I should have drowned you in a bucket the day you were born." As Guinevere exudes calm, Morgana is a storm of power and rage. She positions herself in front of the queen and glares at Arthur. "Would you allow yourself to be so easily manipulated by a pup? Don't you see what's happening here? Surely you've not become so blind? Banish her if you must! But he means to destroy your court. Think of everything we've built, Arthur, *brother*!" Her tawny eyes implore him. "This is not the way!"

Arthur is quiet for a long time. I can't imagine how he must feel even though I understand the question he's warring with.

He doesn't truly believe that Guinevere deserves death, but the loyalty of his knights is in question. If he shows weakness, they will defect to Mordred and all will be lost. There's only one way.

"The law is the law." He booms across the hall.

Guinevere smiles, raising her beautiful face up to meet Arthur's. "I'd rather die now than spend another moment in this *crypt* you've created. Our dreams are dust, and it's all your doing, *my king*." She spits the words with more malice than I would've believed her angelic lips capable of. Then she holds her wrists out in front of her.

Two of the armed guards take hold and drag her forward. Morgana follows them shrieking, but I hear no more as the ground spins on its axis, bringing me to a new scene in this horrible circus.

I'm looking out over what I assume to be the castle courtyard. It's cold up here, the arrowhead window letting in a nasty breeze. Below me is a wooden platform, a huge stake

BETRAYED

planted in its middle. There are already people filling up the cobbles, waiting for the festivities to begin. I shiver and thread my way through the thin doorway and down the spiral staircase. At the bottom, I find a wide stone bridge connecting this tower to the body of the main castle.

Morgana, Merlin, and Arthur are staring out, as I was only a minute ago. Their faces are horribly grim.

Merlin notices me out of the corner of his eye and flicks his head, a 'come here' gesture I immediately obey.

"It's madness, Arthur." Morgana says. Her young face is twisted with emotion —anger, grief, hope —thin white hands clutching at the king's coat sleeve. "This is Guinevere we're talking about!"

"You know the law as well as I, Morgana." Arthur doesn't turn to look at her.

"What's the point of being king if you can't do what you want?" She huffs. "Let's speak plainly. We might as well. The way you're going, Camelot will be gone by Winter's end—"

"Morgana." Merlin warns.

She ignores him, barrelling on. "You already knew about Guinevere and Lancelot. You've known for *years*! You can't mean to punish them now, they're your most loyal—"

"*Loyal?!*" Arthur roars. His voice is picked up on the wind, carried so that the peasants below snap their heads around. "They started their affair the second I left."

"You should *never* have gone!" Morgana starts, then she pauses and pulls in a deep breath, dropping her voice to a vicious whisper. "And you well know why that affair began. To provide you, my king, with an heir seen as you don't deign to do it your—"

A gust of wind rips the words from her throat, and Merlin raises himself to his full height. "You will stop."

Morgana nods, and he releases her from his magical grip.

"My point is, you knew before. And Guinevere has kept your secret all this time. She'll keep it now even if you—"

"Nobody else knew before." Merlin grumbles. "Now—"

"Oh well, then!" Morgana screeches. "Oh well, if *nobody else* knew! Is it only treason if the entire court's aware, Arthur?"

"It meant I could hide it! If she'd have denied it, even *attempted*!" He shakes his head, his lips a thin line as he sneers. "We wouldn't be here! I know she's your friend."

"She's your queen! Your *friend.* She's been with us from the beginning. She built this with us Arthur, she's stood with us the entire time! She and Lancelot have *never* shown disloyalty to you as a king. Guinevere has ruled Camelot and made it strong. Even now they'd stay true! If you allow this to happen, Lancelot won't fight for you, and a war is coming! He won't come back."

"Perhaps that's best." Arthur's voice is utterly defeated. "If he comes back, he'll have to hang."

Morgana's mouth falls open, shocked beyond words. Merlin shifts uncomfortably beside me.

"You must know I can't let him live!" Arthur turns to her. "I never wanted this! They brought it on themselves! If things were calmer, more steady, then I'd have banished them as you asked. But the kingdom needs a strong hand. Mordred means to challenge me and he's already seen too much unrest. If he promises prosperity, then they'll cast me aside!"

"They'll cast you aside regardless of how you deal with Guinevere." Morgana snaps and a deathly quiet falls over the three. Something they've all been thinking but haven't said out loud.

"No, no, there's still time." Arthur breathes.

A horn sounds in the distance. The king lifts his head and looks to his advisor, who nods slowly. Arthur steps back into

BETRAYED

the walkway and makes his way towards the castle. Morgana and I have to hurry to keep up.

"There's only one way out of this! Burn Mordred, not Guinevere! He's the cause of the unrest, not she! Everything will fall apart, everything we've built! Arthur, brother, please! You can not allow Mordred to manipulate you so, *Morgwese* to manipulate you so."

Arthur stops dead. She's hit a nerve. "Morgwese has been banished from here, and I will cast out her devil spawn before the week is over." He turns his head to her, grey eyes pained but cold. "This is going to happen, Morgana. If you can't keep out of it, I'll have the guards throw you in the dungeon until it's over."

She scowls, but Arthur doesn't wait for a response.

He and Merlin resume their walk, hanging their heads like it's them for the gallows and not the queen. I follow them. Even though I was sickened by the peasants earlier, I'm exactly the same as them. I've come to see the queen burn.

"I'll leave if you do this." Morgana's voice sounds from behind us. There's a trembling note of desperation in it, and when I turn to look at her, there are tears streaming down her cheeks. From her expression, I can tell this threat was a last resort, one she's been saving. She doesn't want to leave, but she will. "I mean it, Arthur."

"Mona don't." Arthur says. "I don't have time for this now."

"She was right, you know. Camelot's become a cemetery, a *graveyard* for old bones, for years now. All those wonderful ideas you had about fairness, honour, *love.*" Morgana hitches a breath. "That's why I followed, and why I've stayed. I would have followed you, brother, to hell and back, for those first ideas of Camelot. Then the Grail got into your head and everything changed. I wish you'd never found it."

202

Even in the heat of the moment, I can't ignore that. King Arthur found the grail?

"This is not my doing!" Arthur roars again. "My hands are tied!"

"I can't follow you now. I *won't.*" Morgana drops her whiskey coloured eyes from his, her voice loaded with despair. "I don't recognise you anymore, brother. You've broken my heart."

"I—" Arthur starts, but he's drowned out by the sound of trumpets and shouting. The time has come, and he must go. "Morgana, please, we'll discuss this after!"

The witch takes three steps forward and puts her hand on Arthur's cheek. "There won't be an after."

He pulls his face away and turns on his heel.

"I'll make sure you suffer for this, my king." Morgana screams after him. "I hope she haunts you when you stand in Camelot's ashes with no one but that conjuror for company! I hope—"

She's cut off by Merlin, who slams the huge wooden door in her face.

Arthur's face mirrors how I feel. The muscles in his jaw are working against tears and he's unable to stop them forming in his eyes. He takes in a deep breath and then runs down the stairs, leaving Merlin and me alone.

"Arthur and I have discussed this endlessly. I can't stop him." Merlin turns his sad golden eyes to me. "Mordred's poison got into him."

"Yes." Is all I can manage.

"It's time, and Lancelot will be along any minute," he muses. "I assume you want to see the rescue, not the fire."

I nod.

"Go back and watch from there. It'll be safer." He puts his hand on top of my head for a moment. "I must leave you now."

203

BETRAYED

"Goodbye, Merlin." I whisper, he ruffles my hair and then storms after Arthur.

Emptiness churns in my stomach as I watch him go. I've imagined him differently, so, so differently in those dark hours of the morning, when I've wondered what he would've done in the positions I've found myself in. I understand the pressures of keeping the monarch's council, that their good must always come first. But what about when they're going to ruin themselves? Is that my job? To stand idly by and obey horrific orders. To do nothing as Merlin does now. As I did with Lux.

Things have been set in motion that cannot be undone.

I head back up as he advised. Morgana's gone, and Arthur is now settling into his seat opposite the platform. A few seconds later, Merlin joins him. I wait for him to catch my eye, but he doesn't look up here again. He's ashamed of Arthur's choice. That much is clear. Ashamed of his part in it. And still content to sit and watch. Just as he did with Uther.

Who is he, this man? This person who's supposed to be my namesake? Why don't I recognise him now?

The crowd parts at the castle doors, revealing the queen being led by knights, surrounded by them. She's dressed in a white smock, the bottom of which is streaked with grime and torn in a few places. Her face looks thinner, she must be terrified of what's coming. She keeps her eyes focused forward, her back straight as she walks to her death. I admire her, more than I think I've ever admired anyone.

When she gets on the platform, one of the knights ties her to the stake, wrapping thick loops of rope around her middle. I recognise the coat of arms on his tunic, Sir Gaheris, Asher's ancestor.

At the thought of her, I close my eyes. I'd forgotten about her, the pain of her loss. I should have been there to save her,

204

as Lancelot is about to save Guinevere. I should have—

"Queen Guinevere Pendragon of Camelot, you, by your own admission, have been found guilty of the crime of treason." Sir Gaheris bellows out over the hush of the crowd. "Your sentence is death."

The crowd holds its breath, all eyes turning to Arthur, the young king of Camelot, wondering whether he'll change his mind.

The king doesn't blink; he doesn't even seem to breathe.

"Do you have any last words, Lady Guinevere?" Gaheris asks.

Guinevere closes her eyes for a moment. When she opens them, there's no more fear on her face. Instead there's fire. Burning hot and ferocious. Anger and shame, grief for what's been taken from her.

"I hope you don't all think so ill of me that you won't take my last words of advice." Her voice sings as she addresses her subjects, in tune with the wind. Somehow she's smiling. "Over the long years, I've done my very best for you. We have loved each other, you and I, we have given our lives to each other, to build something immortal."

Murmurs run through the crowd. So far, they've been caught up in the terrible drama of the thing. Now some of them must be realising they're about to watch a *real* person burn. One who has given them so much. One they love.

"I ask not for your forgiveness and I come here to pay for my crimes. I must, as I'm not sorry, I committed them. I'm not sorry I've devoted my life to the greatest king I have ever known." Guinevere turns her head to Arthur. I'm not sure what's coming, but it's something big.

It's much harder to look at the king's face than hers. His creases with anguish, lips wobbling.

"My advice to you, my loyal subjects," Guinevere's high,

BETRAYED

ferocious voice rings out over the crowd, "is to flee. *Run* from Camelot, as far as you can! For you aren't about to be ruled by a great king, *regardless* of who sits on the throne. I'm glad to die, because it would break my heart to see the depths to which you fall." Guinevere gives the king one last look, full of raw frustration and rage. The only time I've ever seen her look anything but magnificent. The crowd gasps, some people call out in anger. Arthur flinches as if he's been smacked, the misery in him almost tangible.

To speak so boldly against the king is treason, but what has she left to lose?

Even as the thought formulates, I know that isn't why she speaks. She's not angry at Arthur for putting her to death, but angry because he's changed. She's been angry for months, years. That was evident in her furious glare and Morgana's pleas. My lessons with Willow taught me that Guinevere was revered by her people and ruled with a fair hand. They loved her. And they trust her. What do they care for the word of a man that's been gone for years? When their queen has given them everlasting peace.

Guinevere lays her head back against the wooden stake and closes her eyes.

The jeering crowd begin to jostle. Arthur's still sitting with his mouth slack, Merlin motionless beside him. From my vantage point, I can see a black cloak shoving through the crowd towards the podium, encouraging the pushing as he goes.

The first shout of *mercy* is barely audible.

"Your Highness?" Geharis looks Arthur, obviously confused.

"Mercy!" another woman shouts, louder this time.

The word rumbles through the crowd, picking up speed and weight as it travels.

The black cloak is almost in position. I hold my breath, adrenaline coursing through me.

When Arthur doesn't respond, Sir Gaheris takes action. He grabs the flaming torch out of the hands of the knight next to him —a stocky blonde man, so much like Owen Lamorak, I do a double take —and throws it on the kindling at Guinevere's feet. It catches almost instantly, and the crowd howls with rage.

Then, a lot of things happen at once, so fast I almost miss them.

Black Cloak jumps onto the platform and throws himself at Gaheris, knocking him over. The blonde torchless knight, who *must* be a Lamorak, takes a dagger from his belt. I'm sure he's about to help Gaheris, instead, he goes towards the flames and begins slashing at the ropes around Guinevere.

Arthur falls back in his seat, and for the first time since I've been here, a smile spreads over his face.

Seconds later, a horse is barging through the crowd, which flies apart to give it easier passage. It's here to save their beloved queen after all, now they've remembered she's beloved. One man even holds the beast steady at the steps.

The black cloaked stranger is still fighting Gaheris, although he's not attacking, just deflecting the shots of the knight.

"Lancelot! Lancelot, hurry!" Guinevere screams from the back of the black stallion.

The man missteps, distracted by her voice, and Sir Gaheris lunges forwards, seeing his opportunity.

He doesn't, however, see Lancelot's dagger flashing in the grey light, rubies on the handle glittering. In one swift movement, the knife slides into Gaheris' stomach, and the hood of the cloak falls. Lancelot's handsome, I can see that from here. He's got a long, straight nose, an angular jaw, and blonde curls that fall into his eyes.

BETRAYED

Lancelot stares into Gaheris' face while he dies.

As the knight falls, Lancelot bolts, his mouth painted with a grim sneer. He vaults onto the back of the stallion, wrapping his arms around Guinevere and squeezing with his thighs. Then they're clattering across the cobbles and through the streets to freedom. The crowd cheers after them. I get one last glimpse of Arthur before the dream disintegrates under my feet. He looks as I imagine a king would look when he's lost everything he's ever loved, utterly shell shocked. Then the whole scene is gone as I'm dragged back into sleep.

21

I wake to the earthy smell of boiling roots mixed with chamomile, honey, and lemon. My muscles protest as I push myself into a sitting position, but at least I can move. Morgana pokes her head through the crimson drapes, a smile spreading over her face. She's barely aged at all since the day of Guinevere's attempted execution. There's only a whisper of crow's feet around her eyes, insisting that she's thirty rather than two thousand years old.

"Sleeping beauty's finally awake." She muses. "How did you enjoy your rest?"

"Merlin could see me." I say.

"Straight down to business, aren't you?" She's still grinning. There's a mist in her eyes, as if she finds me highly amusing. "Yes, he would've been able to, something to do with a blood bond. We'll get to all that in a minute anyway, Sweetheart. First, you need to get up and have a bit of a walkabout. It'll help with the healing."

BETRAYED

She comes to my side and offers me her hands, which I take. Under my fingers runs the tickle of her magic, something I've never felt before. It hums like a tiny electric current. She must be extraordinarily powerful.

"How long have I been out? Where's Aila?"

"So precious about her! I was the same with Suvi at first. Aila's out hunting. She'll be back soon. And it's been three days since we last spoke. He really did a number on you, that boy." Her face darkens.

I'm already unsteady on my feet, but thinking of Owen makes my legs crumple beneath me. I've dreamt of him in flashes. The horrible livid lines of his face, of falling back into the snow, a sharp burning pain in my side –

"What did he say then, Merlin?"

I struggle for a minute to focus on Morgana's voice. When I look into her eyes, I find concern there. She's trying to distract me and also supporting nearly all of my weight. I stand up properly, my legs aching with the effort. There's soreness in my side and across my cheek, it's tender to the touch.

"You'll have a little scar I'm afraid," Morgana says as she leads me through into the main body of the cave.

The space is covered in cushions, rugs, and throws of red, maroon, and inky indigo. They're fringed with threads of gold, some of them have pictures stitched into them. Along the side of one wall is a miss match of furniture. Tables seem to poke from the rock, with chairs, stools, and pouffes strewn around them in abandon. And on every flat surface available, candles are burning, casting wavey orange light over the cave. I'm in love.

"I *know* about electricity, but I've always preferred this." She settles me onto a pile of purple cushions and immediately pulls a soft woollen shawl around my shoulders. It smells of her: dry lavender, rich chocolate and a hint of citrus.

210

"It's lovely."

"And Merlin, Darling?"

"He told me he'd tried to talk Arthur out of it, but Arthur wouldn't be moved."

"Stubborn as an old goat was Arthur, and Mordred had got to him by then. Serpent's tongue flickering in his ear."

"You said you ought to have drowned him like a sick kitten."

"Did I?" Her eyes widen, then she grins, looking quite pleased with herself. "It sounds like something I'd say. And what did you think of Arthur?"

"I was a little star–struck, I'll be honest."

"And Guinevere?"

"She was magnificent."

"Hmm." The witch pauses and leans in a little closer, examining me. "She was, wasn't she? I thought you'd have preferred Arthur. Merlin always did."

"Arthur was his whole life."

"Is that what he told you?" She raises an eyebrow and leans back in her seat. "Hungry, Darling? We're having soup."

"A little." I say, and now I'm thinking about it, I'm absolutely ravenous. "From what I've read–"

"A reader, are you?"

"What's that supposed to mean?"

"Well, you can't trust those old books, can you? I've seen them, you know. Hundreds of tales about what a wonderful pair they made! Always looking out for each other, saving kingdoms, grand quests. Just think of who wrote the damn things! They're not going to make *themselves* look bad, are they? Not that they bothered preserving my image. God forbid! They made Guinevere a whore, me a spiteful old hag!" she scowls.

"They aren't true?"

BETRAYED

"Why? Do I look like a hag to you?" Morgana's eyes flash dangerously. I'd laugh if she didn't have such a venomous edge on her words.

"I didn't mean—"

"I'm joking, Sweetheart. I know I don't look a day over thirty." Now she flashes a wide grin at me. It contains a few too many teeth. Then she sighs. "Sorry. I haven't had company in millennia. It's hard to know what to say."

I hadn't even considered that Morgana might find this interaction as intimidating as I do. After all that time alone, it'd be hard to deal with someone else.

"Did you really leave after that day?" I change the subject.

Her smile fades, replaced by a much more sobering grimace. "I left immediately. I didn't even know Lancelot had saved Guin until a few weeks later! I went straight up to my room, packed my things and fled."

"Where did you go?"

"Here initially. I created this place when I was a little girl, somewhere to escape to —only for small amounts of time back then. I was grieving for Guin and for Arthur, for all I'd lost. When I came back into the world and realised she lived, I went to her."

"She was your best friend?"

"I loved her like a sister. She was a damn sight better than those other two wretches I got stuck with. That day, when Arthur decided, I mean *truly* decided he meant to go through with killing her." Her eyes glaze over with the memory. "He'd put on that big show in the hall, but Merlin and I thought we could talk him out of it. He never budged."

"Even though he didn't want to?"

"Well, you saw he meant it. You were there!" Her voice rises, then she catches herself. "He'd lost himself by then, all his ideas about ruling Camelot with a fair and loving hand,

212

marred by those idiots he called friends."

"The knights."

I'm sure she growls. "They always wanted something from him! Money, land, title, to go on one quest or another! Arthur would've been happy enough to live amongst the peasant folk, as would Guinevere and I, even Merlin. But not those awful knights."

The hate in her eyes makes me tremble. "When did you go back?"

"I *never* went back. I was *so* angry. Arthur sent word asking for me, but I couldn't face him! Not after I'd—"

"You'd what?"

"Doesn't matter." She says briskly. Then she drops her eyes, tears forming in them. "I saw him only once more after that."

"When?"

"I went to him while he was dying at Camlann. I couldn't let him go alone. Now I could've saved him, but back then my powers weren't fully developed."

"I'm sorry."

"He wasn't." She huffs. "'*I've been hoping this day would come,*' he said. And he had been hoping, after everything I predicted came to pass. He was tired of fighting a losing battle." She sighs. "I loved him very much."

"Because he was your brother?"

"Because he was my *king*. Monarchs might not be the same now, but I was devoted to him! I wanted everything he promised, and I gave myself entirely to the cause."

"Until you didn't recognise what you were fighting for anymore." I muse mostly to myself, but Morgana snaps her head up, eyes finding mine.

"Yes." She proceeds cautiously. "All of us felt it, even Merlin."

BETRAYED

"Was he a good wizard? A good person?" I ask, almost desperately. All accounts say he is, if sometimes, a little arrogant, but Morgana actually *knew* him.

"He was an exceptional wizard, and in Arthur's case, an excellent advisor." She pauses for a moment, thinking hard. "I didn't care for him until a bit later, though. I'd always resented him, and Morgwese, my older sister—"

"I'm very familiar, unfortunately."

"I suspected she was the reason you're here." Morgana cocks an eyebrow. "But yes, she *hated* him, and Arthur, and everyone else who ever paid any notice to them. She couldn't forgive him, you see."

"For his part in your father's murder?"

"Yes. I warmed up to him when he started teaching us magic, but not her."

"What changed?"

"Arthur." She closes her eyes, smiling. "My problem with Merlin, my resentment, had been mostly based on one thing. I liked Merlin. He was good to me and my sisters. He told us stories, kept us out of trouble, taught us everything he could about witchcraft. I couldn't understand how a man like that had allowed Uther to act as he did. To let him commit a murder, *aid* in it. Merlin didn't seem like that kind of man to me, although he never denied he'd done it."

"Uther promised not to hurt Garlois."

"So they say." Morgana cocks another sceptical eyebrow. "When Uther died, Merlin brought Arthur to court, to pull the sword from the stone, and when I saw him for the first time, I understood everything." Her eyes gloss over with fondness, almost awe. "It was a bit like love at first sight, if I'm quite honest, although I was never attracted to him like that. But I knew he was the answer to everything. I felt it in my heart and was immediately and utterly devoted to him. I understood why

Merlin had let Uther run riot in his younger years, because he'd wanted Arthur for himself, to mould into the perfect king."

"But that didn't last."

"I would have set *myself* on fire for Arthur and Camelot, but setting fire to Guinevere, I could never forgive. She was my queen, and I was to her what Merlin was to Arthur. I loved her, and Arthur was wrong." She says the words as if she's said them many times before, as if that's the case closed. "Now we've come full circle. I think it's time you ate some soup and got back into bed."

"Don't you want to know why I'm here?"

"I already know why you're here, Darling."

"How can you–?"

She holds up a bony finger. "I'll have a guess, shall I? My sister's done something horrible, tried to take over something, caused some type of havoc? And whatever it is, you need *my* help to undo it?"

"That's mostly right." I concede. While she's been talking, she's led me back to bed, tucked me in and put a bowl of soup into my hands.

"Well, I didn't think you'd climbed the Alps for a social call." She smiles. "You can tell me the details in the morning. You still need to rest."

"I should send word to the others, at least. They'll be worried."

Morgana laughs. "How do you expect to do that? They won't be able to hear you from here, Darling. No. I'm afraid you're stuck with me." Underneath her smile is an expression I don't much care for, and I see the witch she truly is, powerful and feral. "Good night, Sweetheart." She kisses my forehead. "In the morning, we talk."

22

I dream again that night of Camelot and Arthur. The king is a shadow of himself, a ghost walking the unlit halls. His face swirls with Lux's, and Morgana's with Lore's. They are all very, very distantly related, after all. I also dream of Asher, her smiling face and wicked laugh. I wake up to Aila licking the tears from my cheeks and I bury my face in her fur and sob. What will I tell the others? How am I going to explain her death to them? My stupid, ridiculous idea to come here has cost my friend her life. It doesn't even really matter that we found Morgana. What if she refuses to help us? Then it will all be for nothing.

And Asher's still out there, lost in the snow. I bolt out of bed and storm into the living room to find Morgana perched on her purple cushions, reading a book.

"Good morning, Darling. Or is it evening? I can never–"

"Where is Owen Lamorak?"

"Well, how should I know?" She pats the space beside her

and flicks her wrist towards the teapot, commanding it to pour me a cup. "I had my hands full with you two. Once I'd knocked him into that snowdrift, I pulled you inside and closed the rock face."

"He could still be alive. He could be on his way back to the Templar." My heart is racing almost as fast as my thoughts. I've been asleep for days. He could be there by now, if he survived. Lux and Lore might be in danger. "He might hurt the twins."

Morgana's perfectly formed nonchalant expression flickers for a moment. So she knows about them and she must feel something for them for their mention to have cracked her armour. "Then you better tell me what you came here for, and quickly."

"I came for help." I say. Then, as concisely as I can, I tell her everything. I start right from the beginning, from the first time I opened a faery circle and the Shadows that followed, about Mum and Dad, and how Shelby/Morgwese took me under her wing. I tell her about Ren coming to find me and convincing me of my blood, of Elaine's terrible attack on Lore, and my visit with Merlin. My voice is growing hoarse by the time I get to Morgwese's banishment, even with regular tea breaks. Finally, I tell her about Lore's continued amnesia, Lux's night terrors and Oliver's death. I even tell her about Ren's hunt for *Abrasax*. I leave nothing out and I make nothing up. I don't even exaggerate. Morgana will smell a lie, even a white one. And I can't stop myself from unburdening the load, from letting go of the tremendous weight of it.

"I need you to help Lore." I say. "And I didn't come empty–handed. I brought letters–"

"I've seen them. Oh yes, I know they were in your pocket, but they had my name on."

She's right, they did. I suppose I can't be angry at her for

BETRAYED

taking them. They do belong to her after all.

Morgana is quiet for a long time, slowly processing the tale I've just told her. Then she says something I could have never expected. "Are they *heroes?* The children?"

"What?"

"Well, they either are, or they aren't."

"I don't know what you mean?"

"It isn't difficult, Darling. Or maybe it's you who fancies yourself *as their* immortal saviour?" She rolls her eyes. "I've known a lot of them. Heroes. Always sticking their noses into business that doesn't concern them. I was married to one for a short while. I gave *birth* to one and now there's nothing left of them. Only legends."

"I want to help Lore."

She smirks. "They're a funny breed. They're willing to live for you, die for you, wage wars for you, burn and build kingdoms. They're willing to go on quests for godly objects, slay beings that don't exist. They're willing to die for your affections should you see fit. But have you ever met a hero who lived a peaceful life? Who thrived? Who enjoyed the comforts of a long and healthy life? They can't leave well enough alone."

"What's your point? Arthur was—"

She scoffs and shakes her head. "There's nothing you can tell me about Arthur Pendragon that I don't already know. I grew up with him, helped raise him. And you're *proving* my point. I saw him make countless rash and wrong decisions in the name of duty. I saw him turn Camelot to ashes under the guise of a hero. He would have had his own wife burned at the stake, not out of jealousy, but for the god damn drama of it. Jealousy I could have understood, *rage.* He had his opportunity to rid the world of my sister's devil spawn and instead, he lost everything we ever loved."

"So he wasn't a hero?"

"No. He was the perfect hero. All bark and no bite. All for a quest, but to actually do the hard work of ruling, of thinking of someone other than himself, of sacrificing glory for peace?"

"If Arthur hadn't punished Guinevere, he would have lost face... the knights..."

"Oh yes, the knights. See, you're exactly the same. Gave in to their every whim he did. Never mind whether his people were starving! Never mind if the walls needed building and land needed tending and the crops needed growing! And when the time came, where were they? Where were they at Camlann? Those knights he fought so hard to keep. Half of them were at that traitorous usurper's back. He sentenced Guinevere to death out of pride! He was willing to burn everything we built to the ground. Arthur failed to see the bigger picture, as heroes always do. He failed to see that allowing Mordred to manipulate his actions would kill everything. He cared so much for his duty that he allowed it to destroy our kingdom. Is that what you're here to save? For history to repeat itself? Lore might be better off out of it. The Templar is a disease, and I will not stand by and let it reign. They have betrayed me too many times to count. Ruined my good name!" She snaps her mouth shut, her voice cracking, nostrils flaring as she takes a deep breath. "You want to save Lore because you love Lore. So why damn her and her brother to an existence of never ending turmoil? History is there to be learned from. Why should I help you recreate a path that doomed the greatest men and women I ever knew?"

I bring my hand up to my face, rubbing it across my cheek. The pads of my fingers find a rough scab running down the right side of my face. I knew about the cut, but I'm yet to see it.

Everything she's saying is true. I agree with her. I don't want Lux and Lore to go to Avalon, to fulfil their birth right,

BETRAYED

and be miserable. I want them safe and alive.

"I didn't come on behalf of the Templar," I say. "In fact, they fought me most of the way. They always have. But I don't serve them. I serve Lux and Lore. I want them to grow up to make choices without shame, to be true, to know that they're loved and that they have somebody who will go to the ends of the earth for them. I want them to be strong and answer to nobody but themselves. I love them. Not because it's my duty, but despite it. I don't care if they rule Camelot, or Avalon, or whatever it is they're supposed to do. I want them happy, I want them safe, and I want them whole. But I can't decide for them." Tears drip down my cheeks. "And I can't help Lore alone.

"I know you hate the Templar, they deserve it, they make life difficult at every opportunity." I can't stop the small smile spreading on my face. They *are* idiots, but they're *my* idiots. Years of comfort have made them spoiled, but the Templar could be great again. "I know you want them gone, but that isn't right either. Lux and Lore deserve to choose. When the time comes and they take the throne, they will be expecting a full audit of the knights and their use. You can make your case for abolishment, for reparations, whatever you want! But it's *their* choice."

The witch studies me, scowling, then she nods. "You're exactly like your grandfather. Could get anyone in the world to do anything he pleased."

"Does that mean you'll help me?"

"No." Morgana says, her mouth turned down in a frown. "But I will consider it. I will consider coming to fight at your side again, and whether it's in the children's best interests. But I'll have no part in furthering the knight's agenda, or aiding *them.*"

"We don't have time to waste—"

220

"*You* don't have time to waste." Morgana glares at me with her swirling whiskey eyes. "I'm not committed to your cause yet, Darling."

"Can you at least help me get back to them? Someone needs to warn them about Owen..."

"Hmm," Morgana winces slightly and leans forward to take my hand. "Well, about that, Sweetheart. There's something I need to tell you. And promise me you won't be mad."

My heart leaps into my throat.

"You've been here with me for a good long while now, Darling. Ten days. Time doesn't run in here, like it does out there. It's slow. I slowed it down. So out there, where you came from, weeks could have gone by. Months. There's no way to know exactly. I haven't been out in years."

No. No, no, no, no, no. He could have made it back weeks ago! And what will he have told them about us, the others? What will he have told them about Asher? What if we're already too late? I push myself up from the sofa. "Send me back. You have to. Right now."

"I don't *have* to—"

"Morgana, please." I find a bundle of clothes at the end of the bed. A white shirt and soft deerskin leggings, which I throw myself into. "You've got enough magic. I've seen it. Please. If you won't help me, if you won't help Lore, at least let me try!"

Her face disappears for a moment as I rag the shirt over my head. When I meet her eyes again, they're glassy. "All right. I'll open you a doorway, but that's *all* I'm agreeing to. Nothing more." She gets to her feet, ushering me into the centre of the room. I'm barefoot, my hair unbound, trailing down my back. My own magic fizzes as my anxiety heightens. Ready to be unleashed at the first sign of trouble.

BETRAYED

"Aila, to me." I send to her. The big cat saunters to her feet and gives Morgana a long, accusatory stare before coming to my side.

"Ready, Darling?"

"Morgana," I say. "There will always be a place for you with us. Please don't make Lore suffer because of age old quarrels that she had no part in. Even if it's all you do, please, *please,* bring back her memories."

The witch's mouth wobbles, tears forming in her eyes. Then she carves a rectangle in the air with her finger and I feel the air change behind me. A door opened.

"I told you I'd consider it." She says. Then we're falling backwards in the dark. We're going home.

I drop through the hole Morgana made for me and land on my back in the hall of the Templar. I catch myself with invisible hands before I take the full impact of the drop, but the air still whooshes from my lungs. Aila lands on her paws with a thud. At least Morgana kept her promise. I'm home. I don't know what time it is or what day, but at least I'm here.

I push myself into a sitting position and then get up. I need to find Owen right now. I've landed in the Templar foyer. My best bet for finding someone, *anyone*, will be Joth's office. I start down the corridor—

"Merle?" I whip my head around to find Ren standing at the other end of the hall. Something loosens in my chest at the sight of him. He's okay, back from Scotland, and if *he* is here, the twins will be safe. My breath catches in my throat. I never thought I'd see him again.

Ren shakes his head, raising his hand to his eyes, rubbing them. He looks worn out, his shoulders are slumped, and he's much thinner than the last time I saw him. He turns away, muttering to himself under his breath.

222

"Ren! Ren, wait...!

He stops in his tracks, his body going rigid. He turns back to look at me, confusion flickering across his face, the flame of a candle. His eyebrows are drawn close together, mouth hanging in a wide 'O'.

Then he's moving towards me so fast that he's almost a blur. He brings his palm to my cheek, brushing away my tears with his thumb as he pulls me close to him. When his fingers reach my skin he gasps, "Mer... I thought... he said... are you *real?*" His eyes scan my face, taking in my new scar, all of me. I run my hands up his arms, looping them around his neck, nodding as I bring his mouth to mine. I've been waiting for this for what seems like an eternity. Ren crushes me to him, tangling his fingers in my hair, tipping my head back to deepen our kiss. For a moment, the universe stops as I drink him in. Then Ren's hands press on my shoulders, pushing me back. He looks down at me, breathing hard, his eyes burning like hot coals, his lips are pink and the rest of his face flushed.

"I can't believe it's really you..."

"I don't know what you mean,"

"You've been gone for so long." his eyes go dark. "Owen said you were... dead..."

"Dead?" I choke, reaching up to brush his cheek again. No wonder he's so pale, why his hands are shaking. Owen had tried, though, tried to kill me, sliding Carnwennan through my shield and up into my heart.

"He said that there'd been an avalanche, and he got buried in the snow. When he finally dug his way out, you were gone. Asher tried to convince him it was an accident, but he didn't believe her."

He's talking so fast he's halfway through his sentence before I really register what he's said.

"Asher?" My breath catches in my throat. I saw her

BETRAYED

disappear under the snow, I felt her light go out. The room starts to spin. "No, *Asher* is dead. Owen let go of her hand. Morgana *saved* me."

Ren jolts like he's been shocked by a loose wire. "no... that's where I was going. Asher's here. Alive. Being tried by the knights for *your* murder. She woke up two weeks ago and couldn't remember anything—"

"Take me to her," I beg, leaning into him, unable to control my shaking limbs. I have to see her. I have to see her with my own eyes. "Ren. Take me to her, please."

He grips my hand, lacing his icy fingers with mine, and pulls me down the hall.

23

REN

Merle is barely holding herself up as I haul her along, Aila racing beside us. Mer's gripping my fingers so hard they might break, but it does nothing to stop us trembling. I can't believe it. She can't be alive. She can't be. Owen said. Owen said she wasn't, and Asher couldn't remember anything. I feel like I'm underwater, my whole body on autopilot.

Are you real?

All this time, I've believed her dead. Gone. It's been months since Asher fell through the ceiling, her broken body clattering onto the stone. Bedivere didn't think she was going to make it. She's been in a coma, only coming around a couple of weeks ago. Despite mine and Willow's desperate questioning, she's not been able to remember anything.

"I remember getting out of the tent. I remember the avalanche. Owen let me go. I didn't hurt Merle. I don't know where she was."

BETRAYED

We heard something had gone wrong almost straight away, that Rory had broken her arm and most of them were on their way back. Then there was no news for days and days. On the second night, the whole Templar had shaken when Asher appeared. There was nothing else, no *one* else. We didn't know how she got there, what had happened to Merle and Owen. It was almost two days after that when we heard any real news. Eddie and Sir Tristen had gone up to find them. Owen was the only one who'd come back down.

"*She fell. Owen said she fell.*" Sir Tristen told me over the crackling phone wire. He was crying. I could hear it in his voice.

Joth ordered them back here immediately, but the explanation we got upon their return was wrong. *Lies.* All of it.

"*Asher was working with Morgwese from the start, plotting against us. She volunteered so she could go up there and kill Morgana. Merle got in the way. Now they're all dead.*" That's what Tristen and Eddie had whispered to Joth, bloodless faces and swollen eyes.

Willow had got up and left Joth's office without a word. Joth didn't take them seriously, anyway. Asher hurt Merle? *Never.* Never ever. So we knew there was someone else. *Owen.* But they've been protecting him. Lawrence and Tristen. Insisting he's innocent.

I stop when we reach the doors that lead into the Knights Hall. A grim smile flits across Mer's lips. She's still shaking, a thin pink line etched into her cheek that wasn't there before, so close to her eye she's lucky she's still got it.

There's shouting from the other side of the door, specifically *Joth* shouting. Fury boils through my blood. All this time, someone has lied, covered their tracks to frame Asher. And now she's about to be punished for an act of high treason that someone else committed.

Mer is nearly green, swallowing great gasps of air. I put my hands on her shoulders to steady her. And she's there, she's real. Really, truly alive.

"*It's going to be chaos when I open the doors.*" I send.

"*I found her.*" She sends back.

I run my hands over her skin, tracing her collarbones with my fingers, my palms resting on her cheeks. I bring my forehead to hers and she straightens her shoulders under my touch. "*Then let's go in there and destroy them.*"

There's only a moment before the fallout as the huge oak doors swing wide. Joth is standing at one end of the hall, his face red, a vein pulsing in his temple. Lamorak is also on his feet. They don't matter, not right now.

As Merle pushes past me, scanning their faces, searching for the one she wants, the *only* one that will do, the cries of disbelief start. Amalie practically faints behind Sir Percival's chair. Eddie Pelleas in the seat next to them puts his head in his hands and starts to cry. From the Mountain Party, he's been the one to suffer most. He blamed himself for what happened, guilt and grief hounding him.

Merle's knees tremble when she finds Asher, her mouth twisting in a grimace. Then she's storming forward, tears streaming from her eyes as she jumps onto the table, Aila snarling at anyone who might attempt to get in her way.

I'm aware of the silence now descending, falling upon us like rain. In three strides, she's on her knees in front of Asher, throwing her arms around her neck.

"Merle?" Asher sobs, grabbing at Merle's shirt so hard she must rip through it. "I *knew* it. I *knew* you weren't dead!"

I steal a look at Joth, who is slack jawed, tears of his own dribbling down his cheeks. Even though we knew Asher wasn't responsible for Merle's death, we still thought she was gone.

BETRAYED

We've *mourned* her. I close my eyes, swaying on my feet. This can't be real, it can't be happening. This whole thing has been a nightmare, an endless, horrific dream.

There's another thud and I open my eyes to find Merle rising to her feet and spinning on her heel. Whatever the truth is about Owen, she knows it.

My eyes feel too big in their sockets, teeth vibrating in my skull.

When her gaze lands on Lamorak senior, she snarls. Lawrence is standing like a statue, his own face almost as pale as hers. At least he's not running, at least for everything that he is, he's not a coward.

Sir Lamorak squares his shoulders and looks right into Merle's eyes as she turns on him. For just a moment, they flick to Aila, the lethal predator snarling at her mistress' heel. Sparks flutter to life around Merle's fingertips.

"Where is Owen?" She says.

"He would never–"

"The more quickly you give him up, the less likely I am to kill him." Mer's voice is like steel. She means every word she says. And she doesn't look like a novice now. She's terrifying, beautiful and cruel. " I'm not afraid to go inside your head and find out where he is, but I make no promises for what will be left of you afterwards."

"I won't," Lawrence shakes his head.

Merle raises her hand. She's not bluffing. I know her well enough to know that. Lawrence stares her down, holding his breath. When another second goes by, so quiet I can hear my own heartbeat, she rolls her shoulders and a swirl of light begins to form in her palm.

"Stop!" Sir Tristen's shout echoes around the hall. "It's not the boy you want."

Merle's whole body slackens as if she's taken a physical

228

blow; her face creasing in anguish . That expression quickly fades as she turns to Sir Tristen, a mask of bone chilling emptiness washing away her pain. The air in the room rushes towards her, gathering her strength for whatever it is she's going to do. Sparks erupt from her shaking fingers. She's going to turn him to dust. She could do it. With one flick of her wrist, he'd be ashes in the wind.

Merle stops, squeezing her hands into fists. They stare at each other for a long, silent minute.

"You better have a good reason for betraying us, Greg," she finally says. I feel the arrow in her heart, the deep and sickening wound of his betrayal. "And it better be much more convincing than the bullshit Lamorak was about to spill." With a wave of her hand, she forces Lawrence back into his seat, pinning him there.

"Yes." Sir Tristen jut's his chin forward. I can only admire the surety in his voice. "I do. It is."

There's a second where the world is so quiet I can hear my own heartbeat. Then the entire hall erupts into madness.

All the knights, aside from Lydia and Lawrence, jump to their feet. They're shouting over each other, at each other, at anyone who will listen. I'm trembling all over, barely in control of myself. The noise blurs into one long, painful thrum.

"Quiet!" a voice screams through the wall of sound. Usually it's Joth, but when I turn my head, I see Willow scrambling over the table. She's struggling to get up. Her face is grey, eyes wide and bulging in their sockets. "Quiet!"

She's trying to get to Merle, so desperate to reach her.

Merle snaps her fingers as she did all that time ago, robbing the words from the throats of the knights. The room goes immediately silent, so quiet I can hear the wind whipping over the slate roof outside. The mouths of the knight's move noiselessly, opening and closing like fish.

BETRAYED

Willow throws her arms around Mer, sobbing into her shoulder. I take a deep breath and look away, trying to compose myself as Willow's hollow sobs rack through her chest. I can't swallow the lump in my throat, the blood rushing in my ears.

Merle squeezes her tightly. The lines of her cheeks are pinched, lips pursed together in a snarl. Her glittering hazel eyes are full of anger, hatred. Something changed. I understand the torrent of emotion she's feeling. How furious she is, anger so white hot her blood is boiling. Grieving for what this supposed holy order has come to, burning through her resolve like acid through bone. I understand because I feel it too.

Now Merle looks to Joth, whose eyes compel her to free his lips. He breathes a sigh of what I can only assume is relief as she obliges. The rest of the room copies him as she releases them, too.

"You are the guardian of this Templar. What's the precedent here? What do we do now?"

Joth shakes his head slowly. I can feel the rage baking off him and the shame. His mouth is a hard, grey smear across his chin. There's a deep flush on his cheeks, and he can't even bring himself to look at Sir Tristen. "I have failed you, or at least, those of you who remain true. Our law won't serve us here."

"Then turn this ridiculous mockery over to Merle." I say, to hell with them, to hell with protocol. "In this, let her decide what to do with them."

Merle turns her gaze back to Joth, who nods again. Mer pinches the bridge of her nose, thinking, sifting through her choices, each one worse than the last. Selfishly, I'm glad I'm not her. I wouldn't be able to bear the responsibility of it, the heartache. After a moment, her eyes snap open.

"Find Owen Lamorak." Her voice carries through the room. "Then take him and Sir Tristen to the cells."

"Where have you been?" Lydia asks. Her voice is quiet, and she has dark bags under her eyes. "We thought you were dead."

"I must hold council." Merle's says, ignoring the question. She looks a hundred years old standing there, but she must have a plan, a risky one, if she wants to discuss it first. "Go back to your rooms and wait. I'll call you when it's time." Then her roving eyes find mine.

"*Find Owen. He can't get away.*"

I give her a grim nod and turn on my heel. He can't be far, even if he heard her command, even if he's tried to run. My heart thunders in my chest as I race down the corridor, door after door whizzing by. I needn't have worried. Owen is exactly where I left him, oblivious. His face sours in an instant, and he must know something is wrong, that his lies are undone. He doesn't even try to bolt. Instead, he drops his head into his hands and starts to cry.

24

ila and I wait for the knights to file out before jumping off the table and racing to Joth's office. She chases some of them out, snapping at their heels. I'm still reeling from Tristen's confession.

"Stop! It's not the boy you want."

Those words echo in my ears, so loud they make me want to throw up. How could he? How could he do that to me, to us? He's my friend.

I feel, all over again, like a fool. Shame burns in my throat so hot and bright I can't breathe.

"Ask yourself why a man of such good standing might suddenly turn traitor?" It's Dad's voice, quiet and calm. *"What could they have on him?"*

It doesn't matter. I can't forgive him. I won't.

Before dealing with Greg and Owen, there's a more important matter at hand, my friends waiting for me.

As soon as I'm safely inside Joth's office, the old man

wraps his arms around me, then Willow is sobbing into the crook of my neck. I comfort her as much as I can, but really, I'm not up to the job. After a few moments, Joth pulls away, taking Willow with him.

Asher is slumped in the chair behind the desk. She's staring forwards, eyes glazed over. She's far away somewhere, thinking dark thoughts. Her lips are twisted in a grimace.

"I knew you weren't dead. I *knew* it." She says again.

"I thought *you* were. How did you survive?" I cringe as I remember the horrible, wet crunching of her bones hitting the ground. "How can you be here? I saw you fall."

"I don't know. I only woke up two weeks ago. I've been in a coma." She pulls her lips up into a tight, mocking smile.

"She fell through the ceiling." Joth says quietly. "One moment, nothing. The next Asher was in the hall with numerous broken bones, all but *dead.* We didn't know anything until Greg called about Rory's arm. Nothing more until Owen came down the mountain."

"How long have I been gone?" My voice wobbles. For me, it was only ten days ago that Asher fell, since Owen tried to kill me.

"Six months." Ren's voice is soft from the doorway. I turn to him, and he gives me a small wan smile.

My knees buckle, but before I can fall, Ren's arms are around my waist, holding me upright.

Six months?

Now I understand their faces, why Ren looked like he'd seen a ghost. Why they truly believed I was dead.

"I was only with the witch for ten days." I whisper under my breath. "Twelve at the most."

Ren's grip on my waist tightens. "No Merle. It's September."

"It can't be."

BETRAYED

He takes my hand and leads me to the window. Outside, the leaves of the trees are gold, bronze and red. The flowers are wilted. The sky is grey like iron.

"Lydia's child will be six months old soon. Oliver Avery Geraint." Joth whispers.

I gasp and almost choke on the breath. Everything slows down, grey stars falling across my vision. It can't be so. We were already running out of time! What about Lux and Lore? Where are they? I lick my tongue around my lips to wet them. They're dry and hard, like sandpaper. I know they're all waiting for me to speak. I don't know what to say. What I need is guidance, and it turns out, a certain witch owes me another huge favour.

"I'm going to buy us some time, get us some help." I croak. "So I can tell you everything, so you can tell me what's gone on and decide what to tell the knights. How to fix this."

"Did you find her?" Joth asks.

"I did."

Willow starts to cry again, with what I assume is relief.

"Did she agree to help?"

"I'm going to reach across time and space and drag her here by her hair, if that's what's required." I say.

"Wait." Joth says going to the shelf behind his desk, reaching behind a stack of books. When his hand re—emerges, he's holding a pointed stick carved with ornate swirls, running with orange and red and gold. It's beautiful. It sings. Abrasax. "Maybe this will help?"

I let out a shaky breath and hold out my hand. As soon as my fingers close around the wand, it jitters with power, its magic recognising my own, coursing into my veins at the close contact. The gem in its base starts to glow.

"I'm going to summon the witch. Brace yourselves."

As the others crowd towards the back of the room, I go

to the far wall, eyeing up a particular chunk of wallpaper I've always hated. I don't really know what I'm doing, but I'm livid enough to not let that stop me. And hopefully, Aila and the wand will pick up the slack if I wane.

I close my eyes, trying to focus the swirling storm of rage and magic in my heart. I can do this.

Standing on my toes, I carve a straight line from as high as I can reach, all the way down to the floor. At first the wallpaper holds fast, then it comes away in little flakes, peeling as my magic opens a door between realms. I drag Abrasax back up the other side and then join the lines at the top. Then I take a step back and place my hand in the centre of the rectangle. I picture the inside of Morgana's cave, the heavy red drapes made of velvet, the strong smell of incense and musty perfumes. I see her face, the soft lines of her mouth, and molten liquid fire in her eyes.

"*Aperiam in porta.*" I say.

It would be just our damn luck if it's been a thousand years on her side and she's become nothing more than bones. The thought startles a horrible, croaking laugh from me. That would be nothing less than catastrophic.

"Something funny, Darling?" The sweet rich tones of Morgana's voice meet my ear.

I let out a happy sound, something between a sob and a snort. I open my eyes and stare straight into Morgana's tawny gems. A smirk is playing around her mouth, and I know she's trying not to laugh. There's a collective holding of breath behind me, all of them awe struck apart from Asher who whispers, "*Holy shit.*"

"I didn't know if I'd be able to find you."

"I didn't know if I wanted to be found." She cocks an eyebrow, first assessing me, then the others.

"I need you." I say. I've already made my plea, already

BETRAYED

begged. Now it is time for my words to cut. To really hammer home what the cost is if she refuses. "If you truly loved Arthur like you claim, if you truly want to make amends for letting him die at Camlann, you'll come through this door and help me."

Morgana reels, flinching as if I've slapped her. I see the conflict in her eyes, how she wants to come over, even if it's only to end the age–long solitude she's had to bear. She doesn't trust us, though. That I'll keep my promise to her. Then she looks over my head. I watch her, her eyes scanning past Willow and Ren, pausing a moment on Asher's face. Then they set firmly on Joth. I'm sure her expression softens for a moment, then she scowls.

"If you lie to me again, I'll take the children and end you all." Her voice is calm and icy, a threat and a promise. It's not me she's speaking to, not really, but Joth will have to answer for his crimes another time.

"It's now or never." I say.

She drops her eyes back to me and then grins. It's a beautiful grin, full of wonder and adventure and promise. She turns her back for a moment and picks up a battered old leather sack. Then she fastens a travelling cloak around her neck as if she's going a great distance rather than a single step. Perhaps to her it feels a great distance. She tucks a crystal ball under her arm and throws one last look around the cavern she's called home for almost two hundred years. Then Morgana Le Fae steps through the door.

"I'll seal it up. No point going back until this is all over. Can't risk it." She waves her hand, and the brickwork moves back into place. Morgana doesn't even break a sweat when she uses magic. "Now, tell me what you need."

She goes a little pale as I explain everything that's happened since I got back only an hour ago. It feels like a hundred years. "We need some time to get our bearings, to plan a course."

"Well, that's easy peasy, Sweetheart. Put the Templar in stasis for a day. *Stop* time."

"Oh yes, wonderful." Asher drawls. "Why didn't I think of that?"

Morgana turns to the knight, "You would think, seeing as I *saved* your sorry carcass from certain death, you might find it within yourself to be polite."

"What?" All five of us snap.

Morgana lets out a long breath. "Let's just deal with this first, shall we? My magic is somewhat depleted, so you'll have to help. Give me your hand and where's that familiar of yours?"

"We've got this too." I say and hold out the wand for her inspection.

Morgana raises an eyebrow and turns her gaze to Joth. "Well, well, well, you are assembling *quite* the army aren't you?"

Joth's expression doesn't change, neither does he speak.

The witch turns back to me. "For now, Aila will do."

I whistle to the big cat, who pads to my side and I place one hand on her head and give the other to Morgana.

"Now, Darlings, I'm going to freeze time outside of this room. Anyone else inside this place will stop exactly where they are. No harm will come to them. We won't be able to hold the web for long. It takes too much power..."

"Twenty–four hours will do." Joth says.

Morgana rolls her eyes, then closes them. She says nothing as she casts the spell, but I feel the threads of her magic weaving with my own, pulling it into shape, throwing the blanket of her charm over the whole of the Templar. I sway on my feet, dizzy by the time she stops. I don't remember the last time I ate a full and proper meal, days and days ago.

BETRAYED

"That's that then. All done, for *twenty–four hours.*" Morgana drawls, wiggling her eyebrows at Joth. He blushes, the deep red staining his cheeks.

I let go of her hand and open my eyes and look around at my friends. They're all here, all safe, all alive. We're together again and Morgana is here. I might be six months later than expected, but it might still not be too late. I can't stop the tears as they form in my eyes and stream down my face. After everything that's happened, it's almost too good to be true. I step around Joth's desk and crumble into Asher's arms.

An hour later, we're back in the library. I've showered and eaten a huge slab of cake, Ren never leaving my side. Now I'm curled up in the crook of his arm on the sofa, Aila by our feet, soaking up the heat of the fire. Even though I'm bone tired, my freshly healed wounds murmuring with pain, there's no time for rest, not yet.

Asher and I begin, starting our story from our arrival at Chamonix. Asher fills in the bits I've missed, only stopping when we reach her fall. I tell them of Owen chasing me up the summit, and I gloss over as many horrible details as I can as Ren starts to shake beside me. There comes a point that I can't remember, so Morgana takes over, explaining how she pulled me from the snow and sealed the doors of the cave after Aila raced inside.

"I didn't check to see whether the boy was alive." She says. "I was hoping he wasn't."

What I find much more interesting is the story from the others.

First, Ren talks. He tells us about their search for Abrasax and how Lux found some old ring that seems to be important, although they haven't worked out why yet. My heart skips a beat when he describes Elaine in the chapel and how Rab

238

McGavin saved the day.

"For the last six months, we've been in a constant state of reaction." Joth says. "We've closed down most of the estates, redistributed staff and brought everyone to the main Templar houses. There have been a few sightings of faeries, one more attack in which luckily no one was hurt–" he adds as I tense in my seat.

"And what of Lore?" I say when everyone has finished talking. "How is she?"

Joth is quiet for a long time. Then he looks into my eyes and says, "She's different."

"Different how?"

Joth sighs and shakes his head. "You'll have to wait until we wake them up. It's not something I have words to explain."

I let my eyes wander to Morgana, who is chewing on her lip thoughtfully. Asher is almost asleep in the chair opposite. Even Willow isn't focussed. I close my eyes too. At least time is frozen for a little while, at least it can't get any worse.

"Time for bed," Joth says. "We can resume in the morning."

The others grumble in agreement, but I don't. I have an aching heart that won't rest until I've spoken to Greg. I never even suspected him and his betrayal twists like a knife in my gut.

"We knew you never would." Morgwese's voice cackles in my ear.

Anger washes over me, a rage so red and deep I tremble. I trusted him and he deceived me. But that isn't the thing that's causing this crashing tide. It's my frustration that I *still* like him. I want his reason to be enough so I can redeem him, so air tight I can trust my judgement again. I was so focussed on Owen, so *sure.*

Owen was involved. I remind myself. *You weren't entirely wrong.*

No. But I was wrong enough. And I have to know why.

25

"There's something I have to do before I sleep." I say, stretching as I get to my feet.

"You mean to see Greg?" Joth asks.

"I have to know."

He nods solemnly. I squeeze Ren's fingers one more time and then head out into the hall. Aila prowls beside me, a low growl rumbling in her throat. She didn't detect him either. Maybe she feels as stupid as I do. I rub the space between her ears.

"Not your fault. You're new to this. You're perfect." She winds her way between my feet, nuzzling my knees.

The walk down into the cold takes an age. With each step, his confession weighs heavier and heavier on my heart. I feel like I'm the one awaiting punishment instead of him.

"And how will you punish him?" Merlin's voice. *"He's made a mockery of you."*

Even though I'm angry at that, I know deep in my soul I

can't hurt him. I should make an example of him, show anyone else with mutiny on their minds, what will happen to them should they deceive me. It's what Morgana would do. What Arthur would do.

And where is Camelot now? I ask myself. *Ashes.*

By the time I'm at the door to the dungeon, I'm shaking with cold and nerves and rage. Owen is in the first cell, laying on his side in the cot. His frozen face is a mask of misery and confusion, as if he doesn't understand what he's done to deserve his place here. Two doors along is the traitor. He's sitting up, his face in a scowl, hands draped over his knees.

"Surgere." I whisper and wave my hand.

His breathing fills the chamber. He doesn't look up at me, but he knows I'm here. "I didn't know if you'd come."

I unlock the door and step inside, sitting cross—legged on the floor a few metres back from him. He isn't stupid enough to run. Not with Aila waiting to pounce should he make one wrong move.

"I wasn't sure I was going to." I have so many questions, a thousand things I want to know, but now I'm numb with the shock of it, exhausted at the thought of having to decide what to do next.

"It was while you were in the cave, almost a year ago now, won't it be?" Greg starts when the silence gets so thick and close, I think we'll suffocate. He's wearing a bitter smile, like he's truly disgusted with himself. "Well, it was then I made a deal. I went to check on Elaine while you were down in the catacombs. She told me who she was. She said Morgwese wanted someone on the inside, someone to feed her information if her plan to kill you failed."

I say nothing. So long his deception, so painful. The newly healed wound in my side aches.

"I said no at first. Whether or not you believe it, I'm a

BETRAYED

good knight. I was. And I *never* would have made a deal with one of those *foul creatures* that killed my Lila. Not if there was another way." His voice breaks on her name. I almost feel sorry for him.

"But you *did* make a deal."

"Yes." He's weeping now, his mouth trembles as he battles with whatever it is he has to say. "They have her, Merle, they have my Lila."

I snap my head up, dizzy with surprise. *No, no, no, no, no.* It can't be. Lila was killed before I got here. Joth said so. *Tristen* said so. *She was killed by faeries, though, wasn't she?*

"You're lying."

"No." He looks me dead in the eye and I sense no lie in him, but that means nothing. Not when he's deceived me all this time. "She showed me. I spoke to her. To Lila. Elaine said that if I didn't help her, she'd kill her and I couldn't, Merle I couldn't—"

As he breaks down again, I have a moment to think. I'd be crazy to believe anything he says, crazy to trust a word, but I *want* to. I snap out my arm and extend my fingers.

"Show me."

He looks at me as if I've got two heads.

"Give me your hand, find the memory, and show me. If you do that and it's exactly as you say," I take a deep breath, "I'll believe you."

"Thank you." He tumbles forward onto his knees and clasps his fingers in mine.

"Close your eyes and show me."

His eyelids slide shut. I copy him and search for the door in his mind. It's green and battered, covered in scorch marks and soot. It's a guilty brain, a treacherous brain. I have to go inside. I pull aside the door, the haze of the memory wavering in front of me.

242

Being inside Tristen's head is truly terrible. It's freezing cold for a moment, then as hot as flames. He's shivering uncontrollably, swirling from self loathing and disgust to relief and despair. Not wanting to wait here any longer, I step into the mist.

When I materialise, I'm still in the dungeon, although now I'm standing behind Greg. He's peering into the first cell, he doesn't know which one the faery's in. I know that, because I know everything. I'm not only seeing the memory of what he saw, but also the dark, looming weight of everything he felt and thought. It's suffocating.

"Over here, Sir Tristen." A female voice coos from the third and final cell.

Greg shivers. He's not sure why he came. He just wanted to properly see one. To look at one of the awful things that killed his little girl, to see the thing that—

A tide of almost painful grief washes through me. I've never felt anything like it, not even when Mum died. I walk forward and take hold of Sir Tristen's hand. I don't think it'll change the memory, but it might let me communicate with him.

"You have to stop that. I need to concentrate." He can't respond, but the temperature seems to level out a bit.

Elaine comes into view, and it hits me again how arrestingly pretty she is. Her face is symmetrical, small nose and plump lips encased with perfectly sculpted cheekbones. I know her human eyes are honey coloured, but now they're full black. The skin around her features is tinged with navy. A trickle of dark red blood has dried on the side of her neck, a souvenir from where I clubbed her with the lamp.

Once Greg is looking properly into her face, he's enraged. Not a monster then, that killed his only daughter, but a beauty. A perfect creature, and one he despises with every fibre of his

BETRAYED

being.

"I'm glad they sent you, Greg." Elaine tips her head to one side. Her voice is mocking and musical. "I needed someone with a backbone that would be easy to break."

Sir Tristen says nothing. He's smart enough to know she's baiting him.

"Not very talkative, are you?" She sniffs and raises her pointy nose in the air. "Well, that's all right. *I've* got a lot to say. If you've not worked it out already, I am Lady Elaine Garlois, and my sister Morgwese is somewhere up there about to wreak havoc on your snivelling little party."

Greg's intention to run upstairs and warn the knights sweeps through the memory.

"Well, you could do that, yes. Run off and tell like a spoilsport. Not that it'll do you any good. She's going to destroy you all, regardless. Or, you could do what I ask, make me a deal."

"I would *never* make a deal with you!" Greg lunges forward, rattling against the bars. "You sicken me!"

"Bet Lila didn't like it when you shouted like—" Elaine starts, but she's cut off when Tristen slashes at her throat through the bars. He grips her so hard dark blue welts appear on her neck. The faery laughs, wheezing chuckles that sound terrifying and painful.

"Going to kill me, Greg?" She rasps.

"Don't you ever talk about her! Ever!" He squeezes harder. I reach out to stop him, even though it won't make any difference. I already know the end of this story.

Tristen releases her neck and turns on his heel. He's going to tell Joth immediately. He might not believe that Merlin's Heir will be found today, but—

"I've got something of yours, by the way." Elaine calls again. Her voice is still oozing with smugness, albeit a little

244

hoarse. "Something I expect you'll want."

He doesn't know what makes him slow down, but he does.

"Lovely Lila isn't dead."

At her words, the memory starts to shake. Cracks appear in the walls, dust raining down on us. The flood of emotions – shock, grief, shame, confusion, rage –courses through him so fast he almost howls. Her confession has rocked him to his core. He's not stupid enough to rule out a trick.

"You lie!" He hisses, turning on his heel and racing back towards her cell.

"Never found a body, did you, Greg?" Elaine cocks an eyebrow, smirking.

With a wave of her hand, the back wall of the cell vanishes. Replacing it in another set of iron bars, and what he sees behind them, makes Sir Tristen fall to his knees.

A small and thin blonde is crouched in the corner. Her face is streaked with dirt, pale rivers where her tears have forged a path down her cheeks. She's cupping her elbows, knees drawn up to her chest. At first her eyes, so like Greg's, are staring blankly forward. Then recognition flickers in them, and she flies to her feet.

"Dad?! *Dad!* Dad, help! Help me!" She thrusts her arms through the bars, reaching for him. Her voice is so strained and sharp it pierces straight into my heart.

Elaine clicks her fingers as Greg lunges forward, trying to get to her. But Lila is already gone.

For a moment, there's nothing in Greg's head but overwhelming despair.

When he comes back around, Elaine is leaning against the wall, arms crossed over her chest. She's staring down at her nails, blowing on them as if she's just had them manicured. If this were real, I would crush her.

BETRAYED

"Would you have her back?"

The question is pitched perfectly, mostly sincere with a tiny amount of amusement and a large dose of hope. With a sinking feeling that matches Sir Tristen's own, we both know he's going to accept. I don't blame him. If it had been Lore screaming in there, I would have accepted, too.

"Yes." He croaks.

"My sister wants an informant. You." The faery points a long, blue finger at him. "If something goes wrong tonight, you'll get close to her, the heir." She sniffs again in distaste. "God knows what all the fuss is about, even Ren's bewitched! I got a good laugh out of seeing her face when I kissed him at the party! Had to use a little love potion, but the old ones are always the best, aren't they?"

She drugged Ren? I have a second to wonder before I file the information away for later.

Cold, haunting despair is dragging Sir Tristen down like quicksand. He knows he has to do it, whatever this despicable creature asks of him. What kind of father would he be to refuse? What kind of knight is he to accept?

At that moment, I feel the fabric of his character begin to tear. The two fundamentals in him so strong they're going to rip him apart.

"You're going to get close to her, and then you're going to wait. And when my sister wants something from you, *whatever* it might be, you're going to do it."

"And Lila?"

"You'll get her back when Mags is finished with you. Now run along. And if you tell anybody about this, I'll slit Lovely Lila's throat myself."

The memory shivers again, this time though it's signalling transition rather than emotion. The walls change from dark grey stone to trunks of tall trees and green leaves.

246

And mushrooms. With a gut wrenching feeling of disgust, I realise he's in my faery circles. His betrayal deepens, cutting at me like a dull knife. He's taken everything I held dear and ravaged it, even the happy memories I have of my own murdered father.

Sir Tristen is pacing up and down, rubbing his hands together and blowing hot air into them. He looks older that he did in the last memory even though it's only been –

I take a second to take in my surroundings. There isn't snow, but there are glimmering patches of frost and Greg's breath is visible in the air. There are no leaves on the trees, and the clearing is littered with blackened dead sticks and wet amber leaves. The ground trembles, and cracks appear in one of the smaller rings. The earth crumbles away, falling in on itself to create a hole.

A wisp of smoke appears, solidifying, just like the Shadows that used to haunt me. It takes a while though, much longer than I've ever seen it take. Finally, the face materialises and I recognise it as Morgwese's. She looks older too, older and worn out. I know from my studies that she's rejuvenating. Tristen isn't scared. He isn't even surprised. He must've met with her this way before.

"News?" she barks.

"None."

Greg's holding back. We've just announced our plan to find Morgana.

"Don't lie to me, knight."

"I'm–"

Morgwese squeezes her smoky fist together. From somewhere behind her, somewhere we can't see, a woman screams.

"All right, stop!"

The faery relaxes her hand and the noise stops. Her lips

BETRAYED

wrinkle in distaste when she speaks. "The Lamorak Boy's eyes showed me differently."

Guilt rolls through him.

"It was a good idea, having Elaine spell him. And you're sure you can keep him in check."

Greg nods reluctantly. He hates that he's had to bring someone else into this, especially a child. But Owen was the only one he could lure away, the one who's most mistrusted by his peers, the easiest to manipulate.

That explains a lot.

"They were talking about another witch at breakfast." Greg's voice cuts into my thoughts. "Someone called Morgana? I–"

Morgwese shrieks, throwing her head back and raking her hands down her face. "My damned sister! The crow who put me here! *Damn* her! What do they *want* with her?"

Tristen hadn't been expecting that reaction, but her horror fills him with glee. "They want her to come and kill you, I expect."

Morgwese hisses at him, gnashing her teeth together. "You *must* stop her, knight! Stop My Merlie from finding her, she can't come here, she can't–" Morgwese breaks off suddenly, raising her hand to her face, dragging her long, pointed nail across her chin. "In fact, Sir Greg, leave it with me. You've done *exceptionally* well."

"No, wait–!"

Morgwese disappears in a puff of smoke, the ground swallowing her up and then healing itself, leaving no sign of her existence.

As the scene fades, I sense a hundred different memories I could look into. Some in France, some on the mountain, some from the last six months. All the lies he's told. All the guilt and the shame, and the tiny, shimmering flame of hope that he fears I'm about to snuff out forever.

That he'll see Lila again.

I don't need to see anymore. It'll all be the same. Morgwese making demands and Greg reluctantly giving in to save his daughter's life. There's no question about whether he was forced.

The question now is whether being forced is enough to warrant mercy.

I slip out of his head and back into my own. I've never been so glad to be myself. My mind is comfy, warm, and secure compared to his shivering madhouse. I open my eyes and stare straight into his.

"I'm sorry about Lila." I say. "Truly I am."

"So you understand?" His voice is full of relief.

I pause for a moment. "I understand. But that doesn't negate everything you've done."

"They would've killed her, and this isn't her fight!"

"And she'll not pay for your sins." I snap at him. "I'm not like them."

"I know you aren't."

"You should've told me." I reach across and lay my hand on his forearm. "I wouldn't have let it continue."

"I couldn't risk it."

With a squeeze of my fingers, I rise to my feet. There's more to do, but this revelation will be enough to deal with now. It's enough for *me* to deal with now.

"Whatever happens to you, Greg, and I don't know exactly what that'll be, I'll fetch Lila. And because you've been my friend and I–" my voice cracks and I have to swallow back a lump. I'm glad he can't see my face because I'm crying. "I care about you. I'll make sure you get your wish. But after that I don't know what'll happen. I don't know if I can forgive you."

There's muffled sobs from behind me, but I don't turn

BETRAYED

back to look.

"*Revertere.*" I whisper and the sound of him slumping forwards echoes round the walls..

I consider for a moment whether it's worth waking Owen. See what he's got to say about it all. I probably shouldn't. Right now, I don't have the emotional capacity to carry the weight of his reaction. I don't know whether I can forgive him either, even if he truly didn't understand what he was doing. Aila rubs her side against my thigh in comfort.

At the top of the stairs, I lean my forehead against the cool, dry stone. I've had enough for one day. My best friend is still alive, another friend has betrayed us, we've brought over the witch, I've even risen from the dead. So to speak.

But now, I'm not the only ghost to haunt these halls. Lila's screams echo in my ears.

"Get what you wanted, Darling?" Morgana's silken voice invades my thoughts.

"Yes, exactly what I wanted. A reason *so good* that I completely understand why he betrayed us!"

"Yet you don't seem happy about it." Morgana smiles sarcastically at me and then puts her arm around my shoulders, leading me back down the hall. "If you want my advice, I'd not worry about it until the morning. Get a good night's sleep, spend some time with that handsome boy of yours while it's standing still."

Those are the most beautiful words she's ever said.

"He's the Du Lac boy isn't he?" Morgana's face takes on a wistful quality. "Lancelot and Guinevere's?"

"Well," I'm about to launch into a Willow sized explanation about bloodlines, then realise I can't be bothered. "Something like that."

"He looks exactly like her, you know? Same jaw, same nose, beautiful she was, well you saw her! Arthur never really

250

was up to scratch in the looks department. He'd have been fine for a plain princess, but with Guin being an *absolutely gorgeous* demi–fae, and not exactly his type," she nudges me with her elbow. "She was always much more suited to Lancelot. I was glad when they finally got away." Her words trail off, and her face softens at the fondness of the memory. "Anyway, off to bed with you. I'll wake you in the morning. Go on."

"Goodnight, Morgana." I say over my shoulder and then pause. "And you're sure you'll be all right?"

"This Templar was my home for a hundred years." She reminds me, and with a wolfish glint in her eyes she says: "and besides, I've got true prophecy to unravel, and Merlin's cave to explore."

Then she turns on her heel, long skirts swirling around her ankles. I think about stopping her, not sure I should leave her alone with the Golden Book. In the end, I don't bother.

Ren is much more important, and he's waiting for me in bed.

My room is exactly as I left it, even down to the colour of the sheets. As I go to him, he sits up and opens his arms, pulling me into his lap. I throw my arms around him and bury my head in the crook of his neck. His nails dig into the flesh of my back. He's pulling me so close he almost cuts off my air.

"Thank god you're back." He whispers in my ear, his voice thick with tears.

I say nothing, my throat aching with the effort of keeping in my sobs. We stay sitting, limbs entwined and foreheads pressed together. Our cheeks are full of tears. Tears of grief, shock, relief and happiness. Eventually, when we're cried out, I lay down beside him, my arm draped across his chest, his folded around my waist.

"When I got back from Scotland, everything was already

BETRAYED

uneasy, as you know. The other Templars weren't happy about the new law, and we'd not heard anything from you for a while. Then Asher appeared. She was in bad shape, didn't wake up for months. Then Owen came and said—" his words tumble out of his mouth quickly and with growing panic. "He said Asher pushed you over the side. They obviously didn't know she was here. But it didn't matter because she wasn't awake to defend herself! I knew it was a lie, that Asher wouldn't ever, but we couldn't convince the knights with no evidence. Owen said you'd been killed, and there was no sign of a witch on the mountain, that he'd had to leave you there..." he takes in a great hiccoughing breath and squeezes me tight. "And all I kept thinking about was you emerging from that cave, a little bruised up still here! That you'd turn up at any moment... As the months went on though, I started to —and defending Asher was so hard, Willow and I were completely overwhelmed."

"On the second day, there was an avalanche that cut us off from the others." I say. "Pelleas and Tristen went back for help because Rory broke her arm. I wanted to get to Morgana so badly, so we carried on. There was another avalanche in the night and by the time I got out of the tent, I was too late." Now I'm the one who has to stop. The sound of Asher's body hitting the ground has haunted me since I heard it, and it rings through my ears now. "I knew he'd killed her, let her go on purpose, but I was already too late. So Aila and I ran. Cassandra told us about Carnwennan, so I suspected he was going to murder Morgana. We ended up in a fight. We tried to kill each other, Ren. He almost succeeded." I push myself up and lift my t–shirt to show the silver scars under my ribs. Then I turn my face. The thin scar from Carnwennan's blade still shimmering on my cheek. "I don't remember much after that. Not until she woke me a few days later."

"Then I'm forever in her debt." He kisses the top of my

head. "I was barely making it by these last few months. We knew there was a traitor running amok in these halls. I started to believe you weren't coming back and I just, I can't do this without you." He kisses my cheek, brushing the hair off my face.

"Well, that's not surprising. You can't even find matching socks on your own." I'm still crying, and if I dwell on this sadness any longer, I'll never stop. Ren offers me a watery chuckle before pulling me backwards and wrapping his arms around me.

"I love you." I say.

"I love you too." He kisses my cheek again, then lays his head down, pressing it into the back of my neck. I waste no time in following suit and settling down beside him. Tomorrow there will be time to talk. Now I only want to sleep.

26

I wake up to Morgana rattling on the door.

"Are you decent, Darlings?" She calls, but doesn't wait for our answer before barging in. She's changed from her full skirts into a black maxi dress and smiles as she catches me staring. "Your friend Asher has been teaching me *all* about modern fashion, conjured this up about ten minutes ago. Fascinating, isn't it? No stockings or anything!"

There's a tray levitating behind her. With a flick of her fingers, two coffee cups zoom towards us. Ren almost drops his.

"What time is it?" I ask.

"The same time it's always been." She throws open the curtains to reveal the grey half–light of mid afternoon in Autumn. "Couldn't leave you any longer, though. Breakfast is ready.

"Five minutes then." I swing my legs out of bed. Morgana nods approvingly and bustles out of the room.

"It's too soon!" Ren says and throws his head back into the pillows. Aila growls beside him and snuggles closer. "Come back to bed."

"Nope. When the most powerful being on earth tells you to get up, you get up." I offer him my hand and pull him into a sitting position. "And the sooner we do this, the sooner we get to come back and stay here."

"Sir Tristen betrayed us because Lila's alive and being held prisoner by the fae." I announce to a room of disbelieving faces.

We've just had breakfast. Morgana conjured up a feast of pastries, coffee, and fruit. We all sat around the big table after moving the frozen knights out of the way. For a while, it almost felt normal, but then, when the plates had been cleared, reality descended again.

"Impossible." Joth shakes his head.

"A lot of impossible things have happened recently, Joth. Let's not forget that." Asher chimes in. She looks a bit better today, more colour in her cheeks, but she's still not herself. So far, I've resisted the urge to cling to her, which I know she wouldn't want.

Yes. You've missed a lot in six months.

"I've seen her." I say before my mind can run away with itself any further, rubbing the fur between Aila's ears for comfort. "He's taken me for a fool. I wasn't stupid enough to believe him again without proof."

"Memories can be altered." Morgana interjects.

Yes, they can be. I wouldn't put it past Morgwese or Elaine to try something. The emotion, though, the grief, the rage, he wasn't faking that. "You'll have to check, too. Just in case."

"If he's hiding behind my sister's magic, I'll be able to sense it immediately. I thought I detected Elaine, only the

BETRAYED

faintest touch. Maybe he's spelled."

"Maybe. Owen Lamorak *definitely* is."

At that, the whole room shifts. Willow gasps, Ren's and Asher's backs straighten in their chairs.

"Very interesting." Morgana muses. "And you got this from Tristen, too?"

"He had Elaine spell Owen, so the suspicion landed on him. An excellent plan, as it turns out." The bitterness of my words burns my tongue. "It explains a lot, why his actions were so confusing. How it seemed he never knew what he was doing–"

The earsplitting screeching of wood dragging on stone cuts me off. Asher is on her feet, glowering at me. "He *killed* me, Merle. He threw me over the side! And I–" Asher looks at her hands as if she's never seen them before. "He killed me."

"And don't, for a single second, doubt my loyalty to you." I say. My heart thunders in my chest, my ears ringing with its beat. "Don't for a *single* second believe I'd not see him punished for that! If you want him as dust in your palm, you'll have it!"

Asher's eyes lock on mine, assessing me. I don't know why there's a strange rhythm surging between us. Something wrong between us.

"Dying doesn't make you special, Knight." Morgana drawls, but there's a deadly note underneath. "Owen killed the Little Witch too, and you don't see her crying about it. Got her right under the ribs with Carnwennan. Repairing that damage was some of my best work, not to mention what I did for you!"

"You didn't tell me she was alive." I say, my voice trembling. I feel sick, thinking about the ice icy edge of the dagger sliding into my skin. Aila rubs her huge head against my thigh, comforting me.

Morgana's expression clouds over like thunder rolling in. "I didn't know for certain. I knew I'd managed to break her fall, kind of, and that when I portaled her back here, she was alive. I didn't know whether she'd make it."

"So it is true, you can bring people back from the dead." Ren whispers.

"No, not quite. But I *can* stop them from going over, hold on to their souls until their bodies heal."

"I remember." Asher sits down slowly, glassy tears balanced on her lower lashes. "Not the actual– I remember falling. I'm still falling, well sometimes I think I am–"

"Damn it." Morgana hisses. "That's your problem, is it? No wonder you're so bloody miserable!"

"What are you talking about?" I ask her.

"Some of her is stuck somewhere."

"*Stuck somewhere?*" Asher says with disgust.

"You better stop with the attitude." Morgana points a finger in her direction. "The spell I performed to keep you alive was the greatest spell cast on this earth in *five hundred* years! Magic this one won't be able to even dream of for a decade! I felt the grief in her heart, from all that way, and *that's* why you're standing here alive. Remember that."

Asher flushes and clamps her lips shut.

Morgana gets up and walks around the table, passing by me and giving my cheek a squeeze. "You were a piece of cake, though, Darling. All that lovely magical blood."

"She seems to have taken quite the shine to you." Ren mutters out of the corner of his mouth.

"Are you ready, Lady Gaheris?" Morgana asks her.

"Ready for–?"

And before the rest of the question is out of her mouth, Morgana barks a word and Asher goes rigid in her seat.

"Best to just do it, not give them time to worry." The

BETRAYED

witch smiles at me and then, "oh! There it is." Asher tumbles forward in her seat. Willow lets out a small shriek and pulls on Asher's shoulders. "Oh, don't fuss. Look, she's waking up already. How's that Gaheris? Better?" Morgana puts her hands on her hips.

Asher scrambles out of her seat and flings her arms around Morgana's neck. "Thank you! What *was* that? What was wrong with me?"

"As I was saying, *very* complicated spell, and you were miles away, in distance *and* time. So your healing might have had a little blip. Left a bit over there." The witch thrusts Asher to arm's length and then puts her palm to her forehead. "Been feeling moody, have you? Like the world is going to end, no joy in anything?"

"She *was* on trial for murder—" Ren cuts in.

Morgana looks at me and rolls her eyes. "He's exactly like her, I'm telling you."

"Like who—?"

"As much as I'm enjoying whatever this is," Joth speaks for the first time, his voice is friendly and there's a twinkle in his eyes. "We need to speak quickly and plainly. Our time is almost up. We'll work out any details later." He looks sternly at Morgana, a warning not to cause anymore havoc. It seems in the last few hours they've reached a cautious truce.

"If a bit of you got left in the underworld, it would've affected your mood. Dark and cold down there, you see, terrible place. But you're all back together now." Morgana smiles at Joth and then at Asher.

I cast my mind back to our earlier conversation. Owen. "Like I was saying, Owen's been spelled, so while that doesn't excuse his behaviour, it explains it somewhat, and might mean a less severe punishment."

"And what of Sir Tristen's punishment?" Joth asks.

258

"Lila first." I haven't had time to think properly about his question. I'm too bias to decide.

"You want to rescue her?" Ren asks, quicker to understand my intentions than the rest.

"We can't leave her there—"

"It's *absolutely* out of the question." Joth cuts us off. "We need you."

"Lila can not stay there." I say again, slowing down each word, staring between them.

"And she might not have to." Morgana says. There's a wicked glint in her eye, cunning beyond what I can imagine.

"Go on." I say.

"If you want something from Mags and don't want to fight her for it, you'll have to do a trade. Something in exchange for Lila." Morgana's eyes meet mine. "Something special, something she's always wanted."

"Madness." Joth throws his own hands up. "Madness, Morgana! And you know it."

"And how do you know she'll accept?" I ask.

"First, I'm her darling baby sister and I *always* get what I want. Second, we'll offer her something she can't refuse, worth a thousand times what the life of Lila Tristen is."

"Morgana," Joth warns. "Enough."

"If you're all still alive, that means my sister's powers are depleted, that she isn't strong enough to take proper revenge. *Yet.* She won't want to fight either–"

"So what, offer to give her powers back in return for Lila?" Asher scowls, wrinkling her nose. "I'm all for rescuing her, but wouldn't that be a bit stupid?"

"And what could we even trade her for? Is there even anything that could do that?"

Willow sits up straight beside me, brows creasing together. I know that face.

BETRAYED

"There is something that could." She starts slowly, looking at Joth who is taking deep, heavy breaths. "But there's no guarantee it exists, let alone that we could find it—"

"And what is it?" I ask, my mouth dry.

"The Holy Grail." Willow turns her big brown eyes to me, her face serious. "We could trade Lila Tristen for the Holy Grail."

Joth throws us all out of the room aside from Morgana. He's angry. I've never seen him this way, aside from when Lamorak pushed him to knight Ren on the spot.

Even through the closed doors, his bellow's carry. *"Furthering your own agenda at a time like this!", "madness!"* and *"absolutely out of the question!"* are all common themes of the conversation.

We wait in the hall outside, waiting. All of us have our backs against the wall. After a second of comfortable silence, I offer my hand to Asher on one side and Ren on the other. Nothing's changed between us, nothing at all. I've never been so grateful for anything in my entire life. Ten minutes later, the doors to the hall burst open and Joth storms out of them, muttering under his breath. Morgana is leaning in the doorway, looking down at her nails again.

"And?" I ask.

"I told you, Darling. I always get my own way." The witch grins at me. "I've got to help you figure this mess out first, of course."

"You'll fix Lore?" Willow whispers.

"You have my full powers at your disposal." Morgana turns her honey coloured eyes on Willow. "So yes, I'll wake her."

I go to her, taking both her hands in mine. "Thank you."

"Yes, well—" she splutters, embarrassed. "All right

enough. First, we've got the traitors to deal with, and we'll have to wake up the knights soon, unfortunately. After that, we'll plan our next stage."

I go with Morgana to wake Sir Tristen again. I suppose I could check if they've spelled him myself, but she'll be able to sense her sister's magic, if there's anything to sense.

I stop by the cell of Owen Lamorak. My task will be to visit with him while Morgana deals with Greg.

"Oh yes, I can smell Elaine!" She cackles. "She's put him under some kind of controlling charm. As always with Elaine, though, it's mediocre at best." She sniffs the air, so much like the faery in Tristen's memory that a chord of unease quivers in my mind.

"*You'd do well to remember they were sisters.*" Merlin's voice grumbles from within. *"Her loyalty might not lie with you."*

She's helped us before, though. She was the one who banished Morgwese in the first place.

"She's done something to his memories. She always *did* favour memory charms."

"Like she did something to Lore's memory?"

"Yes." Morgana glides through the cell door, unlocking it with a wave of her hand. After a moment peering around Owen's frozen form, she says; "Oh yes, I see what she's done. Manipulated his dealings with you so that *you* looked like the enemy and the commands from her appeared as the natural order of things. She's done a sloppy job, though. As per usual."

"Can you reverse it?"

"In three seconds flat." She grins, then the smile falters on her face. "When you hear what he's got to say, you'll want to show leniency. You can do what you want for me, Darling. But a little advice, too much mercy, and you'll appear weak. There's a war coming, and if your subjects aren't bound to you

BETRAYED

by loyalty, then they need to be bound by *fear*."

She stares at me for a long moment. My eyes start to water, but I don't look away.

"I'm but a humble servant of the throne," I say, injecting as much humour into my voice as I can manage. "The king and queen will decide what to do with them."

"Very well then." The witch grins and then snaps her fingers, the crisp click echoing round the walls. "He's all yours."

"Thank you."

Morgana breezes past me, but I grab her arm above the elbow. "Make sure he isn't lying to us."

Make him suffer. I want to say. *Make him hurt in a way that I cannot.*

But it would be wrong to ask such a thing, even if Morgana would do it willingly. She inclines her head, receiving my message loud and clear, then exits the cell.

That just leaves Owen and I. Again.

I asked Asher if she wanted to be here, to look into his face and cast her own judgement. I don't know if she'll come.

"Surgere." I whisper, and Owen's frozen face jumps to life.

He sits bolt upright, then looks at me with wide eyes. So wide I think they'll pop out of his head. He draws in a great whooping breath.

"Hello Owen." I say, Aila taking guard by the door.

He brings his wide-eyed stare to meet mine, still breathing in and out rapidly, panicking.

"Stop that. I need you to talk. I know they spelled you. I don't intend to hurt you."

At my words, relief surges through his whole body. His muscles relax, his breathing evens out, even his eyes go back into his sockets a little. "I didn't mean it, any of it!"

262

"That might be the case. But you tried to kill Asher and me. If it weren't for Morgana, you would have succeeded both times."

The colour Owen's cheeks have gained runs out of them until he's the same grey shade as old cream.

"I need to hear your side. Everything."

"You won't be fair! You've never liked me! I–"

I lunge forward at him, grabbing at the scruff of his shirt and slamming him backwards. "Listen to me, you spineless traitor. You killed my friend! You killed her! And you didn't even hesitate when it was my turn. What I should be doing is burning you to *ash*. Instead, I'm giving you a chance to explain yourself, but *only one*." I lean in as close to him as I can manage without touching his skin. "So you'd better not waste it. And if you lie, if you lie to me even once, you'll be dead before the last of the words leave your mouth." I've wondered before whether I'd ever have it in me to kill someone, and I'd always been sure I couldn't. Since finding out I'm Merlin's Heir, something's changed. No wonder he looks petrified. I'm a little scared myself.

I drop him down to his seat and step back, sitting cross-legged on the floor as I did with Sir Tristen.

"Just before Christmas I'd started to feel strange." Owen begins with a little shudder, his wide, terrified eyes staring straight at me. "I hated it here. I was having lots of bad dreams. There was a woman in them. She had blue skin and bug eyes. I couldn't get away from her. Every night she was inside my brain just–" he makes a scratching motion with all ten fingers, a look of misery on his face. "I couldn't sleep, and I was just so *angry*. With Joth, with you, with Dad for making me stay–"

"What were you angry about?"

"Anything, *everything*!" He leans forward a little. "But it wasn't my anger, it *isn't*. At first I tried to reason with myself.

BETRAYED

I knew I didn't hate you or wish you ill, even though sometimes I'd catch myself in a rage over nothing. It got too hard to control. In France there were so many times when it wanted me to–" he stops, avoiding the words balanced on his tongue.

"You already stabbed me to death, Owen. I wouldn't get quiet about it now."

If it's possible, he gets paler. "The anger, the dreams, they were telling me I had to kill you and that witch. I knew she was going to help Lore. I *want* her to. But that other voice was talking all the time. I couldn't fight it anymore. I just wanted it to stop. Then on the mountain, I saw my chance. I knew you suspected me, and Asher wanted to get rid of me."

Did she? Maybe she'd wanted to send him back with the twins, but kill him?

"Turns out I'd've been right to strangle you in your sleep." Asher's voice sounds from behind me, and she slinks out of the shadows and into the cell. I turn my head to meet her steely gaze.

"*You good?*"

She only gives me a small nod in response.

"I couldn't stop it." He says glumly. "I tried to fight it when I realised what was happening. It took me a while. I kept getting blank spots, missing time. Eventually, I realised I wasn't always in control of myself. Like when I found that dagger in my bed. I *knew* I'd stolen it. I just didn't know when or why."

"Why didn't you tell anyone?"

"When I got back, Tristen and Eddie were already looking for us. That's when I found out it was Greg. But he already had a story. He told me if I didn't go along with him, he'd kill me anyway." There are tears in his eyes now. "I didn't know what to do! Then we got word that Asher was alive, and

264

I knew I was done for."

"But then you accused me instead?" Asher's face is dark.

"Yes." He meets her stare again, even as tears crawl down his cheeks. He looks young now, and how old is he, sixteen? Seventeen? "That was Greg too, though. At first, it didn't look like you were going to wake up at all, and we certainly didn't have any idea how you'd got back!"

"The witch did it."

Owen lets out a long exhale. "You found her?"

"I did." I say.

Owen nods as if that explains everything. "I was glad when you came round. So you could tell everyone what happened. I knew what I'd done was wrong. I knew attacking *you* was wrong." He motions to me. "But I wasn't strong enough to fight." His voice is bitter and full of self loathing.

"And you never thought of coming forward? Of telling Joth what was going on?"

"Of course I did!" He snaps. "But I *couldn't,* and she couldn't remember anything other than me pushing her off! Greg would have got away with it. Nobody, not even Joth, would've believed that Sir Tristen was *really* the traitor!"

He's right there. Tristen's now admitted it to me multiple times, and I still can barely believe it's true.

"You would've cast me out." Owen looks down at his feet. "And I was too terrified to go. I was ashamed to admit that before, but I'm not now."

"Why?" Asher asks before I can.

"Because now I know you're going to kill me! And I hope you do! Carrying around all this... all this..." He throws his arms out in front of him and leans back against the stone wall, sobbing properly now.

I believe him when he says he's been struggling with the weight of everything, and that he lost the battle. The dark

BETRAYED

circles under his eyes and hollows in his cheeks tell me that. He's wound as tight as a string about to snap. I reach forward and put my hand on his calf, then I offer my other hand to Asher.

Going into his mind is like being submerged in icy waters. Sir Tristen's brain was deceitful and worried. He'd known why he was betraying us. Owen is just terrified. He still doesn't really understand what's happened to him, only bits and pieces of what he's seen and what Greg's told him. He really thinks we're going to kill him, and he really means it when he says he's glad. He doesn't want to live with it anymore, this double life they've forced him into, and he can't see a way out. He wanted to be a good knight like his father, his mind tells me. Then, "*I really miss my dad.*" Then, "*I want my mum. She would've known something wasn't right.*"

I snap my hand back from him, the colour of his grief the same shade as my own. I know what it's like to lose a mum, how the wound still aches in my core. And she probably *would've* known that something wasn't right, that her son, who had longed to grow up like his father and serve his king and queen, had plotted against them. Constantly warring with himself.

I should've known. I should've acted in France when I suspected him of more than 'practical joking'. I look at Asher, whose face is grim and almost grey. She also has tears on her cheeks, thinking hard about something.

"How did you do it?" She finally asks.

"I already told you—"

"No." The tone of her voice is soft and precise, as if she's exerting a great deal of effort keeping herself calm. "How did you make the death knocks?"

"The what?" Now he opens his eyes, his nose wrinkled in puzzlement.

"The knocking I heard. The legend. How did you make me hear them?"

It's a good question, and one I'd very much like to know the answer to. Owen's looking between our faces, completely baffled.

"Tristen copped to that one, actually." Morgana says from the doorway, making the three of us jump. "He never planned to kill you, you see. Thought that if he scared you enough, with the legend and all that, you'd just turn around and go home."

"But I–" Asher protests.

"Elaine gave him something to put in your drinks, *terribly* predictable–"

"I died though."

"I know." Morgana nods sympathetically. "It really was a coincidence, though, Darling. A huge 'practical joke'."

Asher looks like she's going to open her mouth to argue, but then thinks better of it. If she wants to have it out with Morgana, it can wait. It seems we've come to the end of our horrible conversation, at least until we've shared the information with the others.

"What do you wanna do, Ash?" I send to her.

"I've half a mind to give him what he wants." She responds, the ghost of a smile on her face. *"He deserves to be punished, Merle. But not like that,* never *that."*

I couldn't agree more, I realise with a sigh of relief. Even as Morgana's earlier words echo through my head, I know it's not right to kill him, not when I believe him.

"You're going to live another day yet, Lamorak." I finally say, climbing to my feet. Morgana huffs disappointedly in the doorway. "But you'll be staying here until we know what to do with you."

The boy starts to cry again. I don't know whether it's relief or grief that causes it.

"And I'll send your father down."

His grateful sobs follow us all the way up the stairs.

27

"I was going to do it, you know." Asher says to us as we resurface into the hallway. It's much warmer up here, and I can't say I'm sorry about it. Ren's waiting for us at the top and he slips his hand into mine, affectionately scratching the spot between Aila's ears as she approaches. He's been keeping close to me all morning, as if I might disappear again.

"Going to do what?" He asks.

"Kill Lamorak," Morgana answers on Asher's behalf. There's a smile on her face, ruthless and coy.

Asher nods. "That last night we were there. I had such a bad feeling about him. I'd seen him staring, muttering under his breath. Angry. He was waiting as soon as I left the tent, and for a moment, when we were fighting, before the avalanche... I would have."

"He said he could hear Elaine talking to him, like scratching on the inside of his skull." I mimic the motion he used earlier, all ten digits like claws. "Although he didn't know it was Elaine. She wanted him to kill us sooner, and he said he was trying to fight it."

"Apparently not hard enough," Morgana says.

I shrug. She's not wrong. But Elaine had a hold of Owen for a long time. That would take a toll on anyone.

"I knew he had the knife, the Witch Killer." Asher looks between Morgana and me, her face blanching a little. "I thought he was planning to kill you both, Morgana at least. I knew I'd have to do it if it came down to him or us."

"So what stopped you?" Ren almost growls. While she's been talking, we've wandered into one of the sitting rooms. I fold down onto the floor beside Ren's armchair, my eyes never leaving Asher's face as she sits.

"He was already waiting to attack whoever came out of the tent. I thought I had a chance, but then the avalanche started. I hesitated—"

"So did I." I say.

"And yet I found Rhongomyniad cast on the mountainside." Morgana looks at me pointedly while cleaning dirt from her nails with a small knife. Where the hell did she get that?

"Cassandra gave it to me the night before we left. She knew Owen had Carnwennan and thought I might need it." Had I been ready to use it to defend myself? I cast my mind back to that awful desperate race for the summit. How empty I'd been, how distraught at Asher's falling. Like nothing would ever come right again. With hate in my heart. I didn't care if he was spelled then. Had I been prepared to use it in revenge?

Morgana raises her eyebrows, and then she sends, "*It's nothing to me, sweetheart. I wouldn't have let him go.*"

"I knew what needed to be done, and I thought I could do it. You wouldn't have known until it was over, and I could

BETRAYED

face my consequences when I got back. But he's so young and I just–" Her voice wobbles, and I know she's thinking of Eyrie.

"Ever killed anyone before?" Morgana asks.

"No."

Morgana nods knowingly.

"Stop making excuses for him," Ren spits suddenly. "At some point, he knew to do his duty. Maybe not on the mountain, but after. He could've told us then! He knew Asher hadn't killed you. All those months he let me think– he let me mourn you–" Ren's breath catches in his throat, fingers clenching at my shoulder. "And he could have told somebody."

"Makes it easy. Deciding what to do with them. Give the boy a warning, keep him close, and off Tristen." Morgana says, still picking at her nails. "It's what we would've done in my day."

"But not what we will do in ours." Joth's rough voice sounds from the doorway and makes us all jump. I breathe a sigh of relief, the decision taken from my hands. Not that it was ever really in them. "Tristen betrayed us, yes. But we won't sink to his level, we won't put the burden on the children."

"No," Morgana agrees, cowed.

"Have you seen them?" I ask.

"No, not yet."

We're all silent for a moment, thinking of the twins. It dawns on me that we've actually done what we set out to do. Not only did we find Morgana, but we brought her back here, and she agreed to help us.

"It's time to wake them up." I say, getting to my feet. "The knights, and Lore."

Morgana grins at me wolfishly, "lead the way, Wild'un."

Back in the knight's hall, Morgana instructs me to close my eyes and search for the threads of magic holding the Templar in stasis.

"I did most of the heavy lifting through the night," she says. "Couldn't sleep. I was so excited! All the books in that cave! And the prophecy's really something, isn't it?"

Willow huffs exasperatedly. Even with my eyes closed, I know she'll have crossed her arms over her chest. "I can't solve it."

"Well no, but I spent years solving his riddles, didn't I? I'm sure we can—"

"How about we deal with one problem at a time?" Ren says.

"They're literally exactly the same, let me tell you, Darling. Guinevere was always rushing about." Morgana whispers in my ear and I can't hold in a tide of giggles.

"Get on with it, please." Joth's voice booms over the top of us.

By threads, I assume Morgana means the magical sparks of the net thrown over us. If I close my eyes and send out my consciousness, exactly as I would when searching for auras, a shimmering criss–cross mesh of power weaves around us. I can seek out the individual lines of that power and focus on the interconnected strands. I send out a trickle of magic and the line hums where I meet it. "I've found the thread, Morgana. What now?"

"Unravel it. Let it go."

Very helpful, I think to myself. But once I start to think of those glowing points as knots, I can actually untie them. One by one they wink out, time resuming its usual march.

"It's done." I say as the web dissolves. "They should wake up any moment now."

Two seconds later, there's a rattling sound as Monty Percival slips from his chair and onto the floor.

"Very good, Darling." Morgana says and pinches my

BETRAYED

cheek. "Now, take me to my niece and nephew. I've been waiting an age to meet them."

"And you'll wait a moment longer," Joth speaks before I can. "It'll be shocking enough having Merle back. There's already so much to explain, and throwing you into the mix straight off the bat might overwhelm them."

"You asked me to come!" Morgana throws her arms over her head.

"Yes, and I'm very glad that you did." Joth takes a step forward and puts his hands on her shoulder. The touch is affectionate and tender, and her face softens a little. "First, we'll tell them Merle's back, after that we'll announce your arrival to the knights, and then—"

"Well, at least that'll be fun," she huffs. "Go on then, be quick about it. If the girl's still spelled, I want to get it off her as quickly as possible."

Joth reels some quick instructions off to Ren, to call for the other knights and settle them, to ask Etta for tea, and to hide Morgana until we're ready to make our announcement. Luckily, only Percival and Bedivere were in the hall when they awoke, and they won't have time to spread gossip under Asher's watchful eyes. As soon as that's done, Joth and I head upstairs to the third floor.

"They still have their own rooms," Joth says. "If things aren't the same, or if they're angry or cold, you mustn't take it to heart. It's been very difficult for them. I've shielded them as much as possible, but there's only so much I could stop them from hearing."

"I understand."

"And they're different, too." His eyes bore into mine, worry etched into his face. "I don't know how they're going to react."

272

They've believed me dead for a long time, lost. Now I'm returned to them, and they also have to process Morgana, Asher's freedom, and everything else that stemmed from Tristen's deal with Morgwese. It might overwhelm them entirely. I cross my arms over my chest, feeling for my elbows and squeezing. I wish it was easier, that I could erase everything that's happened. There's no more time for wishes as the door swings open. I hold my breath as Joth lets out a gusty sigh.

Lux Pendragon stumbles into the hallway, bleary-eyed and at least two inches taller than I remember. His face is squarer, accentuated by flicks of hair which is in desperate need of a cut. He's got slightly broader shoulders, and long gangly arms. Not a child anymore, but showing the shape of the man he'll become. He opens his mouth to speak as he recognises Joth, probably to ask him what the hell's been going on, but then he freezes.

I don't look any different, but the shock wave that rolls through him is tremendous just the same.

"Merle?" His word is a breath, full of complicated high and low notes.

"Hello, Lux." It's lame, it's not enough. Certainly not enough to explain my long absence, or why I've returned now. He stares at me, mouth hanging open, bottom lip beginning to tremble. In two steps, I'm by his side, holding out my arms, which he folds into. The wetness of his tears smudges across my cheek, his papery breath catching in my ear.

"Is it really you? Really?"

"It's me."

He tenses in my arms, his spine going rigid. Because of the closeness of him, I see the thoughts flash across his mind in quick succession.

"She wouldn't have come back without the witch. Did

BETRAYED

she find her? Can she fix Lore now? Is it over?"

"It's not over," I whisper. "But Morgana's here. She's agreed to help us." I take a step back, placing my hands on his shoulders. There's something he needs to hear, something gnawing at him. "You did exactly the right thing, sending us to find her. Exactly the right thing."

Lux's eyes brim with tears, glassy drops balancing on his lower lashes. "They said you were dead. You've been gone for so long—"

"I know." My voice cracks and I raise the pads of my fingers to wipe away the water on his cheeks. "And I'll tell you everything. But I'm here now, for good, I promise."

"Morgana is very eager to meet you," Joth says from behind us.

Lux nods and squares his shoulders, his face setting hard like the surface of a stone. Yet another show of the man he's on the cusp of becoming. "All right then. We'd best get Lore."

I nod and assume Joth does the same behind me as Lux steps back from us both and goes to the heavy door opposite his own. He knocks, a flurry of taps, a secret message probably, something no one but the twins will ever understand. Then he waits for a moment. The door bursts open with such force I expect it to fly off its hinges. Standing before me is a girl I barely recognise.

Lore is also taller, perhaps even a little taller than Lux. She's as thin as a rake and as pale as moonlight. Her hair hangs around her face in a golden halo, grey eyes encircled with dark shadows. She's beautiful, as if she's been carved from marble, the solemn heroine of a Greek tragedy. Lore barely remembered me the last time she saw me, but as her eyes find mine, recognition dawns in them. She looks tired, old beyond her years, the strain of it all wearing her down to the bone. I offer my hand to her and she entwines her fingers in mine.

They're icy cold and as delicate as the bones of a bird.

"I know you, don't I?" she says. "You're the one I've been waiting for?"

"No," I shake my head. I've not been the one who can fix her, and that thought has been like a shard of glass in my heart. "But I can take you to her."

Joth and I leave the twins outside the hall to await our announcement. Ren claps a hand on Lux's shoulder, inclining his head at Lore. Something is strange, something I've not been here to witness. Lore is better and worse at the same time. More aware of her surroundings, but less herself, darker and withdrawn. Ren's eyes meet mine and there's a shadow in them. I don't have time to get to the bottom of it now, but I will.

There's trouble ahead, a little voice in my mind whispers. *Never mind that,* I spit back. *There's trouble right now.*

"We'll call for you in a moment, when we've announced to the knights that Morgana is here. Then we'll explain everything as best as we can." Joth gives both the twins a nod, then swings open the door for me to enter the hall.

The knights are all assembled, waiting for instruction. I look around to find Mona standing behind Lydia's seat. She's already staring at me, her blue eyes piercing and icy. She grins, showing far too many teeth, and how I've missed that grin.

"I always 'ad faith in ye." She sends.

Lawrence is looking at me too, but his face is not stern, resigned to the facts of what's happened. As long as he keeps his mouth shut, I don't care what he thinks. Eyrie gives me a small wave from behind Asher's seat. She's grown tall too and is the spitting image of her sister, aside from the fact that her braids are black, woven with teal and blue.

Joth takes a seat at the head of the table and I stand

BETRAYED

beside him. Everyone is anxious, the hum of it running through my blood.

Joth clears his throat, a hush falling over the room. "Thank you all for being so patient with us, but it was important that when we made this announcement that everyone was present—"

"I don't need an introduction, Darling." Morgana's rich, high voice rings out as she appears from the shadowy corner of the room. "I'm certain that my reputation precedes me."

Eddie gasps, an enormous grin breaking out on his face. He climbed the mountain with us, after all and is more invested in Morgana than most. Lawrence has his mouth hanging open. Morgana drops a wink at me as she floats into the centre of the room. She's beautiful. Her deep auburn hair falls in ringlets to her waist, whiskey eyes peering into each of their souls. All of them stare back, and why shouldn't they? She's the stuff of legend.

"Didn't expect me to come, did you?" She grins, mocking them.

The doors at the other end of the room rattle and there's muffled voices from outside before they fly open. Lore's standing with her arms wide, pale cheeks flushed pink. She's breathing hard as she stalks into the room.

For a moment, Morgana looks stunned, eyes wide, nostrils flaring. It's the first time I've ever seen her rattled. Then she looks over the girl's head to find Lux. At that, the witch's bottom lip trembles. Like Lore is the image of Igraine, Lux is almost identical to Arthur. With the same eyes and young square face, it must be like seeing a ghost. He comes to stand beside his sister, taking her hand.

"Merle said you've come to help us, that you can fix Lore." He says.

Morgana takes a deep breath, gathering herself, "yes. I've

276

come to serve the line of my brother King Arthur Pendragon, and to love you as I loved him."

"Your sister caused this," a voice rings out. After a moment, I locate Percival, slowly rising to his feet. Amalie is standing behind his chair, scowling. "How do we know your intentions are true?"

"If I remember correctly," she glares at him. "You were the ones who came for me. You need *my* help. If I wanted to hurt them... Monty, is it? It would already be done."

Percival trembles under her gaze but doesn't sit down. Unrest ripples through the room and I hold my breath for an outburst.

Joth clears his throat again, a low rumble in the quiet. "If memory serves, it was also *us* that betrayed Lady Morgana, wasn't it? And not only that, but we've got two traitors sitting in the dungeons, neither of which are her."

I bite my lip against a smirk, and Morgana flashes a sly smile in Joth's direction.

"That doesn't mean—" Monty starts, but he's cut off by another voice.

Lux raises his head and looks at us, one by one. We all feel it, his magnetism, the pound of royal blood in his veins. It used to feel like that, to look at Lore, but she's a ghost of herself. Somehow cold and bitter.

"You're either with us or against us, Sir Percival." His voice doesn't wobble now. It's strong and full of grit. "Morgana's going to restore Lore's memories, and then she's going to help us find peace." His eyes flick to the witch. She nods almost imperceptibly. "If you're against us, you know where the door is."

Percival pauses for a moment, stunned, then he inclines his head at the king and goes back to his seat.

"Okay then, Sweetheart, let me get a good look at you."

BETRAYED

Morgana bends down and looks into Lore's eyes, pulling the lids up with the tip of her thumb. The girl bears it, stiffening her shoulders. "I can certainly restore your memories. You might feel a bit off for a few weeks, Darling, lots of food and rest. Are you ready?"

Before Lore has time to speak, Morgana presses the heel of her hand between the queen's eyes, twisting her fingers in her blonde hair. She spits something, not a word I've ever heard, and a dull pink light pulses from her palm. Lore's knees sag and Lux catches her under the arms. After another moment, Morgana draws her hand away. She motions for Lux to lower her to the floor, which he does, cradling her in his arms.

Morgana sit's Lore up, whispering to her and helping her sip her drink. Lux is taking deep, steady breaths. I can tell he's trying to stop himself from crying in front of all the knights, especially while they're all staring. I look to Ren and then to Asher and Willow. Asher's smirking. Willow has her hands over her mouth, waiting for the moment of truth. To find out whether the queen has been restored. Morgana stands up from her crouch and offers Lore her hand, which she takes, and she shakily allows herself to be pulled to her feet. Lux gets up, standing beside his sister. The room is silent, which is something of a wonder.

Lore steadies herself. Her face is still a little pinched, but she seems lighter, as if a weight's been lifted from her shoulders.

"How do we know it worked?" Sir John Alymere croaks.

"*Same shit different day.*" Asher sends to me and it takes all of my energy to stop myself from laughing.

Thomas Alymere stands behind Sir John, acting as his squire. I bet he was hoping to be sitting in the seat himself by now, being almost fifty.

"She'd've been restored much sooner if it wasn't for your endless prattling." Morgana scowls at him. "And by 'yours', I mean all of you. Your inaction almost caused –well, perhaps it's best not to dwell on that. In my day, the health of the king and queen was of utmost importance. The knights of old would've come to me themselves to save their monarch. They would've done *something* other than sit on their arses and–"

"Morgana," I warn. *"This is not the time."*

"Forgive me," Sir Alymere says with a smile, "I am old and could not have made the climb."

"Then what use are you to me, Sir John?" Lore speaks, her voice brittle like old bones. And cold, so cold. "What use are any of you to us?"

"My queen, I never meant–" Alymere flushes.

I see something flicker in Lore's eyes, something dangerous. The flash of a silver blade in the moonlight. Deep and viscous steel. At that moment, I understand the look that Ren and Lux shared. Her memory might be better, and now it might be restored, but she's still not exactly Lore. Before the spell, she was bubbly and bright, inquisitive and kind. Now it's as if she's encased in ice, hard and unyielding. I catch Ren's eyes, which are dark and concerned.

"I think that will be quite enough for one day." Joth says, rising from his seat. He's noticed the tension and is nothing if not a master of smoothing over tumultuous situations.

"What about the traitors?" Eddie asks, voice trembling.

He calls them that, but he doesn't really believe it, I think.

Rory and Richard stand behind his chair, both wearing the same grim expression. The others are so quick to denounce Sir Tristen, but we saw him on the mountain. He was as good a knight then as any around the table, perhaps better. And I know the pain that twisted him, the dagger in his back.

"We'll deal with them tomorrow. You will all hear

BETRAYED

testimony and then we'll decide how to proceed." Joth answers. "Until then, eat, sleep, enjoy the day. I've asked Etta to prepare lunch for those of you that are hungry. She'll serve in thirty minutes."

Joth doesn't need to say that this might be the last day we can enjoy for some time. That black cloud looms over us. Always.

Lux and Lore leave first with Ren and Morgana. I follow, only waiting behind to tell Asher where I'm going and what I want her to do now.

"Got it." She says and goes about her task.

I catch up with the others as Morgana is tucking Lore into bed. Despite it being only lunch time, Lore looks shattered. "I'm going to give you something to help you sleep, all right, Darling? You might feel strange for a week or so, but you've been under a spell for a long time."

"Will you stay?" The girl reaches for Morgana's hand. "And where's Lux?"

"Lux is–"

"Here." He says, moving past me with an arm full of blankets. He piles them onto his sister's bed and climbs in beside her, arranging a pillow behind their heads.

The sight of them together, both finally *present*, is a blessing I don't deserve. Tears threaten me and I squeeze my arms around my middle to hold myself together. Morgana takes a deep breath, apparently battling with the same flood of emotions.

"I'd hear about Arthur if you've got stories?" Lux asks Morgana. "Was he truly as brilliant as they say in books?"

"Oh, yes." Morgana's eyes sparkle and she sits at the end of the bed. "Even better, for the most part."

"Don't tell a story about a boring quest though," Lore chimes in. "I want to hear about a dragon."

"I've got *hundreds* of stories about dragons. And I remain on quite good terms with Tayldryn, well she doesn't try to set me on fire anymore."

"You *know* a dragon?" Lux says, his eyes as wide as saucers.

"I know exactly three dragons, although I've not seen a tooth or claw of Bromeodanth in over a century. Now get comfy and let's see where to start."

I desperately want to stay with Lore, to make sure she's okay, to let her know how much I've missed her, but it's best not to disturb them now. I mouth my thanks to Morgana, and she drops me a wink as I leave, closing the door softly behind me.

I go back towards my room to find Ren. It's surreal walking the halls now, as if I'm a stranger again. I'd got to where I could find my way around the Templar with no problem, and it's only been a short time in my memory since I left. But the reality is, I've been gone for a long time. Nothing, and everything, has changed. The others, the ones who were left behind, have experienced a terrible ordeal. Ren and Willow have been under tremendous amounts of strain, trying to hold everything together while Asher was accused and I was gone. I slow my pace and take in a couple of deep breaths. It's not my fault, but I should've done more.

"Well, don't worry Sweetheart," Dad's voice whispers in my ear. *"There's plenty more to do."*

And he's not wrong. When I suggested the crazy plan to find and recruit the witch, I hadn't thought properly about what might come afterwards. I truly believed I could bring her here and that she'd fix Lore. But after that? Now, though, there's not only her to consider and what her presence means, but Tristen and Owen and Lila.

BETRAYED

How terrified she must be, trapped alone in a faery prison. Nobody knowing of her existence, nobody looking to set her free. My heart aches against my rib cage, a knot growing in my throat. I believe I could make myself overlook what might happen to Sir Tristen if it wasn't for her. If he were to be exiled or left to rot in the dungeon, it would hurt and I would grieve for him as I grieved Shelby. But in the end, the pain would pass and I could move on.

He'd deserve it, anyway. The horrible, spiteful part of me whispers. I wish the voice wasn't there, that I could think good thoughts all the time. *Fair* thoughts. One's unclouded by fear and anger. But I can't, no one can.

What future would he really have at the Templar now anyway, branded as he is? *Traitor* stamped on him forever. I don't think I could ever trust him again, even if his intentions were honourable.

Owen we might yet save. He needs compassion and a firm hand, both of which Joth can deliver. And the twins' kindness will be met with loyalty. I can feel *that* in my bones. But the choice isn't mine to make, not alone anyway. No, now it's time to hold council and be reunited with my friends.

28

REN

"You summoned us?" I ask Merle as she comes back from settling the twins. I can't help the warmth spreading through me just to see her. When her eyes meet mine, her lips break into their very own smile.

"Yes." She says. "You, Asher, Willow, Rory and Amalie, Richard and Eddie. The other knights weren't there. They didn't see Tristen. He didn't dig them out of the snow or carry them back to safety, or—" she breaks off.

"So the betrayal has been harder for them to bear." I offer her my hand and she squeezes my fingers. I wasn't there and I feel it. The knife twisting in my gut. We don't always see eye to eye, us and the knights, we never have. Long before Merle, we argued around that table relentlessly, even Joth often failing to call the most boisterous to heel. But that was different. Families argue all the time, that's normal. Selling your kin to a faery witch, however, is *not.*

"It's not fair to make them wait until tomorrow. They

BETRAYED

deserve some answers. And I want to know what happened after we got separated." Mer says, bringing me back into the room.

"Then let's find out."

By the time we arrive at the Mews, everyone is already waiting for us. Asher and Willow are huddled together, staring out over the grounds. It *is* pretty. The September leaves turning red and pink and gold. Amalie and Rory are beside them, their thin fingers locked together, braced for whatever news we have. Richard stands with his wife, and Eddie is waiting apprehensively on Asher's left. When Merle steps out from behind me, he lets out a small cry and rushes towards her, gripping her into a hug.

"Thank *god* you're all right! All this time I thought you'd–" he swallows. "And I've not been able to stop thinking about it. If only I'd prepared you for the climb better, or if the avalanche had hit the other way, or–"

"It's okay, Eddie. It wasn't your fault, it wasn't anyone's fault."

"Oh yes, it was." Amalie says. Her voice is low and cold, the bitterness in it driving her strong French accent to the surface. "It was 'is fault, that *traitor.*"

Instead of responding, Mer pushes Eddie off and goes to her. Amalie throws her arms around Merle's neck, burying her head into her shoulder. Mer strokes her back while she sobs, whispering in her ear that everything is fine. We're all back together, and we're all safe. At least for the moment. When Amalie's sobs have finally subsided, she wipes her eyes and goes back to her sister. Somehow Rory seems much older, even though they're exactly the same age.

"I've got something to tell you and it couldn't wait." Merle says when everyone's shuffled back into position.

There's not much space up here, but at least it's warm with so many bodies. "And I want to know what I missed."

"Have you seen Greg?" Eddie asks.

"Yes, and Owen."

"Is it true?" There's hope in his eyes that Merle will tell him it's all a cruel joke. That he can't have been deceived by someone he's called his brother. I know the feeling, the twin to it, residing in my own heart.

"It is true," Merle says and his face falls. "But it's not all there is."

"What excuse is good enough?" Rory spits. "To let us believe you were dead and Asher 'ad murdered you? 'Ow could he 'ave?"

"Morgwese has Lila."

Dead silence. I expected gasps of surprise, but we're met with empty, slack faces. Eddie is as white as a sheet, Richard bracing as Rory leans into him.

"It can't be so," Amalie whispers, tears tracking down her cheeks. "Lila is *dead.*"

"She's not, Amalie." I say, trying to keep my voice soft. I know how difficult this is, too. I knew Lila, I felt her loss. I saw what it did to Greg,

Amalie slumps back against the wall. "If Lila's alive, it changes everything."

"What if he's lying?" Richard asks.

"I've seen the memories. And Morgana checked..." Merle starts.

"She could be lying too, to protect her sister." Eddie mutters under his breath.

"There are plenty of liars in our walls, and none of them are her. Joth told you that." Merle's voice is cool, and a knot of tension forms in my stomach. "Morgana came here with the sole intention of breaking the curse on Lore, which she's done.

BETRAYED

She saved Asher's life and mine. I'll vouch for her. I trust her with my life."

"Me too." I say.

"And me." Willow.

"And me." Asher finishes.

"Then we trust her too," Rory says, and the others nod in agreement, Eddie included.

"What will 'appen to Tristen?" Amalie asks. Her voice is still thick with tears.

"I don't know. That's why I wanted to talk to you—"

"I know." Willow whispers. She's staring out over the grounds again, watery sunlight glinting off the frame of her glasses. "I know the law, anyway. It isn't... there isn't really a good outcome for him—"

"There must be something we can do!" Eddie throws his hands in the air.

"The law says we *should* kill him, no matter the reason for his betrayal. He's no longer fit to be a knight, you see. He swore an oath to the king and queen, and that oath should be stronger than familial blood." Willow continues.

"You can't possibly be suggesting we execute him?" Rory says.

Merle grips my hand more tightly, my heart hammering hard against my rib cage. I'm not sure what Willow *is* suggesting, but I certainly hope it's not that. I would follow her, any of them, to the ends of the earth, but I couldn't follow this.

"No." She shakes her head, hair rippling in the half light. "But ultimately that will be on the table. God, Alymere almost lost his *own* head today. Don't think he won't be out to show his loyalty! When a knight commits an act of high treason, which this has been, whether or not we like it, they can't ever be a knight again! But, like I said, I know the law, and I know it better than anyone else alive. With the extenuating circumstances, we can make a case to save his life. He'll lose his title, his land, everything–"

"That might be worse than death." Eddie says.

"The main priority here is Lila. We need to get her back before we do anything else." Amalie's eyes are green and focused. "Everything else can come later."

"Yes." Merle nods. "And we can't decide exactly *what* we're going to do until everyone agrees–"

Asher snorts and we all turn to her expectantly. "The other knights don't have to agree. You all heard her earlier, Lore. '*Then what use are you to us?*' She said, or something like that. Terrifying. *Brilliant.* Can you imagine? She'd have *their* heads along with Tristen's."

A cold prickle runs down my spine. But Asher's right. What she said rattled them, and we already know most of them are cowards.

"And the *Animus Nostari Salvari* is still under effect." I say.

"So what now?" Rory asks.

Everyone falls silent, and after a moment Merle realises we're all looking at her, all waiting for instructions.

"It's going to be for the king and queen to decide in the end." She says carefully. "Right now, we all need a break, some time to digest what's happened. Tomorrow we'll explain the situation to the knights, and to Lux and Lore."

"It's a lot to put on the children." Rory says, chewing on her bottom lip.

"Only they can decide." Merle says back.

It's late and we've been in bed for a while when Merle turns to look at me. It's surreal, having her back, reaching across the space and finding a soft, warm body instead of cold sheets.

BETRAYED

I've been out of my mind the whole time. Unable to believe without proof. But as the days turned into weeks and then into months, what else was I supposed to think? I run my palm along the smooth curve of her waist, pulling her close so that our noses touch.

"Why aren't you asleep?"

She smiles. I feel the pull of her lips against my own, then she says, "I want to know about Lore. What Joth meant by 'different'?"

I let out a long sigh and twist onto my back. I don't know if I can explain it. There were signs of it before, the distance between her and Lux, the sharpness to her words, but now it's deeper. As if Lore's amnesia was eating her soul from the inside out, and she couldn't keep it at bay any longer. "Well, you've seen her now. She shares a room with Eyrie, but they don't play together anymore. They don't even really hang out together anymore although Eyrie still tries. She's mean to her brother. But not in a *mean* way–"

"That doesn't make sense," Mer huffs, tracing her finger across my chest, goosebumps forming in its wake.

"She doesn't understand it's mean, well, I don't think she does." Maybe it's because she doesn't have a filter anymore. All the codes of how to act like a friendly human being got wiped with her memories. "If Lux makes a joke she doesn't think is funny, she'll tell him off and sulk. Or if they're training together and Eyrie beats her at something, she'll scowl and call her names and storm off."

"She's eleven–"

"She made Willow cry."

Merle bolts upright, the sheets pooling around her waist. Her bright hazel eyes find mine, full of confusion and anger. "What do you mean?"

"To keep the three of them out of the way, keep them

distracted, we've been working on the prophecy. We've made some headway, but not a lot–"

"So?"

"*So,* after one of the study sessions, Lore thought she'd solved something, some part of it, but it didn't make sense, really. When Willow questioned her about it, she called Willow an idiot, that she didn't know anything, and if she was really any good at her job, we wouldn't be in this mess. I know it doesn't sound like a big deal now, not like I'm telling it, but–" I shrug. "The Lore I know would never do that."

"No, she wouldn't." Mer pushes her hair off her face, then puts her face in her hands. "Which part of the prophecy did she think she'd solved?"

I groan and throw my arm over my face.

"Just tell me, then I promise we'll sleep."

I cast my mind back to that day in the library, Lore with red cheeks and clenched fists, Willow stunned into silence. "Lux said something about the '*wings of death*', he thought it could mean a dragon. As soon as he said it, Lore got this strange look on her face, blank and cold. She agreed with him, kind of, but she said the dragon in the prophecy was a man, a man who would come and rain down fire on us. The wings of death are not *actual* wings, but the shadow of his rule." At some point, I start to shake. It had seemed stupid when Lore had stamped her foot and demanded that we take her seriously. Now, in the dark, it feels entirely different. "But there isn't a man like that."

Merle is quiet for a moment, her full pink lips turned down at the corners. Then she closes her eyes and shuffles back down the bed to lie beside me. I thought I'd seen something on her face then, just for a moment, something like recognition. Maybe it's just the light.

"Now Lore has her memories back, things will be

BETRAYED

different." She says. "They have to be."

"They will be." I wrap my arms around her again, unsure whether her comment is a question or a plea. "But there isn't anything to do about it now. Not until tomorrow, at least."

"All right." She says, kissing my cheek, then she snuggles down under the quilt. "I love you."

"I love you, too."

More than anything. More than my duty, and fixing Lore, and fighting this war. More than anything.

29

By the time the next day comes around, it seems everyone has settled, becoming more accustomed to the news of Sir Tristen's betrayal and Morgana's arrival. After breakfast, we file into the hall, quietly taking our seats. Last in are Lux and Lore. They both sit at the head of the table together, Morgana standing beside them. I'm too apprehensive to sit, it is me after all, who has to tell them what we've found.

When everyone has finally finished shuffling, Joth clears his throat and looks at me. "The Heir of Merlin has requested this meeting to discuss the fates of Sir Gregory Tristen and Sir Owen Lamorak, and some evidence that has come to light since his confession."

"I'd also tell you everything that happened on the mountain—the avalanche, when we were separated, when we found the cave— all I can remember." I say.

For a wonder, no one makes a sound. Instead, they lean

BETRAYED

in closer, waiting for my words. I talk for a long time, occasionally looking to Asher and Eddie for reassurance. Finally, I come to the fight, my voice shaking as I explain how we were almost at the top of the mountain when he turned on me. Or maybe I turned on him? Now I can't be sure, but it doesn't really matter.

"He used Carnwennan to cut through my magic and—" I stop. I can see Owen's face looming over me. Bright green eyes bloodshot and full of tears. Then I thought it was the cold, but now I recognise the battle in his eyes. Still, he slid the blade into my chest, delivering what would have been a fatal blow. "Then—"

"I swooped in to save the day, as per usual, and here we are." Morgana finishes. "Two of your best still alive, your queen restored, and not a single word of thanks from any of you."

"We are in your debt." Joth says and the other knights sound their agreement.

All of them apart from Lawrence, whose face is sheet white. There are dark crescents under his eyes, his lips bloodless. He will have already heard some form of this story from Owen last night, maybe even some of the truth. Lawrence is a good knight, even if he's miserable. He's been with the Templar his whole life. That means he knows the law. He knows what's going to happen to Owen. Hearing the words from my mouth, of his son's treason, and knowing what happens next, it's a wonder he's in any way composed.

"*There's only one thing you can allow to happen to Owen, and you know it,*" Mum's voice whispers through my head. "*Mercy.*"

"When I came back and Tristen confessed he was behind it—" I take a second to choose my words, and to knock the wobble out of them. "I couldn't believe it, that he and Owen would willingly—"

292

"He confessed!" John Alymere bangs his palm on the table. "We all know the law!"

"Owen was spelled." I ignore Alymere and look first at Lore, then to Lux. Their identical grey eyes are trained on my face. "I spoke to him. He knows what he's done, but he's not entirely responsible for it. Tristen and Morgwese manipulated him—"

"He is a traitor! Just like Greg Tristen!" It's Alymere again, red faced, watery blue eyes bulging from their sockets.

"If you interrupt Merle again, Sir John," Ren says, his voice cool and lethal. "I'll drag you out of this hall and into the dungeons to join them."

"Wonderful!" Morgana cries, clapping her hands together and dropping a sly wink in my direction. "A fight already!"

"Enough!" Joth shouts, rising from his seat. "Is this how you'd all behave in front of your king and queen?"

Alymere grumbles under his breath, but says nothing more. The twins look at me again, waiting for me to go on. Nerves spin uneasily in my stomach. If everyone's reacting badly to this news, I dread to think what will happen when I announce the rest.

"Before I go on, because there's more," I say. "I'd like to vouch for Owen, and ask the king and queen for mercy." Thankfully, only the surprised gasp of Lawrence Lamorak echoes through the hall. Lux's eyebrows shoot up, obviously surprised, but by my request or being addressed so formally I'm not sure. Lore's face stays still and pensive. She knows what it's like to be spelled, to be trapped against your will in a mind that's no longer your own.

"I'll vouch for him too." Asher pushes back her chair and comes to stand beside me.

"And us." Willow rises from her seat, followed by Ren.

BETRAYED

Pride swells in my chest. I wasn't sure if he would stand for Owen, if any of them would. There's the scraping of more chairs as Rory and Amalie get up, then Richard, then Eddie. Even Lydia Geraint gets to her feet. Lawrence looks around the room, silent tears dripping off his face. I can only hope he remembers, in the coming months, when the times get hard, who is vouching for his boy's life to be spared. And with even more ferocity, I hope he remembers the faces of those who remain in their seats.

"I know some of you would deal out awful punishments. I know you're hurt." I search for Sir Alymere among the crowd of faces. His cheeks are still flushed, red lips pressed together. I suspect that's why he's being so vocal, because Tristen's betrayal has cut him and doesn't know where else to focus his pain. "Owen deserves to be spared in this. He needs guidance, he needs *friends.*"

"And you're sure he won't try to hurt us again?" Lux asks.

"I swear I won't let that happen. We all do."

"I think Merle's right." Lore says. "Now the spell's been lifted, he'll go back to normal won't he?" The question is loaded and I think we all know it.

"In time, the effects of my sister's spell will entirely fade," Morgana answers. "He'll be right as rain."

"I agree with Lore," Lux says. "And with Merle."

"That's settled then." Joth takes over before anyone else can speak. "Owen shall be spared punishment unless he breaks the terms of his rehabilitation. Those terms will be ironed out more specifically at a later date."

"You said there was more, though?" Lux asks, the soft skin between his eyebrows furrowing with the question.

"Yes. It's about Sir Tristen. It's true that he's been working with Morgwese, and he's been doing so for some time. I went into his head, into his memories. I've seen the full extent

294

of it, what he agreed to and what he did. The reason I went into his memories at all was because of the reason he gave me, the reason he'd betrayed us."

"What did you see?" Lore asks. She's shuffled forward in her seat, eyes wide. I wonder if she's looked into my head already, whether she knows what's coming.

"Lila Tristen is alive."

Now gasps ring off the stone from every direction. I wait for the sound to settle.

"Impossible." Lydia Geraint says, her voice a harsh croak. "I remember when she died. It was terrible. Greg was in pieces for months."

"The faeries didn't kill her, they kidnapped her. That's why we never found her body." Ren says.

"She's still alive. I've seen his memories, I've seen *her*. I swear it. He made a deal with Elaine, that he'd feed them information about us and what we were doing, that he'd deliver us to them. All in exchange for Lila's safe return."

"He still betrayed us." Sir Percival whispers. "He almost cost my nieces their lives—"

"And we're not suggesting he go unpunished. But Lila is alive, and she's down there, being held captive. Can't you understand his reasoning? Would you have turned your backs on your own children?"

"I would have betrayed you all for Owen." Lawrence says. He still has shallow rivers of tears running down his cheeks. I can't believe he's speaking on our behalf. "I would leave with him if you cast him out. I am bound to this Templar, to my duty, and I *love* that duty. I would do nothing else than serve the Pendragon line, as did my father and my grandfather, and all those that came before them. I wouldn't give it up, or trade it for anything other than the life of my son. I'll swear to that however you want me to. I understand what a terrible choice

BETRAYED

it must have been."

"So do I." Lydia agrees.

"Even so," Peter Lucan's voice joins the chorus. "Sir Tristen must be punished."

"And we don't know for a fact that Lila is alive." Alymere's watery blue eyes meet mine.

"I told you I've—"

"Seen his memories, yes. But memories can be altered, and he might truly believe Lila is alive and that she's a prisoner. The faeries might have tricked him into it. If she's not alive, then he betrayed us for nothing, which would negate the need for leniency."

"Wouldn't it be enough punishment to find out she's dead?" I spit.

"If I remember correctly, he had no qualms about killing you, or Lady Gaheris. If Lila isn't alive, if she is, it doesn't matter! Sir Tristen is a dangerous traitor and a threat to all of us!" Sir John's voice becomes louder, booming through the hall.

"If we exile him now, while Lila is in faery hands, he'll do anything Morgwese wants! He'll go *straight to her—*"

"I wasn't suggesting exile, Young Witch."

"Then what is it you're suggesting?"

"We all know the punishment for high treason," he drawls.

"At least 'ave the decency to say it!" Amalie joins in, the calm in the room descending rapidly into a storm. "If you mean to put a man to death, at least 'ave the decency to say it out loud. You coward!"

"Enough!" Joth shouts, but his voice is overshadowed by ten other voices, all of them jumping over each other.

I turn my attention to Lux and Lore, the king and queen, to see what they make of the arguing. Their faces are still, not paying attention to what's going on. Instead, their hands are linked, eyes glazed over. I slowly realise they're talking to each other, or communicating somehow, in a way none of us can hear. It's eerie and brilliant.

"Enough!" Joth shouts again, banging his fists on the table. That seems to shock them a little, quieting the shouting to hissed whispers. "You're supposed to be adults! We have a horrible and complex decision to make, lives are at stake! We'll never get anywhere if all we do is scream at each other. Everybody will get a chance to—"

"We've made a decision." Lore cuts him off.

Joth blinks twice, shocked into silence. Then he gives me a grim smile and motions for them to speak.

"You're all right." Lux continues. "Sir Tristen betrayed us, and he is dangerous, but if Lila is alive, then we can't leave her behind. We believe that Merle's telling the truth about Sir Tristen's memories, and that they really do show Lila being alive. But—"

"We're not sure if his memories really reflect the truth. We don't know enough about faery magic to know whether it's possible." Lore finishes.

It's strange, the way they interact with each other. They've never been so in tune in my presence, so clearly two halves of one perfect whole.

"So, how shall we proceed?" Joth asks.

"We don't want to give a sentence until we know for certain. It wouldn't be fair." Lore's face is pale, her mouth set in a determined line. Every time I look at her, she reminds me of a marble statue. Beautiful and cold. "We want to know if Lila is alive, and the only way to be sure is for you to bring her to us."

"If Lila Tristen is presented to us, we'll allow Sir Tristen

BETRAYED

to stay here, he will be demoted to squire, and Lila will take his seat at the Knight's Table." Lux is looking directly at me, I think he's waiting to see what I think of their judgement. It's more than I could have hoped for.

"How long do we have to present her?" I ask.

"You have 100 days."

"If you can't find her by then," Lore takes over. "We'll have no choice but to exile him from the Templar, and Merle will wipe his memories as an added precaution."

"Because we won't kill him. Not under any circumstance, not even if the law says so." Lux says, his eyes roving the faces of the knights. Only looking for one face in particular, and when he finds those eyes downcast, his mouth twists into a sneer. "I'm talking to you, Sir Alymere, although you're now so conveniently quiet."

The knight flushes red but doesn't speak, only nods his head in acknowledgement. I'm glad he's embarrassed. He should be given his earlier behaviour. Amalie was right about him being a coward, hiding behind his title, but never driven to *act.*

"Thank you, your highnesses." I say. The twins have given us a gift. From a terrible situation, they've somehow come up with a compromise that can only benefit us. No matter what happens, they're going to allow Sir Tristen to live, *and* they've granted permission to retrieve Lila. I scan the room, first looking for Ren, who gives me a shallow nod, then Morgana, who does nothing. I don't even think she's realised I'm trying to get her attention. Her eyes are clouded over, thoughts somewhere else.

"I know there's more to discuss regarding the terms of Owen's release and of Lila's rescue." Joth says. He's smiling, obviously happy with the twins' decision. "But I think we all need a day to decompress, and our queen has been restored to us, something we've yet to celebrate."

"A party?" Lore asks, her eyes lighting up. It's easy to forget that they're only eleven years old, still children.

"Will a feast do?"

She beams. It's the first proper smile I've seen on her face in months. It makes her look like the little girl who led me through dark corridors with the promise of cake. Maybe hope isn't lost. Maybe everything will be exactly as Morgana said. In a week from now, Lore might be herself again. Still, I can't get the look that Ren and Lux shared out of my head, the look that said something was certainly wrong.

"That's settled then. We'll reconvene in a few hours if that's agreeable to everyone?"

There's a grumbling of consensus as chairs scrape back and knights get to their feet. They wait for Lux and Lore though, no one moving until the king and queen have left their seats and exited through the heavy double doors.

30

"That was quite something, wasn't it?" Asher asks.

She's laying on my bed with Aila, head hanging over the edge. I can see her through the mirror as I'm applying my mascara. She's been restlessly rolling around on my sheets for about thirty minutes, crinkling her immaculate tunic. My own is waiting for me in my wardrobe, and I'm thrilled to be wearing it again. I haven't had the chance to do so since I retrieved Merlin's magic and it's my favourite item of clothing. Joth kindly had the shirt remade for me after the last one was left in tatters.

"It was."

"You're very quiet about it."

I turn to look at her properly, "I'm happy if that's what you mean?"

"What else?"

"Don't know, I can't put my finger on it. I mean, it's exactly what we wanted, *better* than that. No matter what,

Greg will be spared, so will Owen, and they've already directed us to rescue Lila, so Morgana's plan might actually work. She's agreed to stay, Lore's memories have been restored. And you saw them working together in there! It's perfect, they're perfect."

"But?"

"I've got a bad feeling I can't get rid of."

"Feels a bit like a stomach ache? A knot in your heart you can't unravel?" Asher swings up right and crosses her legs beneath her. "I've got one too."

"Good."

"Is it?"

"It's better that we both feel it, that we're together."

"True."

"I wanted to thank you for standing for Owen, you didn't have to."

Asher smiles, maybe it's a grimace. "I would stand with you in everything, Merle. No matter what, no matter where or when, whether I think you're wrong or right. Publicly, in front of them, I am *always* with you."

"Do you think I'm right?"

"Yes." She nods. "I think with Joth's help, he'll be a hell of a knight, it also keeps Lawrence on side."

There's a sharp knock on the door and then it swings wide as Ren lets himself in, Willow's only a few steps behind him. They're both dressed smartly, Ren in his own tunic emblazoned with Lancelot's coat of arms, and Willow in a calf length black dress. They both look wonderful.

"Why aren't you dressed?" Willow asks, wrinkling her nose at me. "They'll be starting any second."

"Too busy gossiping." I say, getting up and going to the wardrobe. It only takes me a moment to pull on the tunic, then I'm ready. "Let's go."

BETRAYED

The feast is nice. Etta's made me my favourite pasta dish, wild mushrooms and cheesy sauce. For dessert there's carrot cake and sweet wine, which the twins try and screw up their noses at. Then there's music. Lux asks me to dance, as he did at the first ball I ever attended. This time, rather than sheepishly and under his sister's strict instruction, he bows low and then sweeps us onto the dancefloor. When we've spun a few times, he trade's me in for Eyrie.

As I'm returning to my seat, I see Morgana gliding my way. She's dressed in a fine silk gown, her hair tumbling over her shoulders. There are eyes on her as she moves, many of the knights still suspicious of her presence here. That's not the only reason they're staring though. Morgana is, quite literally, a creature of myth, part of the stories they've grown up hearing, the stories they've told their children. She actually *knew* Arthur Pendragon, Lancelot and Queen Guinevere. Legend made real.

"Had enough yet?" I ask.

"I'd had enough of this lot the second I stepped through that door, Darling." She smiles and rolls her eyes, joking I think.

"Joth's got good whiskey hidden in his office."

"Yes, well that's what he wants you to think. Bet he hasn't told you where he keeps the really good stuff. Come one, I'll show you."

As I'm following her out, I look for Ren and find him staring at me with a quizzical expression.

"*Morgana wants something,*" I send. "*You good?*"

He nods and turns back to Lux who I imagine is pestering for more wine.

The witch leads Aila and I through the corridors, stopping by the horrible painting of the ogre eating a knight, to retrieve Joth's secret whiskey stash. The frame swings away from the wall revealing a small crawl space and a dusty bottle with a cork in the top.

"Gave this to him a while ago, straight from Uther's stash. He was always drinking the stuff. Me and Mags used to drive him wild stealing it from the pantry. Elaine was never into that sort of thing, always too quiet for it. She had ambition of being married off to whichever prince our mother chose for her, but it never happened. She lost interest in us when little Anna came along."

"Oh," I stop dead in my tracks. A memory hitting me so hard it's almost unbearable.

"*You have an* Armilla?... *My mother had one just like this. I wanted it, begged for it, in fact, but she left it to my sister, her favourite.*" Elaine had said, all that time ago. She knew that the charm bracelet wasn't 'just like' but actually *was*. That means I have Lady Igraine's faery charm bracelet stashed in my jewellery box.

"Everything all right Darling?" Morgana casts a look over her shoulder, raising one sleek dark eyebrow.

"Yes, fine. I remembered something, well, I actually have something of yours, well I think—" I stop, shaking my head. It's best to go and get it rather than trying to explain. "I'll meet you in your room in five."

Ten minutes later, I manage to find where she's been hiding out. She's made herself at home in one of the rooms at the back of the Templar, out of the way of nosy knights. Its interior decor is much like her cave and I suspect she's conjured up a lot of the items herself, a trick I desperately want her to teach me.

"And Mags gave you this?" She says after inspecting the bracelet. Holding it up to the light, running her fingers over the beautiful and ancient charms.

BETRAYED

"One every year. I used to find them close to the date of Dad's disappearance, well murder." I correct myself. "Elaine recognised it."

"I bet she did. And I bet it drove her *wild*. My mother *loved* it, which meant of course, that all three of us wanted it. She gave it to Mags because she was the oldest, it's strange that she'd give it to you."

"Strange how?"

Morgana sits back in her seat, thinking. "She wasn't always like this, you know? When my father was killed, it devastated her. She was old enough to know what had gone on, you see. It *changed* her. Changed something in her that couldn't be changed back. Before that she'd always been a bit serious, following the rules to the letter, a proper lady of standing. But she wasn't bad. She took care of Elaine and I, brushing our hair, helping us dress, making sure we didn't run amok at whatever fancy dinner our parents were hosting. You know how it is."

"I don't have any siblings."

"Oh, no, of course not." She puts the bracelet carefully on the table, and then snaps her fingers. Two glass tumblers materialise on the table, full of ice, and she fills them with whiskey, oblivious to my awe. "My point is, that after he died, she was never the same. She tried to adjust to life at court, but she couldn't. The only real solace she ever found was when she was studying under Merlin, and even that was tainted. She *hated* him, she hated Uther and Arthur and Anna. She despised everything that had played a part in what she, and quite correctly I might add, deemed the worst thing that had ever happened to her. But she *loved* our mother. She loved our mother so fiercely sometimes it was suffocating. So it's strange that she'd give that away when it's likely the only thing left of her."

304

"It's because she killed *my* father." I say. The more I think about Morgana's words, the more it makes sense. I've always believed it was a taunt, something to hurt me. But maybe that's not exactly right. "No one ever admitted that what happened to your father was wrong, no one even acknowledged it—"

"So, in her own twisted way, she might think it's an apology, or her way of acknowledging responsibility. Sending you pieces of mothers jewellery will have haunted her almost as much as it haunted you, although I don't suppose that's much consolation."

"It's not." I say and knock back my drink, the warmth of the liquor rippling through my chest. "Would you like to keep it?"

"Of course I would."

"Then it's yours."

She inclines her head in a shallow nod, then refills my glass. We're quiet for a moment, the silence settling like dust.

"Why did you really come here?" I ask. "After that, after the way you've been treated by everyone. The Templar has been awful to you and your sisters. Why would you?"

Morgana lays back in her chair, thinking for a moment. "It was *his* letter that convinced me in the end."

"Joth's?"

"Lux's," with a click of her finger, a fold of cream paper appears in her hand. She offers it to me. "Four words he wrote. I never thought I'd see it, someone who resembles Arthur so strongly. Mordred never did, he was a little weasel right from the start. Spent too much time in Mags' shadow, too much time—" she catches me smirking and stops. "I could never take to him. And he was the one who caused it all to tumble down. Lux though, that boy has the same charisma as my brother, a man that others will follow."

I open the paper and written there, along with Lux's

BETRAYED

signature and the Pendragon sigil are the four words Morgana promised. *'A new dawn breaks.'*

"Gave me chills, Darling." She nods matter of factly and takes another sip of whiskey.

It gives me chills too, but they aren't entirely pleasant. "And Lore?"

"She's got a curse on her."

Her answer's so blunt it makes me start. Aila jumps beside me before settling back down. Morgana smiles at her wistfully before continuing on. I wonder what happened to her familiar?

"I brought back her memories, and she *is* better, but— have you ever heard the story of the Snow Queen?"

I shake my head.

"Once upon a time, an evil queen made a magic mirror," she grins and curls further into her chair. "The mirror could only reflect the bad and ugly things in the world, and one day the queen smashed the mirror, sending shards flying into the wicked west wind. Of course he blew them everywhere, miserable as he is, and they fell into the eyes of a little boy, Kay. The shards froze his heart like a block of ice, making him cruel and cold to his friends. That's what she's got, a splinter of ice in her heart."

"How did Kay get it out?" I ask with a shaky breath.

"Gurda, his best friend, saved him with a kiss. The warmth of her love melting the ice away." Morgana smiles wistfully.

"What about Lore's?"

"She'll warm up I suppose. Being under an enchantment that long can cause things like this. Magic isn't always exact, sometimes you can't predict the consequences."

She doesn't seem too concerned, but I shiver again. Lux felt it too, that coldness in her, pushing him away.

"Not to worry, Darling. We've got an ace up our sleeve."

"We do?"

"Oh yes." She grins at me now, sly like a fox, eyes glinting in the firelight. "When I left Camelot on that day, I was *so* angry. I'd never felt anything like it, that rage *burning* through my blood. I hated Arthur for his choice and I wanted to punish him, but I couldn't bring myself to hurt him, and Merlin had warned me not to interfere."

"So what did you do?"

"I knew how to really make him sorry." She spits the words, the shadows dancing on her face, her features sharp and feral. "He'd just returned from one of his bloody crusades. Guin and I hated those too! Endless trawling through deserts looking for holy lies. But this time—" she shrugs lazily.

My breath catches in my throat, I know what she's getting at and why she so adamantly fought for her plan. *I wish you'd never found it.*

"Stole it right out from under his nose. By the time he'd noticed, I was long gone."

My mouth is so dry I can't speak. She knows my question though, the one that burns on my lips.

She smirks at me again from over the top of her glass. "Oh yes, I've got it, Darling. I've got the Holy Grail."

About the Author

Gabby is a YA Fantasy author based in Yorkshire. Gabby has grown up reading adventure stories and heading out into the woods, daydreaming about one day creating her own magical worlds and sharing this passion with others.

When she's not writing, Gabby works at the University of Huddersfield as a Global professional Award Trainer, delivering employability and skills training to young people. She spends most of her free time reading, cooking, going to the gym and spending time with her loved ones.

.

COMING SOON

OTHERWORLD

Merlin's Heir #3

For more information, you can find Gabby's website at:

www.authorgabskeldon.com

or follow-on social media:

@authorgabskeldon

Printed in Great Britain
by Amazon

27376898R00182